The Stones of Bothynus Trilogy

BOOK THREE

Triangulate

The Stones of Bothynus Trilogy

BOOK THREE

Triangulate

by

D.K. Reed

Purple Finch Press
1087 Elm Street, Suite 412
Manchester, NH 03101
www.purplefinchpress.com

Printed in the United States of America

ISBN-13: 9781545627228

Contents

PART ONE

Angels

Quote from <u>Perelandra</u>*: He had full opportunity to learn the falsity of the maxim that the Prince of Darkness is a gentleman. Again and again he felt that a suave and subtle Mephistopheles with a red cloak and rapier and a feather in his cap or even a sombre tragic Satan out of* Paradise Lost *would have been a welcome release from the thing he was actually doomed to watch. It was not like dealing with a wicked politician at all, it was much more like being set to guard an imbecile or a monkey or a very nasty child.*[1]

CHAPTER 1

Back to the Swan Hole

Annie almost skipped down the dirt road that ran through the countryside past her grandmother's farm in the foothills of the Smoky Mountains—in fact, a few skips did break through despite her best efforts at coolness and poise. She avoided the few pockets of gravel in the middle and on the sides of the reddish-brown smooth tracks of packed dirt. She loved to walk barefoot on the road, as long as she didn't have to move aside into the gravel and twigs to let a car pass. This didn't happen too often because the only people using the road were the other farmers who lived deep in the valley past Mamaw Jefferson's farm. On the rare occasion that two cars met, one had to back up until they found a wide spot in the road.

She breathed deeply and was enraptured by the rich mud and vegetation smells she so loved about this farm. The last time she'd come to the Swan Hole, icicles had been present, along with a frosty mist—a different, but equally compelling, scene. Today, she knew it'd be ferns, mosses, and birdsong. And hopefully Aaan—oh, how she hoped he'd still be there. Every time she came to visit her favorite apparition, she wondered if he'd be gone away and the whole thing would just seem like some dream of her youth that later in life she'd wonder if she really experienced.

She thought briefly of the contrast between how she felt visiting Mamaw's this summer versus last; last year she'd been anxious about spending the summer in such a remote place, but that was before discovering the hottest guy she'd ever laid eyes on, who happened to be a half-angel and was eons old, but who appeared to her to be about the same age as herself. She had wondered about that, but assumed his manifestation had something to do with the way he saw himself.

She hadn't seen him since her Uncle Alistair's wedding last winter, where, seated next to his Adonis-like manifested form, she'd been in a state of euphoria, stupid with happiness. But then he'd just disappeared with barely a word. She'd spent the past few months mulling over every second of that event and wanting to make it back here to ask him about it.

She was pretty sure his rapid exit wasn't because he'd wanted to get away from her. He had smiled and blown her a kiss and his look had not suggested avoidance; it had been more like a soldier blowing a kiss to his lady love as his ship shoved off for distant lands. She knew she was romanticizing the whole thing, but there was just something about him she couldn't forget. From reading his cave etchings, she felt like she knew him intimately and that he was a truly good being.

And she wanted to ask him about his father. She wondered if he'd share his feelings about his father with her when, or if, she found him again. He'd been through so much. The last line of his epitaph, which she'd copied from the cave and translated from Latin, still haunted her with its sadness: *"After Seya was buried, I stayed in this cave and spent many days creating art, trying to recall the beauty I had seen in the world through sculpture. Then I decided to remain here and sleep, being tired of struggling."* She'd memorized the whole thing.

How did she feel about him having a daughter who'd evidently been older than her ... and a wife, for that matter? In fact, he was *older* than old. But somehow, he seemed still young and vulnerable. And vivacious and handsome and, really, everything she wanted in the love of her life, except that he didn't have a solid human form. She sighed. Yes, she knew this was a problem, though somehow even this didn't matter.

Aaan had occupied her heart and soul for almost a year now. The only people who knew this were her sister, Red; her best friend, Nyah; and Uncle Alistair. Her parents and Erik knew about his existence, but not of her emotional attachment, though Erik likely suspected; her sister was pretty much an open book to him.

She'd given a lot of thought to telling her friend Carrie about Aaan. Carrie was far away in Bucharest, but they kept in regular touch. She'd decided it would sound too hokey if she blurted it out by email and so would wait and tell her when she saw her in person. And this was going to happen soon—she'd been invited to spend two weeks with Carrie in Bucharest.

She was excited. She always loved her annual visit with her childhood best friend, and they'd missed it last year. They were going to go north into the mountains and visit an old castle right out of a vampire novel. Okay, she was *trying* to be excited about it—in truth, she really just wanted to stay with Mamaw all summer and spend every day at the Swan Hole with Aaan.

Under the current plan, she only got to spend two weeks in Tennessee for now, but somehow, she had to figure out a way to return later in the summer when she got back from Bucharest. She almost wished Mamaw needed her all summer, like last year, so she'd have an excuse to stay. She felt a little embarrassed to be so smitten.

She'd come down to Tennessee with only her mom this time. Red had graduated from high school the previous week and had graduation parties to attend and other plans with her friends and Erik for the following week. Her dad rarely spent a whole week at Mamaw's—he just didn't feel like he fit into the bucolic culture, what with his silver ponytail and liberal politics. He was always restless at Mamaw's, too, not content to just sit and visit while breaking beans or silking corn, and he definitely drew the line at quilting. He'd formerly tried bringing his bicycle but farm dogs didn't tend to stay inside a fence and he always had problems with them when trying to bicycle through the countryside. He'd brought his canoe along a couple of times, and loved to canoe on the nearby Clinch River, but that required someone to shuttle him upstream and then pick him up wherever he stopped, really cutting into her mom's time with her grandma and making her grouchy. So he'd stayed in Maryland to work.

Uncle Alistair and Aunt Zsofia had been gone since their wedding. Annie didn't know all the details of the Hamilton's honeymoon, but knew they were to spend time with old friends in London and then have a whirlwind world tour. Annie suspected the couple would spend a lot of time in a ghost transformation, accessible by using one of the Snap to Alternate Grid controls her uncle had fashioned from dust he'd retained from a trio of ancient stones he had researched. Apparently a person didn't age as rapidly, if at all, while in the ghost transformation, and the couple had lost so much together time by not getting married until they were in their seventies.

Uncle Alistair was semi-retired now from Georgetown University. She knew he would keep his foot in the door at the university, at least until Erik and his other research student, Roy, finished their graduate degrees. His research interests were such a huge part of his life and he had grand plans for solving global problems, like food shortages. Annie thought he'd probably string the semi-retirement out as long as possible so he could oversee research, but also spend a lot of time in the ghost transformation, thus making his lifespan longer. Annie wondered how long he could pull that off before people got suspicious and noticed that he and his wife were no longer aging—maybe twenty or thirty years?

The worst part, of course, was that no Uncle Alistair meant no access to the STAG controls, which would have allowed her to transform and actually see Aaan. Her uncle had been a pushover when she needed to borrow a control last winter, but now he was gone and she hadn't even bothered to ask Erik for help, not after the lecture she'd received from him about national security after he learned she had "borrowed" one last summer.

She'd have to rely on getting Aaan's attention in some other way, and hoped he'd appear to her like he'd done at the wedding. She smiled to herself when she remembered how handsome he'd been. The thought made her start to become nervous as she approached the falls.

She hesitated a moment to drink in the essence of the place. It was so beautiful right now. The warm morning sun hadn't yet reached the pool except in spots where the overhanging leaves left small openings. A slight breeze made those lights play on the water's surface. The ferns and mosses were rich and deep green, hanging from the semi-circular ledge above the falling water. And they were fragrant.

The pool itself had a mystical feel. It didn't surprise her that an ethereal being chose it as his home. She wouldn't be surprised even to see an elf or fairy in this magical place.

As she stood entranced in the atmosphere, she heard many bird songs and one of them began to sound more and more like a flute. At first so faint it was almost indistinguishable from the breeze, it grew slowly until she recognized the beautiful tune that had opened her uncle's wedding. She'd looked it up online after the wedding, wanting to remember every detail of the day she got to sit next to Aaan in sheer ecstasy. Pachelbel's Canon in D, she thought it was called.

The lovely strains of music were coming from the top of the falls. She looked toward the sound, and for a moment, thought her eyes were playing tricks on her. There, on the rock where she and Aaan had watched the sunrise last December, was a Pan-like figure, leaning back with a flute to his lips, watching her. She recognized the angelic facial features.

She giggled at his theatrics and waved her fingers in small, intimate, feathery wave. The figure with no shirt and goat-legs nodded to her in recognition. She shook her head at the absurdity and cleverness of Aaan and giggled once more.

She sat at the base of a large hemlock tree, tucking up her feet and lacing her fingers together around her ankles, and enjoyed the show as he serenaded her with angelic music.

She was so relieved he was still here. He'd always been here when she visited. She didn't want to think about the possibility that a time might come when he wasn't here—the possibility he might get reincarnated into another human body and disappear from this existence for a time. If that happened, she'd probably never know where he was and he'd probably outlive her and not return to the falls until after her death and so she wouldn't get to see him anymore in this lifetime. She couldn't let herself think of that. He was here now—her angel.

After some time, the beautiful strains came to a finale and faded softly, leaving only the sound of the waterfall, and the birds, insects, and frogs. She hadn't realized until now that the other critters had quieted while he played, as if stepping aside for one greater. She realized she'd been listening with her eyes closed to fully enjoy the melody.

Now, as she slowly opened them, she saw him as he'd appeared at the wedding, though not so well dressed, wearing only cut-offs this time. He also had the slight glow he'd had at the wedding, before she cautioned him to tone it down, but he looked normal now — at least no goat feet.

She slowly scanned upwards, taking in his muscular legs, stomach, chest, and arms before reaching his much-too-handsome face. He was now the standard of male perfection by which she'd always unfairly judge all male mortals and they'd forever be found wanting. "Hi," she managed, though she wasn't sure he'd heard over the sound of the waterfalls.

He gallantly got down on one knee, took one of her hands, and bowed his head to touch it with his forehead, as if in reverence, then lifted his eyes to hers and kissed the back of her hand in such a way that the flesh on that spot felt simultaneously seared and soothed. "Greetings, Tiny Bold Maiden. I have waited and hoped every day that you would return."

All Annie could do was close her eyes and revel in the sensation of her hand in his for a moment, a slight coolness still lingering where his moist lips had been. Then she opened them and smiled at him. He smiled back, the most beautiful smile she'd ever imagined. In fact, her imaginings fell sadly short of the real thing. This man was exquisite.

Smoothly, not breaking the spell at all, he transitioned into, "Would you like to join me for a swim?"

She didn't trust herself to speak, but simply nodded. He pulled her hand to help her into a standing position, then kissed it again and released it. She was glad she'd worn her favorite bikini beneath her clothes just in case. Without the STAG control to allow her to transform into a more ethereal state where they could fly or go inside the cave, there wasn't much else to do at a swimming hole.

She felt a little awkward unzipping her shorts or just throwing off her top and so stepped behind the tree. He got the hint and turned his gaze in another direction.

Annie knew her figure was one of her best features. Where Red was robust and a perfect image of the strong female form, Annie had always been very slender, with a wasp-like waist but round breasts and hips. Still, she suddenly felt shy, hoping he'd like the way she looked. What if he preferred robust women? She slowly stepped out from behind the tree.

"Okay, I'm ready." She tried to sound nonchalant.

He turned to look at her and she saw that he took in her appearance from head to toe, but he didn't comment. Instead, he took a step forward and dove into the deep pool, so smoothly that he barely made a splash. His graceful form could be seen underwater due to the slight glow of his body. She saw him ever-so-gracefully twist around and come back up with his face turned upward so his hair washed back.

"I won't lie and say the water is fine—I think you will find it is cold. But it is certainly refreshing. Want to join me? You do not have to if it is too cold for you."

Annie was not usually very sensitive to the cold, and still felt warm from the heat of his touch a few minutes ago. So she didn't even bother to dip a toe in to test the waters, but followed his lead by taking one large step and launching herself into a smooth dive—not as smooth as his, she was certain, but pretty good for her.

The cold water was indeed a shock as she submerged and she quickly scrambled to the top, gasping for air and shaking uncontrollably from the cold.

She heard a hearty laugh as she brushed the water from her eyes. "That's my Tiny Bold Maiden," Aaan said good-naturedly.

"C-c-c-cold," was all she could stammer. She heard him laugh again and then felt herself being lifted upward and realized he was carrying her out of the water.

"Do you have a towel? Or blanket?" he asked.

"Y-yes, t-towel." Her teeth chattered loudly.

He set her down onto her feet and helped her retrieve the beach towel from the daypack she'd brought. He wrapped it around her shoulders and rapidly rubbed her arms and back, getting the blood flowing again. He glanced upward. "Looks like a sunbeam has arrived on my favorite spot at the top of the falls— want to sun up there?"

"S-sounds great, l-let me get my sandals." The chattering had slowed appreciably.

"Who needs shoes?" He laughed again, scooped her up, and flew up to the rock.

"Okay," she managed. Somehow it never would've occurred to her that he could fly while carrying her if she weren't in the ghost transformation. In fact, she realized there was a lot she didn't understand about his form of existence. But this was her opportunity to learn.

Annie had two idyllic weeks to spend with Aaan, going to the Swan Hole alone to meet him every day of her visit. It worked out well, because with her mom there to keep her grandmother company, she was allowed a lot of freedom. Both grown-ups thought it healthy for her to go exploring around the farm. She visited her friend Missy a couple of times, but Missy now had a baby and was preoccupied. Plus, since she didn't live so close to the falls anymore, it wasn't as convenient to see her. Rather, she spent every possible moment with Aaan, mostly talking; they were getting to know each other. There was so much to get to know about him.

Annie's first question was about his state of being.

"I have characteristics both of human souls and of angels. Like any angel, I can be seen at any time by anyone who can see spirits. Some people and animals are naturally sensitive. Sometimes a person can have their 'spiritual eyes' opened temporarily, it seems. I do not claim to fully understand how and when this works. But I can choose to be seen if I use my angelic ability to manifest myself. In this state, I can appear pretty much any way I imagine."

"Like when you were playing the flute?" Annie was enjoying this.

"Yes, did you recognize what I was?" he asked playfully.

"A faun?"

"That's right—a well-read young lady. Top marks today for classic studies."

"And top marks to you for theatre," Annie said, clapping.

He bowed.

"But what form are you in right now? You seem to be about the same age as me." She was delighted to be able to finally ask this.

"This is me," he said. "Let me explain. When I am asleep, I assume I am invisible to you. When I want to manifest myself, if I don't think about it, I appear in the form I had originally when I first walked the Earth. That is the form I think of as me. But I was taller than today's humans and must remember to give myself a normal height when I want to blend in. You may know from your many readings that half-angels were recorded to be giants, though this is partly metaphoric in that they had greater-than-human abilities and so tended to be successful in anything they chose, especially anything that involved competing with mortals. It was, admittedly, an unfair advantage and may have played a role in our being banned."

"Wow. So you really did shrink during the wedding when I commented on how tall you were."

Aaan laughed. "I am afraid that is a problem with my manifestations. Also, I tend to glow."

14

"Yes, I remember." Annie giggled and then had a thought. "Is that why you had to leave so quickly, like you were going to glow or something?"

"Yes, that was one reason. I can only hold an acceptable manifestation for short time, maybe an hour, and could feel myself starting to slip."

"But you're glowing now, and are tall. Are you more comfortable that way?"

"Yes, I can hold this manifestation for a long time and am quite comfortable. It feels natural," he said. His face grew serious. "But Anya, there was more than that."

Annie was almost afraid to hear what he had to say, afraid this wonderful bubble would burst.

He continued, "Another reason I had to leave the wedding in such a rush was because of something I share with all angels and demons. You see, in our dealings with mankind, unless we specifically have a task delegated down the ranks from on high, we are only allowed to have direct dealings with mankind if invited. This is not something I have been told, though it is consistent with my readings, but something I have found out through trial and error. It seems to be a hard-and-fast rule, not easily broken, even if one of us tries. I had been invited to the wedding and but nothing after that, and so I needed to leave. If I had not left, I would have likely disappeared at an awkward moment."

Annie felt a pang. "Oh, I had no idea. But the invitation was to the wedding *and* reception."

"My fault," he said ruefully. "I should have allowed you to bring the written invitation. I only heard you invite me to the wedding. My sincerest apologies. I hope this caused no trouble."

Annie could see this now and wished she'd known it before. How wonderful it would have been to get to dance with Aaan at the reception. Instead, she had been worried and sorrowful during that gay event and for a long time afterward.

"In that case, I'll just say for the record that you are always welcome to be with me wherever I go." She bobbed her head emphatically one time to make the point in a playful way but Aaan took it seriously.

"Anya, I don't think you know what you are saying." He seemed a little anxious about the idea. "I mean, if I should ever turn ... evil, like my father, I might try to possess you. You would never want that. In fact, you should recant that right now."

Annie was just beginning to see how serious he was. Though she didn't see how he could ever turn evil—that was laughable. "Okay, okay. Um, I recant that I have asked Aaan to be with me wherever I go. What I meant was that I give him permission to be beside me always, but not to ever possess me. Does that clarify things?"

Aaan smiled warmly. "Very well stated, Tiny Bold Maiden."

Annie smiled back. My, how she liked this man. She didn't care if he was a different kind of being and had complicated her life infinitely.

CHAPTER 2

Daanak and the Fiend

"Oh, but he looked so beautiful, so divine. So like ... her." The deeply tormented voice was filled with unspeakable sorrow. The angelic figure slumped.

"'Oh, but he looked so divine.'" The boyish sneering voice mocked him, then bellowed with laughter. "Is the great Daanak to melt at the feet of his bouncing baby boy? Such a good little boy," the voice now cooed, "good little boy ... like milk toast, no ... like those little ones they used to sacrifice to me." He cackled at his own joke. "All that *purity*." He spat the last word as if it were a loathsome taste in his mouth. "How he glowed."

"Enough!" shouted Daanak. "You can go to hell." Then he looked at his tormentor and, despite his misery, this struck him as hilarious and he burst out laughing.

"Good one." The voice now had a crueler, less jovial edge as the snake-like demon rubbed his narrow chin. "At least you have retained your sense of humor. Yes, that may come in handy ... let's see, what would be the most fun sport to make of the boy?" The voice now had a feminine witchy quality.

Daanak eyed his companion with lowered lids, hoping the subject would drop. Purity was a topic he would not discuss with this devil. Purity was a lost paradise for him—oh how he wished the universe was different. No ... it wasn't the universe, it was him. How he wished *he* were different.

And to discuss my good son with this—this ... He tried to control his rising ire—to resist the bait. "Look, Your Highness. Sir, I thought we agreed to leave each other's, um, families alone. Remember Lilith? I could have—"

"You could—have—done—*nothing*." The voice was now deep but had a hissing quality as he enunciated each word clearly and with cold finality. A fist came down emphatically for each word. "Without me, you would be nothing. Remember that."

The snake-like demon seemed to realize he was getting to Daanak and persisted, gloating on his new find. "Now, let's see. What would be fun? Oh, I know." He now jumped excitedly like a child. "That little Cherokee girl of his. Let's—no, wait." His face fell like a wailing tragedian. "I think she died, didn't she? Too bad."

Now annoyed, he resumed. "Hmmm, likely out of our reach, then. Wait. Wasn't he— no, that was too long ago, too. I may have to do a little research to find his current weakness."

He seemed to be in deep thought for a moment and his self-delight was apparent once more. "It's always fun to watch

them squirm when I get the boys to work on a dear loved one."
He laughed heartily, now living in some memory from the past.
"Oh, please, please. Have mercy," he said in the mocking witchy
voice again. He then burst into relentless maniacal laughter.

Daanak tried to ignore him and move away. The mocker
began encircling Daanak, repeating over and over, "Oh please,
have mercy. Oh please, have mercy. Oh please, have mercy ... "

Daanak kept moving, trying to block the thoughts that came
flooding in, but could see the whole decrepit, hopeless scene.
He was unable to rid himself of the interminable taunting and
worse, the weighty hopelessness that now pulled downward,
ever downward in the pit of his being. *How long must I endure
this?* And then he remembered: *Forever*.

Annie expressed her concern to Aaan about the piece of bot-
tomland that ran alongside Kingfisher Creek opposite the side
owned by her grandmother—she had learned from Mamaw that
it had been sold. "What if the new owner brings in a bulldozer
and builds something that destroys your cave?"

He smiled. "Do not worry, Anya. I already considered this.
The land went up for sale and I purchased it."

She was overjoyed that he owned it, but was not sure how
it could be legal if someone challenged it since he certainly
wouldn't have a Social Security number or birth certificate—
she wondered how he'd accomplished this. As she thought
about it, the whole thing seemed impossible. "Aaan, if you
can't be involved with people without their permission, then

how did you buy this piece of land? You couldn't have put the deed in your name since you don't officially exist. I mean, don't you need a Social Security number or birth certificate or something to buy land?"

Aaan smiled a crooked mischievous smile. "Funny you should ask. Let's just say that I had full permission to purchase this on behalf of a client."

Annie was partially satisfied, relieved to know there was no danger to the cave, but she couldn't fathom what he meant by his cryptic remark. But she didn't pursue the topic.

Another day, while sitting in the shade and dangling their feet in the water, Annie mustered the courage to ask Aaan about the epitaph on his wall. "Who were you writing to?"

"Anya, you probably don't know this, because I don't think you can read Latin. But I have to tell you that I have lived a long time." He looked into her eyes, apparently to gage her reaction.

She giggled. "What do you mean 'can't read Latin?' " She proceeded to quote a line from the text and then translated it into English.

He raised one eyebrow. "I am both greatly impressed and deeply humbled. I meant no insult whatsoever to your abilities or education. I just thought schools no longer taught Latin for the most part."

She admitted to taking the etchings and translating them using computer software.

"These computers sound useful," Aaan said. "I confess to being intrigued by them and would like very much to have an opportunity at some point to learn how they work and how to use them."

Annie blurted out, "I can teach you—well, not how they work, really. That's something someone could only learn by studying both electrical engineering and computer programming. But I'd love to teach you how to use one."

She was beginning to get excited about this and then an amazing idea struck her. "Hey, do you have to stay in this cave? I mean, couldn't you come back to Maryland with me?"

Amusement twinkled in his eyes. "I was already planning to do just that. After all, you invited me. Unless, of course, you choose to recant—again."

Annie was ecstatic. "Oh, that would be great. You could stay in Uncle Alistair's room until he gets back from his honeymoon—if he ever does. Or in Aunt Zsofia's house, unless, of course, Mom's able to convince Mamaw to leave the farm and come back with us and occupy that house now. Aunt Zsofia will likely live at our house if or when she comes back. But it's unlikely Mom'll ever get Mamaw to leave the farm."

"Yes, it does get in one's blood." Aaan looked around appreciatively.

"So, you were just, like, hanging out here, waiting to get reincarnated?" Annie was very curious about Aaan's existence and wanted to know everything, but was trying to be careful not to pry too much or appear pushy.

"Well, not exactly." He took a deep breath, indicating years of frustration. "I have never known really what to expect next. I just seem to awaken approximately every five hundred years in this in-between state and remember a human life I have just finished. But the in-between state is usually a lonely one, and I often sleep for a very long time—even centuries. There really isn't a bible for my kind. I have been mostly on my own during the periods between reincarnations. I had a brother, also a half-angel, but I have seen him only twice since the flood. He is the only one of my kind I have seen in this state, at least, that I recognized. I guess he's just like me, getting reincarnated *in perpetuum*, uh ... sorry, perpetually."

"Does everyone reincarnate?" Annie was intrigued by his firsthand knowledge of the afterlife.

"You will be amazed, Anya, at just how little I know about that." He gazed off into the ether with a wistful look of frustrated acceptance.

Presently, he continued, "I don't think so, though. At least, I have not seen my mother again since the flood. I like to think she went to the place known to many as Heaven. I have wondered if, perhaps, reincarnation isn't something mostly peculiar to half-breeds, like myself. Perhaps we don't have the same afterlife as humans, and yet we are not angels like my father, an immortal being who exists in the same state in every era—only becoming more good or more evil by his choices. Perhaps that is why the practice of angels and humans propagating was so

22

sternly curtailed." He stopped a moment, the topic obviously one of great emotion even after ages of time had passed.

"But I do not see many other souls in the in-between state, only a few. I have read accounts of humans who have had near-death experiences, who go to an in-between state where there are many beings to greet them. This has not been my experience. I am still trying to research the topic. Reading is my chief delight. It can be tricky at times, however. I can easily travel to one of the great world libraries at any time, but cannot open a book without risking detection. Oh, I can wait until dark when any given library is closed, but then where is the light to see the words? Nowadays, there is usually some faint light from exit signs and various electronic gadgets, and I do use them, but, again, it is not the same pleasure as reading in the daylight. So I often read over someone's shoulder."

Here, he laughed. "I guess there is a reason that people often think of libraries as haunted places—they are. In fact, when I think of the other ethereal beings I have seen, that is usually where they have been. Libraries, places of worship, and courthouses. My theory is that places of worship are frequented because of the soothing music, and courthouses because of the fascination with justice and judgment, and, in some cases, revenge. But I guess every spirit—ghost, whatever you want to call them—has his or her own journey."

"Do angels and human souls have a gender?" Annie was really fascinated with this conversation. "I read that you have reincarnated as a female twice—was that strange?"

"Yes, and no, and ... again, I don't know entirely. Yes, I am male, at least in the in-between state, and no, it didn't really feel weird to be female because I didn't know my spirit was male at the time. It was actually very good for me to see how the other gender thinks. And it is really not so different. I think, at least I have read, speculation that in the highest spiritual states, both genders are represented in a single being. But the dichotomy, at least in the human existence, helps souls recognize they have some types of gifts to give and are lacking in others and so are compelled to share and receive so that two together are more whole than one alone. It encourages first a longing for something other than oneself, and then the answering joy in connecting with that other. It encourages ... love."

The way he said *love* made Annie blush and she felt her breathing increase. She nervously steered the conversation back to a more neutral subject so she could retrieve her composure. "What about angels?"

Aaan hesitated a moment, seeming to be in deep thought, and then said, "Well, angels are definitely different. Angels and humans are both beings with the freedom of choice. Most angels are very good and dedicated to their assigned task to a fault. Take guardian angels—I would not want that job. They are intense. I have never seen one that is not totally focused on watching and zipping back and forth to carry messages upward ... or outward."

He stopped a moment and chuckled. "No, I take that back. I did see one totally confused about what to do. That was your guardian angel on the day you visited me in the transformed state, your second visit, where you were normal-sized but ethereal, the one you call the ghost transformation, I think. That angel was very confused. They are not used to being seen by their charges. It seems to be somehow taboo to them. That angel seemed torn between keeping an eye on you and hiding from you."

Annie also laughed, now envisioning this. "Yeah, Red told me about that part beforehand and so I knew what to expect. You said they carry messages. Where? To God?"

"Again, I am sadly lacking in information. I assume there is a hierarchy and they are taking messages to their superiors, but I have never been invited into their confidence. Perhaps it is directly to God, I do not know."

"I thought angels would know everything about us— God, Heaven. For a half-angel, there's a lot you don't know," she teased.

He laughed good-naturedly. "You are right about that. There is definitely a lot I do not know, but one thing I do know is that I know more than you." With that statement he dove into the pool, purposefully splashing cold water onto Annie.

She giggled delightedly and ran around the pool so she was on the opposite side of where she'd been before. When he emerged, he looked around and didn't see her right away. As he eventually looked behind him, Annie timed a grand splash with the heel of her hand, right into his face.

Annie continued this horseplay for several minutes and was delighted that Aaan seemed to be enjoying it too, until he finally said, "I need to get you away from this water, you little nymph." Scooping her up in his arms, he flew to his rock perch.

Upon landing, he took his time in setting her down. He looked warmly into her face and she thought for one heart-pounding minute that he was going to kiss her. But he didn't.

He seemed to reluctantly set her down on the rock, then sat beside her, one arm behind her back. She loved this spot and they were sitting in just the same position as they had the morning last winter when they had watched the sunrise together.

Eventually, their conversation ensued. "Okay, where were we?" Aaan asked.

"You were telling me about angels and how smart you are."

"Oh, yes. It's true, you know, about the smartness." He laughed again in such a warm way that Annie felt her heart melt.

He cleared his throat and raised his chin. "Back to angels. You were asking if angels know everything. And I guess the answer would have to be that collectively, they probably do know just about everything. But individually, they are just another type of created being. They are not little gods really, depending, of course, on how you define the term. In the human world, they are thought of as 'supernatural' because man does not understand the science behind their existence, or materials of which they are made. But they are as natural as humans, just different. True, some have had duties that allowed them to work much closer with God than any human would ever dream of doing, but I am certain no one angel knows everything.

"As for myself, being a half-angel, I do have abilities that are different from yours, except when I am incarnated as a human, and then I am no different from any other human. Once incarnated, I forget everything except my present life. It is just that after each life, instead of going on, I have thus far remained on the Earth in this ethereal form. I am more like an angel at these times. Like an angel, I can travel quickly from place to place, just by thinking of a place and deciding to be there. And I remember clearly what happened in all my lives when I am like this. But I have never been in the angel *clique,* if you will excuse the modern expression. I have tried to talk to them and have only been minimally successful. Case in point—you asked where they go when they flash back and forth. I simply don't know.

"I also believe I never answered your first question, which was, 'for whom was the epithet intended?' I would have to say that I wrote it mostly for myself, for introspection. I have read and pondered a tremendous amount over the years about the nature of existence. I have tried to figure out what I am supposed to be doing—my purpose. I have also wondered if I might not have a purpose because I was not supposed to exist.

"So I tried to sketch out my existence based on the cardinal virtues to see if I might be in training for something greater. I guess I would have to say I don't yet know the answer. I was pleased to see the lessons I learned did seem to fit the cardinal virtues. My spiritual lessons even seemed to be ordered from easiest to most difficult. For example, leading was easy for me but being subservient and humble was hard."

He hesitated thoughtfully and then continued, "I think, too, that I sometimes learned the most important general lessons about existence in moments of mere quietness. In my original life, I once made a little mossy garden and imagined myself a giant, making this garden for a tiny person to enjoy. This made me think of the creator and how he or she must have felt, wanting us to be happy and making the beautiful earth for us to enjoy. I read about someone having a similar experience once—it was by an author named C. S. Lewis."

"No way. That's amazing!" Annie exclaimed, pleased to connect two people she held so dear. "Uncle Alistair's an expert on C. S. Lewis writings. That ceremony last fall he went to in London when he got kidnapped was because of C. S. Lewis. I guess he got a spot in Poets' Corner at Westminster Abbey or something."

Aaan seemed pleased. "That does not surprise me. He deserves a plaque in that beautiful place. And I am not surprised that your uncle is a fan of his writings. He strikes me as someone with a very highly developed spiritual life."

Annie agreed. Looking down on the pool, she thought of how deep and dark it seemed from above the falls. "Were you here when the Swan boy drowned?"

"No, I was away, watching over my daughter, Seya. In my most recent incarnation, I had a daughter, Seya, half-Cherokee—a half-breed, like myself. I felt especially close to her. After I died, I stayed in a shed on her farm while she was alive. Then I came here. I assume the drowning occurred before I came, but I suppose I could have slept through it," he said. "Either way, there are caverns below the pool that cause a dangerous drag, especially after a rain. I have seen boys come here to swim, diving off the falls into the deep pool, but that stopped at some point—perhaps due to the drowning—but in any case, I missed it. Perhaps I could have helped. As it turned out, the drowning caused people to fear swimming here. The only reason I suggested you swim here was because I knew I could rescue you. One result of the drowning is that it allowed me to have solitude. Also, there used to be an opening to the cavern that would admit a human, but I filled it in with stones after people stopped coming and so the cave became very isolated and allowed me to sleep for many years."

"I didn't know angels slept," Annie said.

"Yes, we do, at least, half-angels do. But not like a human. Not eight hours a night. It is more like hibernation. So far, I have always awakened, though I do not know if there is a rule about that. Sometimes, the awakening has been to a new incarnation. As I mentioned already, when that happens, I do not remember having slept or lived before, so the real awakening is after an incarnation."

"Did you ever see Seya's spirit or soul again after she died?"

"No. I never did." He looked wistfully into the distance.

"You know, Aaan, I was worried about you after you saw your father in Italy. You remember that I translated your epithet?"

"Yes."

"Well, you said something about him turning evil or something. I—I thought he might ... convince you to go with him."

"Anya, I am shocked at your accusation."

Annie blushed, fearing that she'd gone too far.

Then he laughed. "Teasing, Tiny Bold Maiden. You would be correct to be concerned with such a risk. That is why I asked you to retract your original invitation."

His face took on a more serious demeanor. He looked upward for a moment and then continued. "Anya, I need to go try to help my father. I need to try to convince him he can still change and choose good. Your uncle mentioned a visionary, a Christian mystic from the fourteenth century, Julian of Norwich. He recommended I read her writings. I have done so and her visions have given me new hope for my father.

"You see, I have assumed in all these centuries that he was a lost soul, a fallen angel, one of the damned, with no hope of redemption. But in the visions of Julian of Norwich, the message seems to be about a redeeming event set in motion by the Messiah that is much more far-reaching than the established church assumed, certainly much more than I had ever considered. I thought the gift of reconciliation was being offered to human beings only, and then only to those who performed certain acts and went through such initiation rites as the established church required. But the message from her visions was

30

that *all* will be well. I may have helped your uncle see through the prison bars of his own making, but he did the same for me. I owe him a tremendous debt for pointing me in this direction."

"That's wonderful, Aaan. So you now think it's possible for your father to change?"

"That is something I need to find out—and fully pursue. I would have gone straight away, but I guessed you might be worried about me. And I confess, I did not want to lose touch with you. I needed to see you again." He reached a hand and stroked her face.

Annie closed her eyes to focus fully on the spot where his hand touched her face.

"Anya, I feel like I need to say something. I want very much to kiss you and I think you feel the same way."

Annie opened her eyes, looking deeply into his, and looked to his lips, hoping desperately that they'd come closer and touch her own.

"Anya, I love you and cannot take a chance of incurring divine wrath upon you by doing this. It is taboo for an angel to make love to a human."

Annie's mind was whirling with conflicting emotions. He had, in the very same sentence, said he loved her but that their love could never be. She opened her mouth to speak but no words came.

"I will, however, figure something out," he said. "I have an idea, but don't know if it will work. Just know that I long to be with you."

31

Annie began to find her voice. "But didn't you have a wife and daughter?"

"Yes, but don't you see? I was human at that time. Now, I am more like an angel than a human. In fact, I am not human at all. I am showing you a manifestation of who I was in my original life. That life defines me. It is how I see myself. But to ... *seduce* you in my angel state, that is forbidden."

Annie's eyes clouded with tears. Anger began to rise in her throat at the unfairness of finding such irresistible love and yet being forbidden to taste of its sweetness. "Why? Why is it forbidden?"

Aaan sighed and looked away, his expression pained. "I think it has to do with the different courses—journeys that humans and angels must take. Angels are immortal, humans are not, well, at least, not in their original state. To breed immortality into humans is just not the plan, Anya."

"Then why all this?" she spat angrily, gesturing from herself to him and back again.

Aaan took a deep steadying breath and ran a hand through his hair in frustration. "I don't know. But I do feel that it is for a purpose. I knew I needed to learn to love more. And it has come."

The intensity with which he looked into Annie's eyes made her heart pound. He continued, "And as I said before, I have an idea. There are ... options, I think. I am looking for certain opportunities. It wouldn't do any good to tell you now. I want you to have the right of refusal when and if an opportunity occurs."

"Are you talking about reincarnation? I don't want to date a baby." Annie laughed at the absurdity.

Aaan was silent as Annie continued with a measure of hysteria. "Are you thinking I'd wait sixteen years for you to grow up? But then I'd be *thirty*-something. An old woman."

Aaan smiled. "Well, hardly an old woman, at least, I don't think your parents would agree that thirty is old. But no, that is not what I am thinking. But I don't want to say more right now. Just trust me. I will be by your side for the rest of your life if you want, and hopefully someday find a way to cross the line between our worlds. That is, unless I do get reincarnated, which I am desperately praying does not occur right now."

A cold, vacant laugh ensued from the snake-like demon as he listened to Aaan confess his love to Annie. *Got him.* He reveled in a feeling of bitter smugness.

He eagerly anticipated the scornful fun he would have in taunting his companion. *I tire of his company, anyway. What better way to rid myself of that sour face? Fresh, innocent blood, that is what I need.* And once again he laughed to himself.

The game of playing keep-away with the stones just got appreciably more fun. This delighted him. First, the discovery that Daanak's son was involved with the enemy. People—how he loathed them. He knew his bitterness had long ago eaten away almost all of what had once been beautiful and good in him. And now he despised it all.

Second, he now had a new lead on the stones. He did not really care about attaining the stones; it was more that he knew how desperately Daanak wanted them and this gave him leverage for sport. But what great sport it was. *The stones, yes.* They had been kept behind an impenetrable fortress for centuries. The ancient order that had hidden them away had not only placed them inside the Vatican, but evoked guardians for them there, where they lay cleverly camouflaged among the other largely unimportant artifacts that seemed to have been carelessly shoved into storage. It was just possible to actually breach the Vatican defenses. He had been working that angle almost as long as the stones had been there and had come close several times by cleverly manipulating someone within by using a combination of fear and uncontrolled weakness—often a compulsion.

He loved to play with people's compulsions. That was one of his favorite things. The whole pedophilia and child pornography compulsion was a favorite; it really messed with the mind of the victim as well as the purveyor—two birds with one stone. The young victim of sexual abuse felt like he or she had done something wrong, something dirty and despicable. And the abuser could be played from both sides; the irresistible nature of sexual deviation gave them feelings of euphoria that made them mad with obsession, while the loss of control in something they knew was wrong made them realize what a monster they were even when they pretended to deny it.

And when the deviant got discovered, that was often when the real fun started. Oh, how he loved that part. Especially when the loathsome old fool hanged himself, as had happened more than once. And then, the icing on the cake was all the self-righteousness that always accompanied such a discovery. Those with perverted desires condemning others for a different set of perverted desires—he loved it.

He knew he had the most control when he manipulated circumstances to the point where humans actually gave him or one of his cronies permission to possess them. He didn't usually bother with the actual possession too often, though—too confining. He needed to be free to move about, orchestrating multiple projects at any given time. His work was hard. He prided himself in his ability to put so much energy and enthusiasm into it. Although he used despair and the accompanying slovenliness as a favorite set of tools, he never succumbed to this kind of drivel himself. He had far too much energy coursing through him from his bitterness and hatred to slacken his efforts in the least. A veritable fountain of hate stemming from so long ago that he didn't even really remember its inception any more. He just felt that his ideas were best and did not want to be confined in any way, not drawn into this confining *harmony*. The last word left such a bitter taste in his mouth that he involuntarily made a face just thinking it.

He had been excited in recent months by one of his subjects that he had been torturing—no, taunting. That was how he preferred to think of it. He loved to torture. He laughed at this thought. It made him feel powerful. Immune from the pressure to even think about playing nice. Yes, he dearly loved to torture. The subject of this particular torture game had let it slip that someone had been taking the stones out of the Vatican to do modern research on them—some university professor.

That had made him almost feel excited in a way he hadn't felt since ancient times, almost as if it felt good to sense progress, rather than destruction. Destruction sometimes got boring.

Progress in a given path—as loath as he was to admit it—did have an exciting ring to it.

Hearing about the stones was probably the most excited he had been since the Nazis were defeated. He sighed, thinking of that era—all the prayers of people worldwide had become so oppressive that the effort just hadn't feel like it could survive much longer, and so he had lost interest.

But now this project—this was fun. He had never actually touched any of the stones. It was hard for him to believe he had never succeeded, given the success he had enjoyed at times in almost completely controlling parts of this world. Alas, it was true. The one called the Angel Stone was supposed to grant an angel a different set of physical parameters, a different state, so to speak, and he thought that with it, he just might be able to infiltrate the parts of creation he was not allowed to enter. He might actually have grand fun with such a tool.

And now—he just may have found his opportunity. A crack in the dike. He thought of something he had once seen on a sappy greeting card: "When a door closes, a window always opens." He laughed derisively. This was so true. This little snip of a girl would be his "window." He would be able to manipulate Aaan, and thus, Daanak, into anything he wanted. Playing with Daanak's desire for the stones was really more irresistible than actually *getting* the stones.

He already controlled Daanak's other Son, Zaak—a worthless piece of offal. He would have this puny son, as well—Daanak could have a lesson in the rewards of love by watching him destroy his precious ones with exquisite slowness and control.

Oh, how he longed to feel the power of having Daanak plead with him while he and he alone controlled the amount of pain inflicted.

Alive—that is what this feeling was. He felt more alive at those moments than any other. Crossing the line. Yes. Lines drawn by someone else—he spat at the thought.

He knew his hatred was vindicated in some twisted way by the suffering of others. Others had to suffer and it was not his fault. It was the fault of the one who created the unwritten rules that so many had tried to write down—the Tau, the Way, the Word, do-unto-others, love, charity, enlightenment. How he loathed the sniveling sheep that went along with this infringement. How he wanted to remove those rules, to cut them out of his own heart. Yet they remained. He knew they were there—they were his impetus for rebellion. He rebelled, he loathed, he lashed out, and someday, he would win and be free from the loathsome, controlling inner voice. Until then, he would take as many down with him as he could. Down into the screaming, gut-wrenching, fetid, burning darkness of torture, into hopeless despair. The dark night of the soul, indeed. He would give them a dark night from whence there would be no dawn.

CHAPTER 3

Back to Maryland

O n the car ride back to Maryland, Annie's mom mentioned that Mamaw had cautioned her about a feeling of foreboding and tried to talk them into staying in Tennessee another week. Her mom had declined, needing to get back to work, but now wondered about Mamaw's feeling.

"Wow, Mamaw's never been superstitious, has she?" Annie asked. "Last summer, she always seemed happy, even though she couldn't do much after her surgery. She's such a practical, down-to-earth kind of person. I mean, she did have me plant by the moon signs, but don't most farmers do that? And that's kind of scientific—not modern science, but the phases of the moon would affect crops, right?" Annie made a mental note to ask Aaan about that at the first opportunity.

"Yeah, but I don't know, Annie—it was really odd this time. Mom had such a worried expression when we left. I just wish

I could have talked her into coming back with us. I think it's mostly her anxiety. She seems to think danger lay ahead for us in Maryland. But I'm sure she'd feel differently if she were securely situated near us so she didn't have to feel so alone all the time. Maybe that's what it is—misplaced anxiety."

Annie was in a very different state of mind than her mom. She'd opted to ride in the backseat, suggesting she might want to put her feet up and sleep. Lounging comfortably, she was anything but anxious; she was elated. She felt like her life was just beginning. She'd found love. She knew some might've worried that the object of her love was not really human and didn't have a solid form, but she wouldn't worry about that. She just didn't see the world that way. To her, the spirit world, angels, and all things related made sense. They didn't seem foreign or out of touch. She wasn't really sure when she knew she believed reality was made up of more than molecules and gravity; she just knew it was. And she was happy about it.

She thought Aaan was likely riding in the car with them but she didn't know for sure. He'd said he'd come back with them. She knew he could just materialize there—wait, would it be called materializing when he wasn't actually made out of real materials? Probably not. Anyway, she knew he could just think about being there and transport himself, but why would he go ahead without her? There were so many things she wanted to share with him. She smiled and thought of hugging herself in her excitement, but she was trying to be cool and not have her mom notice her ecstasy. It'd be hard to explain.

Her iPod was filled with her favorite songs and so she listened with one earbud in and one on the back of the seat beside her in case he was sitting there and wanted to lean his head back and listen. She felt gleeful, thinking with each song that she might be sharing that particular treasure with him.

"Annie, are you all packed for your trip to Bucharest, or do you still need to do that when we get back?" Her mom broke into her blissful world.

"Yeah, mostly." Annie had almost forgotten she'd be leaving for Bucharest in just four days. She hadn't told Aaan and wondered if he'd feel uncomfortable in coming with her to someone else's house.

She added, "Um, I just have a few *new* things to pack. Things I didn't realize I could take with me before but now don't want to be separated from even for a day." She emphasized the words and looked toward the spot where his head would be if he were leaning it back against the earbud, hoping this would soften the announcement that she'd be leaving just four days after inviting him to come home with her.

"Oh, that sounds intriguing." Her mom obviously had caught something in her words.

Annie didn't take the bait and dish any information, but leaned back with her eyes closed, hoping her mom wouldn't ask for further explanation.

"Anything we need to shop for when we get back?"

"A new swimsuit. Carrie's house has a pool. Mom, could we go to Madame Dulop's at the mall before I go? They have really cute swimsuits and you can get the top and bottom separately so that both fit perfectly." Now that she had a boyfriend, she intended to look as good as possible.

"Madame Dulop's? Isn't that a little too sexy for a sixteen-year-old?" Annie knew her mom thought of it as the place with the padded push-up bras.

"Mom, you obviously haven't been there in a while. There's nothing wrong with their swimsuits. All my friends have swimsuits from there."

After saying that, Annie worried briefly that she might sound like a spoiled brat to Aaan, and so added respectfully, "But of course, if you prefer a more traditional store, that's perfectly fine. I meant no disrespect."

Annie saw her mom look in the rearview mirror at her as if to ask, *Is this my daughter?* Annie didn't venture to respond but feigned sleep to avoid any uncomfortable conversations that might be overheard.

The instant her mom pulled into the driveway and stopped the engine, Annie grabbed her daypack and travel bag and started toward the house. After only a couple of steps, however, she remembered she now had someone she wanted to impress with her maturity and went back to the now-open hatch to help carry some of the garden vegetables Mamaw had sent home with them. Even in wintertime, she sent frozen vegetables or potatoes she had stored in her basement on large, flat wooden baskets formerly used in tobacco farming. Annie knew Red would be disappointed that tomatoes weren't in yet. Frankly, the vegetables they'd brought weren't terribly exciting to her but she knew she needed to pay more attention to how vegetables were prepared and how to eat a healthy diet if she wanted to be on her own someday. She reasoned that having a boyfriend made her feel more like a woman now, even though he couldn't eat a meal she prepared. She sighed but didn't allow her mind to go there.

She was way too excited just having him present to think of anything negative and she really wanted to be alone so she could talk to him. So she rushed into the kitchen, dropped off her load of produce, and cut through the dining room, heading toward the stairs.

Seeing that the dining room was empty, she slowed and whispered, "Aaan. Aaan, are you here?" She looked around in every direction as she walked into the foyer but didn't hear a response.

She said a little louder, "Aaan."

She was just beginning to wonder if he hadn't been with them on the ride up. As she placed her foot onto the first stair step, an alarming sound nearby shocked her into confusion as she heard, "Surprise! Happy Birthday-and-a-half, Annie!"

She stood dumbfounded for a moment. Here were her Gaithersburg friends and her friend Nyah, along with Red and Erik. As she realized the warmth and good wishes that were being shared with her, she melted into joyful delight, unable to resist the happy faces of these people she loved.

She was awkwardly aware that she'd been caught talking to an apparition, and was certain she'd been overheard by the guests. But everyone seemed to be focused on greeting her.

First she hugged Olivia, who'd been her best friend at school since kindergarten, and with whom she'd spend countless hours playing on the computer. She had saved her sanity when Carrie had moved away.

And then she hugged her second-best Gaithersburg friend, Stewart, who'd been a pre-school buddy before boys and girls realized they didn't like each other. At some point, they'd avoided each other, during the phase when they both thought the other gender had cooties. He'd really grown and developed into quite a hunk since she'd seen him last. She'd thought him cute when they were younger and probably even had a crush on him. It was funny, though, as attractive as he was, seeing him now didn't elicit a feeling like she got when she saw Aaan, or for that matter, when she just read Aaan's writing on a cave wall or simply thought of him.

The whole gang was here. She could hardly believe it. By the time she came to her newest friend, Nyah, the two clasped forearms and jumped up and down in unison with squeals of delight.

The surprise was doubled by the fact that it wasn't even close to her birthday. What had they said? Happy birthday-and-a-half? She tried to count and didn't even think that was right, but gave up and decided to just enjoy her friends.

She spent several hours catching up, listening to music, eating pizza and cake, and even opening gifts, though the gifts were gag gifts. There was a T-shirt with a picture of a fish that said "Crappy Attitude" and one with a picture of a crab that said "I'm Crabby in the Morning," along with a cake of soap that left one's hands stained, and a couple of very difficult puzzles.

She was distressed to realize a few of them were planning on sleeping over. This would normally have delighted her. Who wouldn't like to introduce their old best friends to their new best friend?

But her anxiety for Aaan was growing. She hadn't heard a peep from him since they left Tennessee. She tried to remind herself that she hadn't been alone for even five minutes for him to have appeared to her. Still, couldn't he knock something off a shelf just so she knew he was actually here? What if he'd misunderstood or changed his mind?

She signed, thinking she likely wouldn't know anything until her guests left tomorrow. She'd wanted to show him to Uncle Alistair's quarters since he'd have plenty of privacy there, as Uncle Alistair would be absent for who-knew how long. She had to content herself with the thought that Aaan was old enough to fend for himself. She felt some wry humor at the thought, despite her anxiety.

She'd just have to play it by ear and enjoy her friends until they left and then she could find Aaan and make sure he felt at home. She couldn't help but feel a thrill in the knowledge that he intended to stay by her side, but at the same time there was a hint of worry that something might go wrong.

After watching two horror movies, Annie was not surprised when the girls decided they wanted to sleep upstairs in her room. She spread a thick comforter on the wool rug in the center of her room and placed pillows and quilts on top. The girls sat or lay on the comforter and joked and giggled until, one by one, each stretched out and succumbed to sleep. In the end, only Annie and Olivia lay awake, stretched on their backs, looking toward the ceiling. Annie was beginning to feel sleepy despite all the excitement and panic about Aaan.

"Olivia, what made you guys decide to surprise me now? It isn't even my birthday-and-a-half," Annie asked.

Olivia answered so sleepily that her speech sounded somewhat slurred, "Yeah, I know. It's just that I had a bad dream about you and told Stewart and ... he said we needed to check on you."

"What was the dream about?" As sleepy as Annie was, she was mildly concerned.

"What? Oh, yeah. Dream. Yeah. Um, an evil demon was dragging you into a dark hole in the ground and you were screaming. And I ... was trying ... " Annie could tell by her breathing that this was all she'd get out of her friend tonight; Olivia was sound asleep.

Annie was touched, thinking of her friend arranging a brigade of friends to come to her rescue. With that warm and fuzzy thought, she allowed herself to succumb to the increasing pressure of her own lowering eyelids and the slumber clouding her brain. She dreamt of no evil demon, but of a very good and loving angel that night.

The next morning, no one seemed to be in a hurry to go and Annie was determined to relax and enjoy her friends. She heard Nyah and Olivia laughing together and thought how nice it was that her old and new friend had hit it off famously—she was sure there'd be many more gatherings involving both.

She was glad when her dad, true to his usual tradition, made waffles for everyone. After breakfast, they all walked the three-quarters of a mile to the neighborhood pool. Annie enjoyed herself and thought this was how summer should be for a teen, but still, she was anxious to be alone so she could talk to Aaan. She hoped he didn't think her rude for ignoring him on his first day in Maryland.

Finally, after what seemed an eternity, the last friend went home and she rushed to her room.

She pressed the door closed with her back, leaning against it and shutting her eyes for a moment, taking a couple of deep breaths to calm herself. She was just going to whisper his name when she opened her eyes and let out a blood-curdling scream.

There, standing in the corner, was the zombie-doll from one of the horror movies she'd seen last night with her friends, its arms outstretched, beginning to walk toward her, zombie-like.

But upon her scream, it immediately transformed into Aaan's image and ghosted to her. "Anya, please, it is me, Aaan.

Please maiden, do not be afraid. I thought you would laugh," he said imploringly.

Seeing the horrified look on his face, she caught her breath and then saw the humor in the situation. She doubled over in laughter, her adrenaline contributing to the hysteria.

A knock at her door sounded urgent. "Annie, you okay?" Red asked.

Annie opened the door just a crack because she didn't want her sister to enter, and yet wanted to make sure she didn't suspect anything. In her giggling voice, she said, "Yeah, sorry for the scream. It's nothing, just a book fell. Guess it was those movies last night—they've got me jittery."

"Yeah, know what you mean. Erik said that one about the doll even gave him the creeps."

Annie closed the door and turned the lock on the knob. "Okay, you, what was that? Actually, that was a pretty good one."

Aaan appeared again, still looking sheepish. "I just wanted to be playful."

Annie laughed. "I know. Listen, sorry I was busy with my friends and couldn't welcome you properly. I was going to show you Uncle Alistair's suite. You'll probably want to stay there because he's gone now on his honeymoon ... um, that's a tradition where the bride and groom go off and travel after they get married."

"Yes, I know about honeymoons. Remember, I have done extensive reading."

"Oh, yeah. So, you can stay there. Mom and Dad don't ever go in there. I mean, I haven't told them about you. And I guess they might freak out."

"No, I understand. That is probably best, at least for now. There is a reason most people do not see angels and those who do often need reassurance like, 'Fear not.' " Aaan smiled an adorable sideways smile.

"I know, you said that before." Annie teased, trying to add a little touch of an edgy attitude, and then softened, remembering to whom she was speaking, "But if he comes back, you could crash in here, or ... in one of the other spare rooms. I mean ... I'm not exactly sure what all you need."

"Not a thing. Your presence is way more than I had hoped for. Remember that I have spent several decades sleeping on that rock ledge in my cave. And I was very comfortable. I like my little cave. But I am very happy to be here where you are. I can sleep on top of the house, under the house, in the basement, in a tree, wherever. And I don't really need sleep like a human. I can sleep for years or not sleep for years. It is different with us. It is more for restoration or awaiting the next adventure."

Annie giggled. "Oh, this is going to be great. So just let me show you where Uncle Alistair's suite is and then you can come and go as you please. You can hang out there when you want to be alone or here when you want company."

Annie walked toward the door and then remembered. "Oh yeah—Aaan, I think I'll tell Red and Erik that you're here, if you don't mind. You met Red, and Erik knows all about you, and I'm sure they'll be happy to know you're here. And Uncle Alistair, when he gets back, I'm sure he'll want to spend time talking with you."

"By all means."

Annie led the way, checking the hallway to make sure no one saw her going into her uncle's suite while he was away. That might be hard to explain. The coast was clear, so she showed him the location and then hurried back to her room.

As she'd hoped, he followed her back. "Well, you said if I felt like company, I could 'hang out' here," he said.

Annie giggled. "Yes, I did. And I meant it. You may hang out here as long as you don't startle me in the shower. That might be a little creepy. Oh, and as long as you don't do that doll thing again."

Aaan laughed. "Deal."

"Hey, Aaan. You know, I was thinking. You did all that beautiful artwork in your cave with just mud and water."

"And mineral salts and time," he added.

"Right. Well, I was thinking. Do you want me to get you some art supplies? If you can do all that with just mud, imagine what you could do with an easel and paint, or real sculptor's clay."

"Oh, that would be lovely." Aaan seemed so touched and his countenance so beautiful that Annie felt her breath being taken away.

"What materials would you like to begin with?"

"Oh, whatever you have. Please do not go to any trouble."

"Well, I have all kinds of drawing and painting supplies here in this box." She opened the door to her closet and pulled a large plastic storage box down from the shelf over her hanging clothes and opened the lid. Inside was a telescoping easel, a sketchpad, pencils, paints, and several miscellaneous items, including a sharpening strap for the pencils.

"Anya, this is perfect. I may use these?"

"Of course. And please let me know when you run out of something or want to try another medium. Red and I both like art a lot and our parents are used to our needing art supplies and wanting to go to the art store. Red actually spends more time sketching than me, well, for the last couple of years, anyway, but I do it sometimes. So, just take what you need and ... let's see." She moved some tossed clothing from a wooden chair in the corner and set up the easel in front of the chair. "How's that? Or would you rather I set it up somewhere else?"

"No, this is perfect. I can watch you sleep as I draw. I can draw sketches of you sleeping." He laughed sweetly.

"Okay, that's creepy. I mean, it's okay occasionally, I guess, but— "

"Teasing. I thought you liked jokes. Well ... teasing partially. Though I probably will at some point do just that, but never fear. I will not do it every night." He laughed but his eyes seemed to shine with a tiny amount of mischief.

Annie frowned and then laughed. "Deal."

The next morning, Annie and Red were alone in the break-fast room after sleeping much later than their parents, who had already left for work. Red eyed Annie suspiciously before remarking, "Okay, dish. What's going on? I haven't seen you this pleasant in, well ... ever. You're like little Annie of Green Gables. Like you've decided to play the happy game."

Annie laughed and kicked her feet, which were resting on the cushion of one of the dining chairs. Then she got up and did a happy dance, stomping and pumping her arms up and down, turning in a circle. She giggled and then plopped back into her chair.

Red rolled her eyes.

"Okay, I'll tell, but only if you agree to not tell anyone except Erik. And Uncle Alistair, when he gets back."

"All right," Red said hesitantly.

"He's here." Annie squealed, guffawed, and then pumped her fists up and down as if drumming on an invisible drum.

Red sat still, her eyebrows furrowed. "Who's—oh my gosh. No. You're kidding."

"No. It's true. Aaan came back with me."

"Annie. That's ... I don't know what to say. I mean, I guess that's wonderful for you. But Annie. He's like ... an angel or a ghost or something. It's not like you can ... I mean, he's invisible most of the time. "

"I know, I know. But I don't care. And I seem to recall a sister of mine, not mentioning any particular sister, who had a huge crush on a Viking ghost. He's here and I'm happy. And I think he's happy. And that's all that matters. But you can't tell Mom and Dad—they'd freak out."

"You're right about Mom and Dad. But I don't remember any sisters being particularly encouraging to the un-mentioned sister in regard to said Viking ghost."

Annie ignored the last dig. "But you can tell Erik. In fact, I think Aaan wants to talk to Erik about the stones."

"Annie, you told him he has to be careful talking about the stones, right? I mean, if word got out ... Erik has already been in danger. And Uncle Alistair—I mean, look at what's happened already."

"Red." Annie gave her a derisive look. "What do you think? I'm not stupid. Of course he knows to be quiet about them. Think about it—who's he going to tell?"

"Yeah, guess you got a point there." Red quickly moved behind Annie and knuckled her head. "On your head. Ha ha ha." Then she smoothly glided away, laughing.

"You—" Annie made a half-hearted attempt to grab her, but knew that since she had dropped out of tae kwon do and Red had stayed in, it was useless to try to catch her sister.

A couple of hours later, Annie re-entered the breakfast room just in time to hear Erik's enthusiasm at learning about Aaan. "Annie, Sonia just told me about Aaan," he said as she walked in. "When can I talk to him? I could really use his help with my research if he's willing."

Annie was very happy that at least one person apart from herself was pleased to have Aaan here. But she wasn't sure she liked the sounds of him helping with research. It sounded suspiciously like Aaan might be the research subject. "You can talk to him any time. Want me to see if he can talk to you now?"

"Absolutely," Erik answered enthusiastically.

Without Annie having to make a move, Aaan appeared in the chair next to the one she'd taken at the table.

"Aaan, this is Erik, Red's boyfriend. Erik, this is Aaan, my ... friend." She blushed at the awkwardness. That one had snuck up on her—she hadn't realized in time that she'd set herself up to define their relationship. She'd be prepared in future.

The two men didn't seem to notice. They both rose and shook hands. "Aaan, I've heard a lot of wonderful things about you from Sonia, as well as from Professor Hamilton—um, their Uncle Alistair." Erik was obviously delighted and a little awed.

"Likewise, Erik, I have heard good things about you, as well. Alistair is one of those rare individuals without a trace of hatred or cruelty in him. Any student of his has to be a wonderful person."

Annie saw a hint of puzzlement in Red's face. Red caught her eye and shrugged. She responded likewise with raised eyebrows. Who knew these two would hit it off this well?

Annie noted Erik seemed to have abandoned his plan to head to the lab, obviously deeming this discussion to be more important. Annie listened as Erik told Aaan pretty much the same information she'd already heard about the stones, Roy's possession, the research, and the details about Alistair's kidnapping that Aaan might not have known—though having been a part of the rescue, Aaan already knew the gist of that episode.

She was a little shocked and dismayed at Aaan's excitement in allowing Erik to experiment on him. Since he and Alistair had learned from Aaan that the Angel Stone was only supposed to work on angels, they were anxious to see what it would do on him. Erik admitted it would be unlikely to help with fixing world problems, like food storage, but it was a good opportunity to learn about the stone's potential. And who knew its potential without experimentation?

By the time Erik left, it was time for their parents to return and Aaan had agreed to join Erik in the lab at Georgetown bright and early the next morning. Annie could only sit and listen, thinking how much she felt like a parent. She'd always heard how difficult it was to watch your children going to their first day of school, or drive off to college. Now, she had a sense of how that must feel. She felt very protective of Aaan. She'd brought him here from the snugness of his own private little moss-covered cave and now he'd be exposed to unknown situations.

She decided to make the most of the evening since it could be their last evening together just in case he ended up getting beamed into another dimension during the course of the research and didn't return until she was eighty. She sighed.

She asked Red to tell her parents she wasn't hungry and was going to turn in early. She then went to her room and talked with Aaan until the wee hours of the morning, listening to stories of his past lives and telling him of her childhood, though it seemed so lame in comparison with his past. She was glad to see he didn't seem to think her stories were lame and was gracious enough to listen with interest and enthusiasm to everything she had to say. She finally drifted off to sleep with her head on his lap, he sitting on her bed, leaning back against the headboard and stroking her hair.

The next day, Annie didn't see Aaan until the evening, when she left her computer to flop down on her bed to mope about his absence. Erik was obsessed with his research. She had a boyfriend for the first time in her life, yet it was like having a brand new toy she couldn't play with. And she was on summer vacation. And her boyfriend was staying in the same house with her, for crying out loud. Yet she hadn't gotten to spend a single minute with him all day. She'd gotten more furious with Erik as the day wore on—and to be totally honest, miffed at Aaan, too. Why didn't he just say no to Erik and come to her?

Just at the point of peak anger, as she lay on her back with one arm over her eyes, she felt a presence. It was hard to define which sense alerted her, but she just knew a presence loomed over her. She moved her arm slowly down and peeked, then swiftly inhaled, ready to scream, but stopped herself when she recognized his beautiful eyes. A vampire-Aaan hovered over her, black caped and fanged. "I vant to dlink your blood," he said in a bad imitation of an old movie vampire.

She burst into laughter, as did he. He flopped down on the bed beside her. After a minute or two, when she was able to recover her breath, she looked sideways at the head on the pillow beside her, now in its usual form, devoid of fangs and cape. "Oh, I get it. My Romanian trip."

"Of course. I need to instill some fear into you before you go visiting any old castles in the Transylvanian mountains."

She propped herself up on one elbow. "But you aren't coming with me?" Disappointment hit her.

Aaan quickly placed one hand on her forearm. "Of course I am coming with you. I wouldn't miss it. Like I said before, I want to spend every day with you as long as it is possible."

Annie was relieved. "Oh, okay. Guess I misunderstood."

"It is just that— " he hesitated. "Well, Erik is convinced he can figure out how to use the Angel Stone on me. He tried several different things today—different combinations of stones, with or replacing the magnet ... but nothing worked."

"You mean the Angel Stone didn't work on you?"

"No. It did not do a thing that I could tell. I am quite disappointed. I had hoped it would allow me to more fully access the angel realm and in some way help my dad and find my mom. At least, I thought it would let me go wherever those angels go when they zip back and forth. I always assumed they were going to either carry information or conspire with their superiors. I think there is a definite ranking system. My father wasn't around much when I had my first life and I didn't get to ask him many questions. Still, there were things he told my brother and me about his world."

"So Erik wants to try more combinations? You know, Aaan, I worry you might get stuck in some other dimension and I'd never see you again."

"Anya—I think that I would find a way back to you."

Annie's eyes teared up at the sweetness of this sentiment. She wanted to kiss him badly and didn't feel like she could risk looking into his eyes. She just patted his hand and nodded to indicate she'd heard. But after a moment, she couldn't help but blurt out, still not looking at him, "But why take a chance? And I thought you said something about collaborations between angels and humans being forbidden."

She felt him squeeze her hand, though she couldn't risk looking up, afraid she'd start really crying.

After a moment he continued and she knew from the sound of his voice he was smiling. "You should know that I always want to be where you are. But I also feel the need to solve this ancient mystery that has colored my existence. This is not collaboration in the sense that we are trying to harness power—Erik is helping me gather information. I want to keep working with him as much as possible, now that I have found this unique opportunity to connect with my parents, and per-haps learn more about my kind. It has been a lonely existence for me, not belonging to either human or angel realms. I think I have to chase down any lead I can that might allow me to learn more about myself, maybe even find my brother and help my father. My hope is that the stones can transform me in such a way that I will be able to learn something more about the angel realm—perhaps they might make me able to go where the angels go when they travel in and out of sight. I do not know what I will find. I just know I must try."

"I don't understand. You said you were going with me, but now it sounds like you're not." Annie was a little dismayed at hearing him refer to angels as his kind—what did that make her? Was he going to go off with the first female half-angel he encountered?

He propped himself on one elbow, mimicking the movement she'd made earlier. "Do you remember that I can come and go instantaneously? I guess you would call it teleportation—I think of a person or a place and it often works that I am there. It is not perfect, or at least, I do not know all the nuances—no one ever taught me, I just do it. Strangely, I have never been able to go to my brother. But I had no trouble going to your uncle. So I should be able to spend my days with you, and the nights while you are asleep working with Erik. The time difference is such that nighttime for you will be the preceding evening for him. I just have to make sure he understands he has to adjust his schedule and work late if he wants to keep the research going."

"Okay," she said, feeling a little better. "But forget the earlier part, 'cause knowing Erik, he likely won't stop his research even one minute before midnight. I'm glad the timing works out at least moderately well. I can't wait for you to meet Carrie—she probably knows me better than anyone except Sonia."

"So you plan on telling her right away? Perhaps, you should ... well, find out if she would be receptive to the idea. Anya, finding out your best friend has an apparition following her around might actually be cause for concern for some less bold maidens." He smiled a sideways irresistible smile.

"Hmmm. Maybe." Annie was quiet for a few moments, thinking. "I guess I thought I'd do it in person. I'll play it by ear."

"Speaking of unwelcome apparitions, Erik told me something interesting today. You will be happy to know I am now a certified non-demon." Aaan smiled. "It seems before Professor Hamilton left for his honeymoon, he had the laboratory blessed by a team of priests in such a way that evil beings are prohibited from entering the research area. Since I had no problem entering, it proves to a degree that I am not evil."

"Well, I didn't need a test to show me that." Annie loved the way Aaan's eyelids lowered with humility, as though he'd have blushed if it were possible.

The two once again chatted until Annie fell asleep, snuggled against his side, his arm behind her head protectively. Her last thought as she drifted off was that this was a part of life she really never expected to actually exist and a habit she could get used to.

CHAPTER 4

Bucharest

WEDNESDAY, JULY 2

O n the flight across the Atlantic, Annie was happy she got a window seat, and even happier that the middle seat was unoccupied. The aisle seat was occupied by a heavyset, middle-aged woman who slept through most of the trip. Annie was pretty sure Aaan was seated next to her but knew he could not appear easily without risking being seen. Annie listened to her iPod and surreptitiously placed one earbud on the headrest of the seat beside her so Aaan could also listen. As the light lowered to almost darkness, she looked around and noted that the people directly across the aisle were also asleep. "You here?" she whispered very quietly.

He appeared for just an instant, gave her a captivating smile and raised her hand to his lips. She smiled back and snuggled as far over against his chair as she could and closed her eyes.

They arrived in Paris late morning. Annie made sure to look out the window as they descended to see the city. She'd love to spend some time exploring, but had to rush through the airport to catch a connecting flight. In the past, her parents had always booked a non-stop flight when she went to visit Carrie, but this time there was no non-stop flight to be had and they reasoned that Paris would be a good place to change planes. She was sure they had no idea of how close the flights were—they'd have been worried sick. She made it to her connecting flight in the nick of time.

Later that day, she once again looked out the window as she descended into Bucharest. The city intrigued her very much. Such magnificent stone architecture—she thought she saw several gothic towers. She'd also thought just maybe she'd caught a glimpse of the mountains to the north just before they began to descend, but wasn't sure whether the grey shapes were mountains or clouds on the horizon.

Traveling north into those mountains was the part of the trip she was looking forward to the most. *Transylvania*. Just the name sent delighted shivers up her spine. Her mom had expressed some trepidation in her visit to a Transylvanian castle, citing Mamaw's foreboding dream. Annie hadn't even bothered to ask what the dream was about, but now, as she approached the ancient land, she wondered for an instant, then shook it off. She wouldn't let fear stop her from anything, ever.

Carrie and her parents were all waiting to greet her. It was so good to see her old friend. Even though they had emailed pictures of their everyday lives fairly often, and she already knew how Carrie had blossomed into a beautiful young woman, it was even better to see her warm face in person.

Annie and Carrie talked non-stop in the car ride back to the house. She knew within just a few minutes of their re-connection that she'd tell her about Aaan at the first opportunity. It was just that kind of relationship. They kept no secrets from each other.

They talked into the wee hours of the morning. Annie made sure to listen to her friend's updates, especially regarding guys, and told her the whole story of meeting Aaan—from the cigarettes with Missy to the stones to the cave etchings to finally meeting face-to-face. She'd been reliving the moment and talking non-stop when she realized that Carrie was staring at her with her mouth open in a most dismaying show of incredulousness.

"You actually think you saw ... a ghost?" Carrie looked pale.

The old Carrie was braver than this, Annie thought. Perhaps being so close to the legendary haunt of Dracula had changed her, turned her chicken. She now wondered if she had shared her precious secret too quickly and tried to backtrack a bit. Giggling, she said, "Oh, I don't know. I guess at the time, I thought I saw something in the cave. But who knows, maybe it was just some reflection from the water and the beam from the flashlight."

Carrie seemed somewhat mollified, but was obviously still trying to process the information in a way she could fit into her concept of reality. "Maybe these stones made you hallucinate. Maybe you just *thought* you were small and invisible. I mean, are you sure that was tobacco that chick gave you in those cigarettes?"

For a moment Annie was tempted to allow herself to be offended that her friend wouldn't believe her. Carrie even had the gall to doubt Uncle Alistair's research. On the other hand, she knew Carrie very well and knew she was nothing if not down-to-earth and practical. Carrie, like many, seemed to have a notion that only what textbook science and our five senses told us was true. Nothing else was possible. She knew she'd need to work to broaden Carrie's perspective. But not tonight. She felt sleep overpowering her. "Yeah, maybe," she answered sleepily. "Carrie, I think I need to sleep now."

The two friends said goodnight and Carrie quietly left Annie in the guest room. As soon as the door was closed, Annie plopped her head on to the pillow with an exasperated sigh.

"I am sorry, Anya," came the familiar voice from the pillow beside her head. "I am afraid having an ethereal being for a boyfriend is not easy. You want to share this joy with those dear to your heart but not all people are in the same place, spiritually or emotionally."

"Why do people have to be so blind? I mean, what do they think is beyond their little universe? I've always thought it more difficult to conceive of infinite nothingness beyond what we know than the idea that all things are in some form of order because we are inside a vast mind."

"Do not be too hard on your friend. People find a zone of comfort in one set of beliefs or another and hesitate to question what is beyond that comfort zone."

"But it's not like Carrie never believed in anything super-natural—or at least, she used to."

"Again, comfort zone. You wouldn't want her to believe everything she hears, would you?"

"No, but I hardly think her lifelong best friend fits into the category of 'everything she hears.' "

"You are right. Sorry. I just meant that in the human state, we have five senses, a brain, and a spirit, and many do not acknowledge the latter. The human brain is perfectly adequate for life on Earth, but only the spirit can really fathom the whole of existence. Of course, some ingenious brains, and especially those whose creativity has been cultivated, can fathom parts of the broader picture. But don't be hard on one who cannot yet see a spiritual truth. Perhaps in time, she will be able to see. Pushing one too hard can cause a backlash or mental illness because that brain is not ready to go beyond certain boundaries of comfort. Why do you think humans so love to taunt them-selves with evil legends that are not 'really true?' "

Without waiting for a response he continued. "It is because they want to ease into ideas that are broader than their own realm of experience without actually losing control. Like dipping one's toe in the water to test the temperature before taking the plunge. Anya, that day in the pool, you did not dip your toe, but dove right in. That is the difference between you and your friend. She may not even be ready to dip a toe. But you can help her expand her horizons gently, as a true friend."

Annie was almost asleep now. "But what you said does take some of the fun out of visiting Transylvania—I don't think I wanted to rationalize that."

She heard Aaan laugh heartily and felt him pat her head. "Ah, my Tiny Bold Maiden—let's hope you are not too bold for your own good."

Over the course of the next few days, Annie and Carrie slipped back into their comfortable constant banter on many topics: music, school, boys, movies, books, clothes, videos— everything except another attempt to seriously talk about Aaan. There was some degree of teasing, mostly in the context of Dracula and their upcoming trip to Transylvania. But Annie steered away from teasing very much about anything related to Aaan—she still hoped to be able to work her friend into a receptive mood and introduce him to her, or at least own up to the fact that he was real.

Annie could tell Carrie had been particularly lonesome since her only sibling had gone away to college. Annie resolved to focus for now on giving her friend some companionship and listening as much as contributing to their conversations. She learned that though Carrie had enjoyed a few crushes and flirtations, she really hadn't started dating yet. She was mostly focusing on her studies. Her brother had gotten into Yale and her parents hoped she'd have similar success.

As the second week of her stay wore on, Annie was getting more and more excited for the upcoming weekend because Carrie's parents had surprised them by announcing they were going to stay in a castle on a Transylvanian mountaintop, right out of the pages of Bram Stoker. And there was to be a costume ball on Saturday night. Annie had known all along they were going to drive into the mountains and sightsee, but this was truly the icing on the cake.

She and Carrie shopped long and hard and each picked out a very cute dress and mask. Carrie's was silver, with an amazing sheen, and Annie's was black. Annie had seen many beautiful dresses of perhaps more interesting colors, but she was still into her Goth mode too much to bypass an opportunity to dress in all black—dress, shoes, feathery mask. But she did let Carrie talk her into silver metallic fingernail polish and a nice, deep, red lip gloss.

Annie, in preparation for the trip, had purchased an audio book version of Bram Stoker's *Dracula* for her iPod. On the drive up in the backseat of Carrie's parents' plush sedan, she and Carrie each used one earbud to listen to the book. By the time they arrived in the picturesque locale, it almost seemed to Annie they were living in the pages of the book.

Annie got the impression Carrie's parents considered this a romantic getaway for themselves and seemed content to allow the young people the run of the castle. Carrie and Annie shared a room with one old-fashioned bed, narrow but tall, with wooden steps to climb up. Annie loved the antique and authentic furniture and the small, cozy room with its own fireplace grate, but was a little dismayed she'd have no privacy from Carrie. How could she converse with Aaan? But this was only for two nights, she reasoned; she'd have to make the best of it.

Once they had hung their dresses in the small wardrobe and unpacked as much as they could into the small drawers of the dresser, Carrie announced she was going to search for the bath, which was shared with other tenants and had been retrofitted with at least the minimum modern conveniences, including a shower.

As soon as she left the room, Annie was almost afraid to look behind her, expecting another prank by her favorite apparition. She was seated on a puffy dressing stool, looking into an ornate oval mirror, when she saw movement behind her. She giggled as she watched a black-caped, sleek-haired Dracula slowly approach from behind, his arm hiding his fangs. His head bent slowly down, his mouth inching toward the crook of her neck.

"Hey Drac, don't think you'll find much there, because I'm famished. I think I'm probably dehydrated, too, but knock yourself out."

He made a growling, ravenous sound as he tickled her neck with his mouth and nose, making her jerk away, laughing. She let her head fall back as though she'd fainted and he took the cue, making the growling ravenous sounds once again against her neck. A tap at the door made her jump and he instantly disappeared.

"Who is it?" she called.

"Hi Annie, it's just me." Annie recognized Carrie's mom's voice. "Just wanted to let you girls know we're going down to the dining room now. As soon as you girls get ready, come on down, okay?"

"Okay, thanks."

Aaan followed her to dinner and seemed to enjoy this excursion. She saw him walk by their table a couple of times, still dressed as Dracula, once carrying a wine bottle and once a tray, pretending to be one of the wait staff. This was possible because a few of the employees were dressed as Dracula and no one seemed to notice one more—except Annie. He winked at Annie each time and she suppressed a giggle.

Annie was a tad disappointed to find the castle was touristy. She'd expected more of a real Middle Ages-type of experience. But this was fun and Carrie seemed to get a kick out of it. And Aaan was certainly having a good time.

Later that evening, Annie realized having the bath outside of their quarters was actually a way to escape from Carrie's constant company and at least speak with Aaan for a few minutes. After her nighttime teeth-brushing and face-washing, she explored further down the hallway, dressed in a flannel gown to take the edge off the chill of the mountain air.

She found a door that opened out onto a balcony and a cylindrical tower with a winding stair descending steeply at the end, furthest away from the modern elevator lobby. She slipped out onto the balcony and saw an amazing lightshow overhead. So many stars.

She realized then just how remote they were up in the mountains. She could see very little of the jagged mountain shapes jutting off to the northeast because of the late hour. But she could see a full moon off to the west reflecting somewhere far below in a silvery sliver of water.

She caught a movement overhead—a shooting star—then felt an arm around her shoulder. She leaned her head into Aaan's neck, under his chin, and they stood silently for several moments, enjoying the magical world of the Transylvanian Alps at night.

CHAPTER 5

Spiritual Infancy

FRIDAY, JULY 11
4 P.M. IN MARYLAND
11 P.M. IN TRANSYLVANIA

"Erik, didn't you learn anything from my hellish experience? I mean, good grief—she's only a kid. Is she even out of middle school yet?" Roy was obviously riled.

"Of course Annie's out of middle school, *Roy*." Erik spat the name, not appreciating this interference. He let out an exasperated huff as if he'd already said this many times. "She's sixteen, a high school junior, and smart as a tack—she could easily graduate early and go to college next year if she wanted. She's very responsible. For crying out loud, she's traveled all over the world by herself since she was a kid. And not gotten into any trouble or become possessed by any demons, unlike some people I know."

"That was low, even for you. And at least I didn't get lost in an alternate universe."

Erik eyed Roy and felt mutual anger seethe between them for a moment and then felt a laugh coming on. He saw Roy break as well.

Erik's wry humor still tickling, he tried again, "Listen, Roy, I know this angel, Aaan. He's okay. Really. He helped Professor Hamilton, didn't he? And he rescued him. You know if he'd been on the dark side, he wouldn't have helped us. You were there. How can you think he's a demon?"

Roy appeared to have calmed down as well and resumed his work at a lab bench, taking weights and measurements of various stones, seeming to want to occupy his hands as he spoke. "I don't trust any of them. Why wouldn't he possess someone if he could? I mean, it's gotta get pretty boring living on Earth as a spirit for centuries on end. In a cave? Come on, Erik. Believe me, comrade. You don't want to let one of those bastards inside you. It's hell on earth."

Erik could see he was getting agitated again.

Roy lay down the stones he'd been holding and looked Erik in the eye. "I mean, Erik, I didn't want to act like that. I was still in there, but it was like I had no choice any longer. It was like being trapped in a bad movie. I had all this anger and hatred and it seemed to be controlled by someone else. It was like someone else was squirting in a dose of rage at just the right moment to make me behave violently in a given situation. I can still remember everything and it'll haunt me to the grave." He banged his fist on the counter and looked away.

"Roy, I know you went through hell. But please try not to think about it. It's all over now. You don't have that nasty thing in you anymore. And believe me, I saw it—it was nasty. It looked nothing like Aaan," Erik said. "Roy, you know how it is in the transformed state, seeing essences. It's like a way of seeing how good or bad a spirit is by how pure or murky the essence is—at least, that's how I interpret it. And Aaan has a pure essence. I'm sure he's okay."

"I'd like to believe that, but I just don't know, Erik."

"I mean, you're studying theology—doesn't anything you've learned teach you that angels have a choice to be good or bad, just like we do? And Aaan obviously chose good—I mean, you were here when Hamilton had that team of priests bless the lab. I don't know how well that sort of thing works, but it seemed pretty convincing to me. I, for one, don't think Aaan would be able to hang around here if he were evil."

Roy appeared to think a minute. He started to speak but seemed to think better of it, then said, "Erik, I hear what you're saying. It was just so horrible I think it'll take time for me to sort it all out."

"Fair enough." Erik smiled encouragingly at his friend. "Guess we'd better end this discussion anyway, since the object of the discussion will be here any minute."

Roy nodded, then stretched. "Think I'll walk over to the grill for some coffee—you want anything?"

"No, I'm good."

Erik looked up from his work to think for a moment now that the lab was quiet. He had made the most of the time he had been given to work with Aaan. Aaan usually appeared each day in the late afternoon somewhere between four and five o'clock, depending on what time Annie fell asleep, then disappeared in time to be back when Annie awoke each morning at seven Bucharest time, which was midnight in the lab. To be honest with himself, Erik had a hard time filling even that much time with new things to try. He was becoming more and more frustrated. He knew he was missing something, and it was probably something very simple and obvious. But he couldn't for the life of him put his finger on it.

Erik's thoughts turned to a conversation he'd had with Aaan the day before, when Aaan had asked him to explain how the STAG controls worked. "Well, what I learned from earlier research was that a magnet is needed to activate the stones; their action is linked to the direction of electron flow." He'd stopped, somewhat embarrassed. "Do you know about magnets?"

"Yes, of course. Why would I not?" Aaan had said this without a hint of defensiveness, just a question.

"Well, because you haven't been to school in modern times, right?" Erik certainly hadn't wanted to offend him. He knew he seemed very wise but wasn't sure how much practical knowledge he'd learned.

"Yes, of course, I see your point. But you do not need to hold back. I have read extensively. I have had much time to do so. And I have attended the occasional class when I wanted to hear a lecture. I have listened to lectures by Socrates, Aristotle, Jesus, two of the Buddahs, Confucius, and many modern lecturers. I have browsed the libraries and museums of Alexandria, Rome, London and New York, to name only a few. But you had no way of knowing this. So, please, do not be embarrassed at your assumption. I did sleep many decades in my cave, but then, I had many decades—nay centuries—to explore, and even when I slept, I awoke from time to time and had a learning adventure."

"Yes, of course." Erik had been awed by this proclamation. He valued learning so very much and this was someone who not only valued it but had accessed information he could only dream of accessing. "Wow."

"You were saying—about the magnets?"

Erik no longer held back then, but explained all he understood about the action on quarks and electrons and the flow of energy being activated by magnets, or reversed by switching the position of the magnets to the opposite polarity. He explained that the three stones were now locked away at the Vatican, but the research team had retained some dust particles from each stone, which they'd used to create the STAG controls. The controls themselves were simple. Each operable button exposed the dust from one or more stones to a magnetic field of one polarity or the other and opened a laser connection between the hand-held control, formerly a television remote control, and the object to which it was pointed. Erik showed Aaan the labeled map of the buttons and their functions.

"I see." Aaan nodded his head thoughtfully. "So, you have tried exposing me to each stone, separately and in combination?"

"Yes, that's exactly what I've done so far. Every possible combination of stones and polarities. And nothing. Then, I thought that just as the magnets were needed to activate the other two stones, perhaps some other type of material might be needed in conjunction with the Angel Stone. So, I've tried many different types of natural stones and even some man-made elements. Still nothing. But as long as you're willing to allow me to experiment on you, I'll keep trying."

"Please do whatever is needed. I, too, wish to solve the mystery. I just don't understand why the Angel Stone will not work on me. Perhaps it is because of my half-breed makeup."

"Well, we aren't going to give up, so don't despair." Erik knew he sounded more confident than he felt. He'd tried pretty much everything he could think of. "I hate to say this, but I guess we do need to consider that someone could've switched that stone long ago. But I don't really think that's it, because the three had identical casings around them. So let's keep trying. Hey, it took a while to decipher the codes of the other two stones as well."

Now, Erik drummed his fingers on the lab bench, deep in thought. Something. Something was just out of reach. What was it he was missing? A few minutes later, Aaan appeared.

Erik beheld the peaceful face. Even without being under the transformation that allowed him to see essences, he could clearly see this wasn't an evil being. "Hello, friend," he said with special enthusiasm, needing to counter some of Roy's bad vibes.

"Hello to you as well." Aaan nodded his head in a sincere way that made Erik think this was the true sentiment modern day head-nodding only implied. His nod seemed to come from an ancient place—the old world, where mere body language could get you crowned or run through with a sword. *How could anyone think this being evil?*

"Ready for more tests? Hey, we're going to crack this code. Solve this mystery."

"Yes, I am ready." Aaan's voice revealed a hint of excitement. Erik looked quizzically at him, but Aaan did not say anything else.

Roy returned from the grill, sipping from a large Styrofoam cup. He usually seemed to avoid the lab when Aaan was there, and Erik was glad he did. But today, he was hanging around. With Professor Hamilton still on his honeymoon, Roy's funding for literature searches had almost played out and he still needed to be at Georgetown at least one more semester before finishing his degree, so Erik had been instructed to give Roy work out of the grant he used for the laboratory part of the research. Erik sometimes wished he'd finish and move on out of the picture. Roy had been his friend for a long time, but something in his own feelings for Roy had been lost when he saw Roy's weakness cause such trouble for others. He just didn't trust him fully yet— perhaps he hadn't forgiven him, either. And the way Roy made no bones about the fact that he didn't like having Aaan around made him somewhat uncomfortable having the two in the lab together. But what could he do? He knew he should forgive and forget. Some things just needed to play themselves out.

Aaan seemed to sense Erik's hesitancy. Glancing toward Roy, he held his tongue until he and Erik walked over to the staging area for the experiments. Roy seemed busy with his task and had earbuds in, so they resumed their conversation.

"What's up, Aaan? You seem bursting to tell me something." Erik smiled.

"I suppose I am. Anya may have solved the mystery for us."

"Oh, do tell."

"Last night we were talking and I suppose I was indulging in a bit of self-pity at the lack of progress we are making and attributed it to my half-breed nature, as I am wont to do for many problems that come my way." He looked down and then back at Erik. "So, my dear one suggested that it was almost like each nature 'cancelled' the other." He looked very satisfied, as though he was waiting for Erik to have an *ah-ha* moment.

"Go on ... " Erik said.

"I think the beams coming from the STAG controls are cancelling each other," Aaan said. "The two states are very different. While the other two stones may be used in the same control together, for the Angel Stone beam to work, perhaps it must not touch the other beams."

Erik's brain was churning. Then suddenly he got it. He almost shouted, slamming his fist down on the lab bench. "*Of course!*"

Roy glanced up at the shout but seemed not to catch the importance of their discovery, and so resumed his work.

"*Triangulate*," Erik cried. "That is what is needed. Three STAG controls, each activated for only one stone, laid in a circle with you at the center point."

"Exactly what I was thinking."

It took only a few minutes to set the STAG controls in configuration to triangulate the three beams to converge on a single spot, with Aaan positioned so the locus was in the center of his torso.

"Remember the plan?" Erik knew he did because they'd gone over it so many times in the past when they had thought they might be successful, but this time, he thought the plan would actually be put to use.

"Yes, return here in an estimated half hour. Since I will have no timepiece, you will focus the beams every ten minutes for one hour. If I do not return, you will do this every day for one week, same time."

"Correct. Good luck, my friend."

Erik noticed Roy look up just in time to see Aaan disappear. This obviously caught his attention and he sauntered over. "So, it worked. Nice going, Erik. Professor Hamilton will be pleased, I guess, though I can't for the life of me see the utility of this. I mean, food storage is one thing, but angel transportation?"

"Does everything have to have a practical use? Can't some things just be interesting?" Roy was getting on his nerves. He didn't feel like having to explain. It just didn't seem worth it.

He decided to make notes on his clipboard of the exact time and settings of the STAG controls. He knew it was so easy to forget numbers even when you thought you'd remember. A distraction occurs and the numbers go right out of your head.

After twenty minutes, he began to get very excited to hear what Aaan would report. He began to look toward the locus of the three beams, drawn there because he knew something really tremendous and important had happened at that spot.

He was still deep in thought when his cell phone rang. He glanced at it and saw the caller was his mom.

"Hello, Mom—what's up?" he said cheerfully, realizing how excited his voice sounded.

His excitement was dashed in an instant when a strange male voice said urgently, "Sir, I'm sorry to have to tell you this, but there's been a traffic accident. I'm a bystander here on the Beltway. A man and woman are being loaded into an ambulance and will be taken to Suburban Hospital. Your number was the first one on this cell phone so I called it."

"Are they alive?" Erik's felt his voice shake.

"Yes, but both are unconscious. That's about all I know."

"Thank you very much. I'm on my way." Erik almost bolted from the lab but then remembered that in eight minutes, Aaan would return. "Roy!"

Roy asked urgently, "Erik, what's happened? What can I do?"

Erik felt breathless as he forced out, "Mom and Dad had a car accident. I'm going to Suburban. At exactly 5:10, please open one beam on each of the STAG controls, each a different stone, for a total of three stones—got it? They are set to triangulate at this point." He walked over to the spot and pointed it out. "Got it?"

Roy nodded.

"If for some reason, he doesn't show, you know the drill—every ten minutes, okay?"

"Erik, don't worry about a thing. Just go to your parents. I've got this covered."

A few minutes later, Roy felt discomfort and anxiety rise like bile in his throat; he didn't want to have anything to do with this. He had never agreed with Erik that they should be experimenting on that abomination. Yet now he was supposed to help out?

He threw his empty coffee cup into a metal trashcan with more force than usual, noticing how good it felt to throw something away—to cast off debris from his life. Then he picked up one of the STAG controls and turned it over in his hands thoughtfully. *I don't think so,* he thought gravely. He laid it back down, looked at his watch, and leaned against a nearby lab bench, considering.

At 5:10, he pushed away from the lab bench and paced around the configuration. Taking a deep breath, he said, "Aaan, nothing personal, but I'm not going to bring you back. I've had enough of your kind. I know what you're capable of. You should leave this place, and leave that little girl alone. We don't want your kind around here." He then picked up the STAG controls, locked them in the safe, and went home.

CHAPTER 6

Transylvanian Night

SATURDAY, JULY 12

The next morning, Annie and Carrie took a nature hike on a mountain trail, and then, after a nice lunch in the dining room, a guided tour of the castle. Annie liked each activity, especially the mountain views; something about looking off from a height made her feel like she was able to connect with the joy of flying. And the castle tour had been a perfect way to get into the mindset of the upcoming costume ball. She got a feel for how people lived during the Middle Ages, how food had been prepared and fires kept. She got to see a dungeon and wondered if it was authentic. She saw a beautiful library with rolling mahogany ladders to reach books on shelves twenty feet up. She even got to tour the stables, where horses were still kept. She hoped they might have time to take a carriage ride over the mountain road before they left on Sunday. She could imagine herself riding in a carriage, hearing werewolves in the distance.

She half-expected to see Aaan appear, but didn't see him at all during the morning, or at least, didn't recognize him if she did. He could take on any form, though, and she was sure he was nearby.

By the time the tour was finished, both she and Carrie were so excited to prepare for the ball they convinced Carrie's parents to dine early with them so they could spend time showering and doing hair and nails.

Annie didn't see Aaan in his Dracula costume or any other guise in the dining room even though she surveyed each and every guest, looking for a hint of recognition. She was disappointed. But she brushed it off, ate up, and rushed upstairs to get ready. No Aaan again—she wondered if he'd gone to the lab early tonight and thought it more likely that he was planning a surprise for her at the costume ball. She thought he might surprise her there as Dracula and smiled at the thought.

As Annie and Carrie entered the ballroom, Annie was pleasantly surprised to see several heads turn. She wasn't accustomed to dressing up or trying to look sexy. Tonight, more than any time ever before in her life, Annie felt a heady power at the unmistakably admiring glances from several people around the room. She imagined herself and Carrie as two enchantresses, one dressed in silver and one in black, gliding down the massive staircase leading into the foyer off the ballroom, their gloved hands moving as smooth as silk on the mahogany handrail.

After a moment's hesitation in the entryway, she began to feel self-conscious and slowly moved into the room. The room was large, with an enormous chandelier hanging from an outlandishly high ceiling. A few couples already twirled to the music from the small orchestra playing on a raised platform off to one side. Most of the ladies in the room were dressed in a style similar to Carrie and herself, with traditional masquerade garb—there was only one Catwoman and one female vampire. The men seemed to be of two kinds—Count Draculas and those who wanted to be different from Count Dracula. There was one Phantom of the Opera, two Elvises, one Hulk, and one red devil. The red devil caught her eye because he stood out with his red bodysuit stretched tight over his muscular frame. He had a forked tail and horns, but the thing Annie noticed was his incredible makeup job—his red skin caused his eyes and teeth to glisten in the soft light. Carrie tugged at Annie's arm to point him out. While both girls were looking in his direction, he looked up and made a slight wave of greeting.

At the same instant, a Dracula turned to the girls slowly. Annie's heart skipped a beat when she thought she recognized Aaan. Of course; she had been right—he'd stayed away today to surprise her and be her dance partner.

Annie would've walked right up to him, but Carrie stopped her with the hand she still had on Annie's forearm. Annie regretted now that Carrie didn't know Aaan and that she still had to pretend he wasn't real. But she was happy with his brilliant idea of interacting with her at a costume ball—what better place to be *incognito*?

Carrie motioned to some seats around the wall, but Annie wasn't about to sit—she wanted to dance.

Carrie shrugged and allowed herself to be dragged to a spot on the edge of the room, where the two stood together in an area where a few other wallflowers were hanging out.

Oh no. Annie noticed an Elvis walking their way. But to her relief, she saw that Aaan and the devil were also approaching now; somehow they managed to arrive first.

"Ladies, if I may be so bold, please allow me to introduce myself and my friend," the Count said. "I am Count Dracula and this is Diavol."

Annie spoke first. "We are delighted to make your acquaintance. I am Noir and this is Argent."

Dracula took Annie's hand and raised it to his lips. "May I have the honor of this dance?"

"I would be delighted." She glanced toward Carrie and was relieved to see that she seemed to be having a pleasant chat with Diavol.

Annie had never before danced with Aaan and, for that matter, had never really done ballroom dancing, but she knew the steps from dance classes over the years and more recently from her Wii dance game. The whole thing seemed effortless and she was amazed at her own confident movements. She was pretty sure in this case, though, that it was largely due to the expert guidance from her partner.

She caught a flash of red moving nearby and had to suppress a giggle at seeing Carrie and Diavol also gliding smoothly over the floor. He seemed to be an expert dancer, as well. It was just that his skin-tight, red body suit looked absurd. She refocused her attention on her own partner and decided to be content with allowing Carrie to fend for herself.

"Who's your friend?" she asked.

"Dunno. Just some bloke I met here and passed time chatting with 'til you arrived."

Annie raised an eyebrow. She wasn't used to hearing Aaan speak so casually. He was usually so formal in his speech. She shrugged inwardly, deciding he was probably just having a good time.

After three songs, Dracula steered Annie to a bar set up on one side of the room. "Care for a drink?"

"Of alcohol? Is that legal here?" Annie hadn't considered it might be legal for her to drink in Romania.

"You have to be eighteen to purchase alcohol, but its consumption is not governed by the laws." Dracula had a mischievous look Annie had never seen before.

"Trying to get me drunk, sailor?" she asked.

He simply chuckled. "What'll it be? Champagne?"

"Okay." It seemed like a fun adventure, but Annie cast a nervous glance toward Carrie to make sure she was okay. After all, she was a guest of Carrie's parents and didn't want to have them angry at her. Carrie was still dancing with Mr. Red Spandex and seemed to be content. By the time she looked back to Dracula, he was already pressing a fluted champagne glass into her hand.

"To a fun evening," he said and clinked glasses with her.

This didn't sound like the Aaan she knew, though she supposed after being around for several millennia, one was likely to have various facets to one's personality.

Annie was glad to have an opportunity to openly dance with Aaan without anyone being the wiser. And yet, something wasn't right. As they gyrated to a jazzy beat, she thought this should be the highlight of her life. But somehow, she really just wanted to be with Aaan back at the Swan Hole, or in her room, having quiet time. She wondered about the change in him and whether he might be changing his attitude toward her. She didn't want to think of that. Despite the difference in their states of being, he was irresistible to her—she'd let him into her heart. She didn't understand this thing between them. He wouldn't even kiss her. And the difference in their ages! She scoffed at the absurdity and had to swallow hard a hysterical laugh she felt threatening to burst from her mouth.

The song ended and she saw Carrie walk off the dance floor, followed by Mr. Red-Spandex, and decided to follow suit. By the time they got to the edge of the dance floor, Carrie had apparently already excused herself from her dance partner and looked imploringly to Annie. "I'm off to the ladies room. Want to come?"

What girl could resist the age-old practice of going to the ladies room with a best friend to talk about guys? "Sure," Annie said, excusing herself from Dracula and following her friend.

Once inside, she noted the ornate and obviously expensive furnishings of the large downstairs ladies room—many times larger than the tiny retrofitted bath they shared with several other guests upstairs. A plush entryway contained a couch, several mirrors, and tissue boxes for dabbing makeup. She excitedly sat and pulled Carrie down beside her, anxious to catch up with all the amazing happenings of this evening. "So Carrie, what do you think about Diavol? You like him?"

"I don't know, Annie. I mean, he's kinda cute, but ... he also kinda, well, gives me the creeps," Carrie said uncomfortably. "What about your guy? Dracula?"

"Oh, Carrie, I really do like him. He seems really nice and he's sooooo hot." Annie stomped her feet excitedly.

Carrie shared her excitement by taking both her hands, shaking them, and squealing before saying, "You go, girl."

They each took a quick inventory in the mirror and Carrie touched up her hair as Annie reapplied lip gloss. Carrie said, "I think I might dance a couple more dances, and call it a night. I don't really want to spend a whole evening with Diavol. Don't you think he's a little odd? No one else is dressed so elaborately in a skin-tight body suit. I mean, his body looks good. Looks like he works out. But I dunno. Maybe he's a narcissist and is showing off. I just couldn't really see myself with him."

As she pushed the door open to return to the dance floor, Annie caught sight of Diavol across the room. He was futzing with a stray lock of hair, and Annie couldn't help but gawk at the absurd sight of his bulging body in the spandex, showing every detail.

"I see what you mean. To be honest, I think I'd ditch him too," Annie said. "I think I'm going to stay a while longer, though, 'cause I kinda like Dracula, but you can go up anytime. I brought my key."

Back on the dance floor, Annie danced a few more dances, and then, looking around, noted that Carrie was gone. She didn't see Diavol anywhere either. She hoped Carrie hadn't had difficulty getting rid of him.

She pulled Dracula off the dance floor at the end of the song and had to shout to be heard over the loud din of the now-crowded room. "Looks like Carrie turned in already. Did you see that Diavol guy leave?"

"No, maybe ... " He said more but Annie couldn't make it out.

"What?" she shouted into his ear.

"Come, let's go outside for a walk so we can talk where it's quieter." She heard enough of that to make out the gist and enthusiastically nodded her head.

He took her hand and pulled her through the crowd out into the opulent foyer and then through heavy wooden doors out into the fresh, cool air. The air was so refreshing that Annie had to just stop a moment and enjoy the freedom to breathe and move without bumping into someone.

She hadn't realized until she looked up toward the stars that she felt a little tipsy. How many glasses of champagne did Dracula bring her? It seemed like she never really finished one, but always had plenty in her glass. She was pretty sure he'd produced a new one a couple of times, placing it into her hand as if it were the same glass and saying, "Drink up." It was a fun lark to be here where the drinking laws permitted her to have a glass of champagne, but she now wished she'd paid more attention to the amount she'd consumed.

Perhaps, given Aaan's different form of existence, he hadn't realized what he was doing. It occurred to her that she hadn't ever asked him about eating and drinking. She didn't think he consumed food while in his spirit form, but when he materialized, he evidently did so because she was certain he'd been drinking champagne, as well.

She almost tripped on a root as he pulled her along a path leading into the heavily wooded area surrounding the northern end of the castle. "Hey, Aaan, slow down." *My high heels aren't intended to be hiking shoes*, she almost said.

"Sorry," he said flatly, not turning to look at her, still pulling her forward.

"Where the heck are we going?" She was beginning to get irritated, in part because a hint of a headache was already forming and she felt tired all of a sudden.

"Just up ahead. You'll see."

They began to climb some stone steps and Annie was glad there was an iron handrail, its posts seemingly embedded into the large stones that jutted up from the ground. Once they got to the top, Annie saw another set of stone steps going down onto an overlook off the eastern side of the mountain. Not hesitating at the top, Dracula pulled her forward, down the steps and onto the platform. Annie felt a cool mountain breeze picking up, as though a storm was approaching.

The same starry sky shone overhead, though this lookout faced east so the rising moon was behind the trees. Annie looked around and drank in the breezy summer air and the dark and light contrasts of the glowing cinders in the sky and the dark, foreboding shapes of the trees swaying in the breeze behind them. It was so similar to last night when they'd been out on the balcony, yet somehow different. Perhaps it was that she'd still been within the safety of the castle, merely out on a balcony, but tonight she and Aaan were out in the Transylvanian night.

She looked up into Aaan's face, hoping for comfort, but something was different. His usual glow, which he allowed to show when no one else was around, wasn't as bright as it should've been; it was more like a fading candle. His eyes held none of their usual loving yearning. He didn't look her in the eyes. His facial expression seemed hard, sad. Something was wrong.

"Aaan, what's wrong? You frighten me." She could only muster a whisper that competed with the sound of the wind, but he heard.

"Anya, I need your help." He now looked into her eyes and then quickly looked away.

"Yes, of course, Aaan. Anything. What is it?" She felt her speech slur, and she swayed a little with the breeze, but the worry of the moment took away the tipsy feeling and replaced it with adrenaline.

"I am to be reincarnated ... tomorrow. But I don't want to be parted from you."

"Oh, no. What can we do?" Annie felt hot tears spring into her eyes. How could she lose him now?

He took her squarely by the shoulders and looked into her eyes. She felt a strange feeling, not the usual loving feeling, but more a feeling of wicked foreboding. And yet, an irresistible draw, like a moth to a flame.

"Annie, you have to allow me to possess you. To live in your body for a while, until we can figure something out."

"But you said—"

"Never mind what I said," he snapped, showing a side of him she'd never seen.

He seemed to be struggling and after a moment seemed to will himself to calm down. "I'm sorry. It's just, the thought of losing you ... it makes me crazy. Annie, it will be all right. Just give me permission and we will always be together."

"Aaan, of course ... but ... "

"Please, Anya. You must do this." His fingers cut into her upper arms.

"Aaan, you're hurting me."

His hands immediately dropped from her arms. He took a moment, apparently to steady himself. He ran his fingers through his hair, then turned away. Leaning on the wall of the overlook, he looked out over the valley below.

Annie focused on trying to calm herself, which was challenging given the ever-increasing speed of the wind. It was getting difficult to talk. "Aaan, hadn't we better go back? I think it's going to storm." She longed for the security of the immense stone castle.

He shouted now over the wind. "You go if that's what you want. But this is it. If you go back, you will never see me again." He did not look at her, but continued to stare out over the valley.

Annie felt her knees go weak. How could she leave him like this? He'd saved her uncle and now she was denying him the help he needed. She felt this whole night was somehow wrong. Ruined. Not fun anymore. But she simply couldn't leave him. She loved him.

"Okay," she whispered. There was no possible way his ears could've heard this over the wind, yet somehow he did hear and his head snapped around.

"What did you say?" His expression was different now, very intense.

"Okay," she shouted, a little angry with herself for giving in when she didn't feel right about it and at him for putting her in this spot. Weeks earlier, she'd have gladly done this, but after he told her it'd be bad to allow him to possess her, she'd believed him. Now why was he taking it all back? Something was different about him. But nagging fear kept saying that this was it—she'd lose him if she didn't act quickly. He was so handsome and knew so much of the world. And he needed her. She didn't know what was happening and didn't entirely trust the situation, but felt she had no choice. She trusted him — at least the Aaan she had known before today. The thing she feared most was losing him.

He slowly approached her. As he looked into her face, his sideways grin seemed to hold a hint of mockery. "That's my girl," he said and laughed heartily, his head thrown back. And then he was gone.

CHAPTER 7

Journey into the Realm of Angels

FRIDAY, JULY 11—THE DAY BEFORE
4:40 PM IN MARYLAND
11:40 PM IN TRANSYLVANIA

Aaan felt a snap and then the world changed all around him. He had already been able to see angels, but now he could see them in a much clearer sense. It was as if before they had been ethereal, ghostlike, but now they were solid—their forms appeared identical to his own. He drifted upward, the lab building extremely faint now, as was the fountain atop the hill and the people. Less distinct than a ghost, more a vague mist. He could still make out essences, but these, too, were faint. He surely was in the realm of angels. He could see them so distinctly that they now seemed much more numerous than before. Or was he seeing further? He looked up and realized he could see details on the surface of the moon, already visible — would it have been visible this early if he were untransformed? He didn't know.

He could still see angels zipping in all directions. He had always assumed they were carrying messages to higher angels or to God. Now he could see the atmosphere was filled with golden paths on which the angels traveled. He looked down and saw two vague student forms walk by, their guardian angels hovering overhead, now much more distinct than the humans. To his surprise, both angels looked at him and nodded amiably. He returned the nods and smiled. They smiled back and glided away, following the path of the students. *Now, this is something that has never happened before. Wow.* He was really in the realm of angels. They could see him and seemed to think him a fellow angel. He had never been treated like one of them before. This was something new and good.

He looked upward, wondering if he had time during his allotted half-hour to pursue one of the golden beams to see where it led. Perhaps he should not take such a chance today. He did not want to lose his chance to return to Anya. He would arrange with Erik for a longer stay in the transformed state so he could pursue the beams.

His objective was to gather information and figure out where his mother was. This was now an even more important consideration because he needed to know if it were possible for him and Anya to go to the same place in the afterlife. It had evidently not been possible for his parents to do so and he thought this was what had driven his father over the edge into the clutches of the evil one. Or perhaps it was an evil realm? He wasn't sure. All he knew was that evil existed. There were numerous stories of evil beings and he had seen fallen angels — they were not a pretty sight. But he did not know the extent or if one particular being was in charge.

He thought about trying to strike up a conversation with the next guardian angel he saw. He stopped a moment to savor the beauty. The land of angels was breathtaking — the golden ribbons of trails, the clarity of far-away vistas, and the sheer beauty of the angelic beings. Their robes flowed and their faces shone. He had never before been able to witness their warm beauty; rather, he had always sensed their scowl of disapproval directed toward him.

He tried to look at his own form to see if he looked like them. Hands and body looked identical to theirs — his robes flowed as if by some magical wind. He wanted so much for Anya to see all of this. Even with the perfect beauty of the angels all around, to him, Anya's beauty was still superior. The angels were pure and glowed with a silvery light, but Anya's essence had something that interested him far beyond the pure beauty of the angels — she was different. Like a work of art.

As he pondered and observed, a movement below caught his attention. One of the guardian angels moved rapidly, following her ward, who was running from the building below to the parking lot. The human looked like Erik, though he could not see him very clearly and he was facing away.

It couldn't be Erik; Erik would not leave the lab with him in this transformed state. Still, he thought his time would be over soon and he had better make sure he was in place for the transformation back. He couldn't wait to tell Erik and Anya all about his adventure and make plans for a lengthier transformation so he could make some progress on his search for knowledge.

He returned to the spot in the lab, but found that Erik was indeed gone. This troubled him, but he trusted that Erik would be back. He was very good at reading essences and Erik was one that could be trusted.

The other researcher, Roy, was working in the lab. His essence was not as clear as Erik's. It was not nearly so murky as many he had seen, however, and he thought Roy was likely on the road to spiritual growth. Not a bad person—more a spiritual infant.

He watched Roy work, placing a test tube from a small wooden rack into some type of meter, then writing something on a clipboard. Then he replaced the test tube and repeated the process with the next tube.

He noticed that Roy kept looking at the clock. Aaan thought that he had been transformed around 4:40, which meant he'd be transformed back at 5:10. He waited and watched as Roy eventually pushed away from the lab bench where he was working and walked toward the transformation point slowly.

He saw Roy take a deep breath and then say, in a way that suggested a mixture of regret and anger, "Aaan, nothing personal, but I'm not going to bring you back. I've had enough of your kind and know what you're capable of. You should leave, and leave that little girl alone. We don't want your kind around here."

Aaan felt shocked as the words sank in. The words did not contain real malice and he could understand that Roy might feel fearful after having been possessed by something evil. But Aaan was not like that; he was not evil. How he wished he could talk to this man! All he could do was watch, helpless, as Roy picked up the STAG controls and locked them in the safe. Roy then walked toward the door, switched off the lights, and locked the door behind him.

Aaan had been through too much in his existence to panic. Problems to him were more puzzles than threats.

He thought a moment. The plan had been to try again every ten minutes for an hour and then try again at the same time the next day. He did not think returning in ten minutes would gain him an entrance back, but perhaps in twenty-four hours, Erik would be back. Surely, whatever had called him away would be over within the week. He would keep returning each day until Erik returned and zapped him back to the normal state.

In the meantime, he would check on Erik, and then would seek information. Anya would still be asleep, so he had a few hours. He hoped he could manifest himself from this state to her side just as readily. The possibility of not being able to communicate with her was something he would have to test. He would try to manifest himself to Erik. Then, if the manifestation did not work, he would figure out a way to go to her—nothing was going to keep him from Anya.

He concentrated his thoughts on Erik, and was instantaneously transported to a hospital, where Erik sat with his head drooped toward his knees, both hands on the back of his head as if in grief or extreme worry. This was not a good sign. Something dreadful must have happened to someone close to him—Red? He hoped not. That would destroy Anya.

He looked around the room and saw several others were present. An elderly lady in a wheelchair with an oxygen tube under her nose sat patiently to one side. A youth sat with both feet stretched out in front, his head leaned back against the wall, and seemed to be asleep. A poorly dressed, middle-aged couple sat deep in whispered conversation. Aaan decided not to try a manifestation here.

He waited, hoping to learn Erik's purpose for being here. After a few minutes, he decided he could look over the shoulders of some of the staff to see the names on their lists. He might be able to decipher the facts this way. He was just moving toward the two women behind a desk when he heard Erik's name called.

Erik quickly stood up and walked toward a man in a white lab coat—Aaan assumed it was a doctor. He heard the man tell Erik that his mother, Minah Wolfeningen, had a slight concussion and would be observed overnight, but that his father, Viggo

Wolfeningen, had been bandaged and was ready to go home. Aaan watched as a wave of relief washed over Erik's face and felt the same feeling himself.

He followed Erik down a hallway to a small room, where a woman was asleep on a hospital gurney, hooked to several beeping monitors. A man, presumably Erik's father, Viggo, was seated in a chair by the bedside. He looked up with a grateful expression when he saw Erik approach.

Erik embraced him and asked what happened. The two took seats next to the bed and Viggo began to fill him in. It seemed that Erik's parents had been run off the road by a hit-and-run driver. They had sideswiped a guardrail and Minah hit her head on the side window, but the accident could have been much worse. Viggo had been able to ease the car to a stop without flipping it or crashing into any other cars. The police had been called and had already questioned him.

Presently a nurse brought Viggo's discharge papers, and after much reassurance that the hospital staff would call him immediately if Minah's condition changed, Erik was able to talk Viggo into leaving the hospital to go home.

Determined to communicate with Erik so he would know that he needed to be transformed back, Aaan rode along in Erik's car.

He thought about his situation. He really did not know what Roy had in mind and whether he might lie to Erik about his decision to not bring him back. He could see Roy was not possessed again—that might have explained his behavior. But this was merely Roy being Roy. No demon involved. He suspected it was something akin to self-righteousness and fear. He had seen that before, frequently in humans with spiritual immaturity. Roy had been stung and wanted nothing to do with ethereal beings. When in doubt, reject. What were his words? Something like, *"We don't want your kind around here."*

Such fear and blame had caused countless atrocities across the centuries, and now Roy was caught up in it. Aaan saw that Roy was a loose cannon to be watched. He really needed to communicate with Erik—tonight.

Erik parked his car in the driveway of a house that Aaan suspected belonged to his parents. Aaan watched him help his father into the house and offer food, drink, and help with his bath. But Viggo shunned the offers of help. Aaan assumed he had been independent too long and was determined to fend for himself. He told his son he was tired and just wanted to go to bed so he could return very early to the hospital. Erik reluctantly concurred. Kicking off his shoes, he lounged on a sofa and recapped the whole episode to someone on his phone; Aaan was pretty sure it was Red.

Aaan decided this would be a good time to try manifesting to him. He concentrated in the usual way, but nothing seemed to happen.

He tapped Erik on the shoulder to see if anything was different. He did not feel Erik's shoulder, which was not a good sign. Erik did not respond to his touch, but kept talking.

Aaan tried again and again, concentrating harder. He remembered that it had taken some practice to learn to manifest well in his prior state; maybe with some practice now, he could master it in this state. He tried for some time, but nothing happened.

Looking at a clock on the fireplace mantel, he realized it would soon be time for Anya to awaken, and he felt anger surge inside him. Poor Anya would not know he was okay or that he was still watching over her. Roy's prejudice was rapidly becoming a serious problem.

He decided to go check on Anya, even though he would not be able to communicate with her. He left Erik, who was still talking to Red, and instantaneously materialized at the foot of Anya's bed.

Anya lay asleep, as he had left her. He tried to hold her, but his present form and hers seemed to be like a dream to each other. The hand he tried to place on her shoulder went right into it without any resistance at all. This was not good. He tried focusing with all his might to make his hand materialize in a different form, but nothing seemed to help.

Eventually, she awakened and looked around, probably for him. Her brow furrowed. How he wanted to reassure her and kiss that furrowed brow!

Still, Anya seemed to be excited about her day. He could make no progress in communicating with her. She showered, dressed, and went to knock on the door of her friend, who answered promptly. He followed as the two went downstairs to breakfast.

Aaan hung around Anya all morning as she and Carrie joined a group on a nature hike. She seemed to enjoy the natural beauty of the mountains, stopping to examine some wildflowers, and used her phone to take pictures of them.

He tried several times to manifest his form in a way she could see—he tried to tap her shoulder, make branches shake. Nothing. He couldn't communicate with her in this form. And worse, he couldn't seem to manipulate solid objects and so probably could not help her in any way if she needed him.

Aaan felt frustrated and realized that right now all he was doing was wasting time. He needed answers. Perhaps he should spend at least part of the day exploring those golden contrails to try and find a being that could advise him, some wise old angel. Somehow, he would find a way back.

He looked at Anya again and saw her giggling with her friend, just as she had done the first time he had seen her splashing at the entrance to his cave. He smiled and looked up, and in the next instant, felt himself become a mere streak of light, like a meteorite streaming upward.

Aaan saw planets and stars streak by in the darkness, but his speed was so great that their appearance blurred into what looked like a glowing tunnel. Presently, he saw blue at the end and was extruded from the tunnel onto a soft, mossy path, with mists rising on both sides, so that the obvious thing to do was walk forward.

Before him, the path climbed a green hill, topped by the most beautiful palace he had ever seen. It had white marble columns and smooth alabaster walls. The roof appeared to be made of green onyx.

He began to ascend the steps leading to a heavy door trimmed in gold with some type of green stones; perhaps malachite or emerald. He gazed at the building; it had more than a physical beauty—it also glowed with a joyful essence, he thought.

He knew he needed to keep making progress on his quest, but now felt a growing apprehension that he was unworthy to enter that grand palace.

He surveyed the surrounding vista. The land stretched on and on in all directions, but it was impossible to tell where it ended due to the mists rising from the ground all around. He saw other castles or grand halls off in the distance, each atop a similar smooth hill. Each looked equally ornate, but with different color schemes. The nearest seemed to be trimmed in rubies, and something glinted in the sun from a distant palace atop one of the hills, as if the whole palace were made of glass or diamonds.

He thought the whole land was beyond exquisite. He was a little surprised to hear birds overhead. He looked up and saw a v-formation of swans pass over him. To his left, there were fewer buildings, but taller mountains jutted skyward, densely covered with dark green trees, much like on Earth.

He took a deep breath and steadied himself to knock. Just as he was about to grasp the large golden knocker, he heard footsteps behind him.

He turned to see the wizard-like figure of a different sort of angel climbing the steps slowly, his attention on a worn copy of a small book he held in one hand. He seemed to be talking to himself as he walked.

"Hello," Aaan tried.

The white-haired, bearded figure raised his eyes to observe Aaan and politely said, "Hello. Peace be with you," and then resumed reading and mouthing the words.

Aaan waited for him to arrive on the top landing, assuming he would enter the castle, but instead, upon reaching the landing, the figure took a seat on a small marble stool placed behind an ornate marble handrail that skirted the landing on either side. He leaned his head back to relax for a moment and took a deep breath of the breeze blowing across the knoll. He looked to Aaan once again, nodded, and resumed his reading.

Feeling that he had been dismissed, Aaan returned to his previous decision to knock on the door.

He made two sharp, deep knocks and felt the weight of the golden knocker shake the door and seemingly reverberate into the inner room.

Presently, the door was dragged back by an angel looking much more polished than the figure reading nearby. Aaan thought he resembled a human butler. "Yes, may I help you?"

"Yes, thank you," Aaan said uncertainly. "My name is Aaan and I have come from Earth to ask some questions, if you please, sir."

"What do you mean, came from Earth? What were you doing on Earth? What is your current assignment?" He snapped at Aaan, apparently annoyed by this interruption.

"I do not presently have an assignment." Aaan had been hoping to find a merciful angel, but this one did not seem to be gifted with that trait.

"No assignment?" The angel shifted suddenly into a defensive stance and jutted his chest toward Aaan, clearly communicating that he was not welcome. "Fallen angels are not welcome here. Go back to your own den of vagabonds."

"No, sir, I am not a—" But the door was slammed shut in his face.

Aaan looked toward the wizard-like angel, feeling embarrassed and bewildered. The grizzled old face was watching him and Aaan saw it break into a smile.

Aaan approached slowly and leaned against the wall beside the seated figure.

"Don't let that one discourage you. I am afraid he still has a little self-righteousness to work through. Remember how a better one than I once said to beware of the leaven of hypocrisy? Well, classic example. But there is also the timing. You see, even though time does not affect this realm in the same way as Earth, when we are working with those living on Earth, we must observe Earth-time. And I happen to know that a very important meeting is going on inside. Some higher-ups are here to help work out some problems going on right now in the Middle East. And it is daytime there—I would say that it is ... " he closed his eyes and seemed to be meditating, "afternoon. If you come back after, say, about nine or ten o'clock Jerusalem time, I would venture to say that you would receive much more courteous treatment."

"If you don't mind my asking, how do you do that?"

"Do what?"

"Find the time in Jerusalem by meditating."

The old angel laughed jovially. "Oh, that. I connected telepathically with someone I know there. I used to be his guardian angel and established quite a connection with him. I have since moved on to a new assignment, and he has another angel. I can communicate with her as well."

"Sir, my name is Aaan. Do you think it would be possible for me to ask you some questions? I am only half-angel and have never been privy to very much of the angel realm. But now I am here temporarily in this place ... oh, it is a long story. But I would dearly love to learn more about this realm, as well as anything you might know about what a half-breed can do to either attain the angel realm or the Heaven where human souls go."

The angel was looking at him and slowly nodding his head. "Well, well. You certainly have a lot on your mind, Aaan. My name is Eriel—that's with an E, mind you." He pointed his finger at Aaan. "Any mermaid jokes and we are done."

Aaan wasn't sure what he was talking about, but picking up on the intended humor, laughed for the first time in several hours and began to feel hopeful. "Deal."

"Let's take a stroll over by the fountain. Since my reading has been interrupted, I might as well show you around." He winked at Aaan.

It was like nothing Aaan had ever experienced, the opportunity to converse with such a wise and ancient being. He learned so much during the next few hours, which he spent with Eriel, lounging around the idyllic fountain. He found it humorous that rather than having an angel statue in the center of the fountain, as he would have expected, there was a graceful swan, its wings unfurled, rising backward, protecting a laughing human child astride its back, water spraying from its mouth.

He listened to Eriel intently as he described the angel realm. "You see, the angel realm is hierarchical. We all have an assignment at all times, as well as one or more superiors we must obey, with committees to resolve any disputes as they occur. So you might imagine why the angel who answered the door reacted with such astonishment when you told him you had no assignment. Commonly, the only angels without an assignment are fallen angels—those who have chosen to reject their assignments."

Aaan was especially fascinated to hear of fallen angels. "Please tell me more of the fate of such fallen angels. Sadly, my father is such an angel."

"Yes, I do know something of this." He seemed to study Aaan a moment before continuing. "You see, friend, angels who chose rebellion long ago sometimes have been able to repent and return to the realm, but this happens only rarely now. I find it helpful to envision that each of us is on a trajectory; those on a trajectory traveling toward evil tend to perpetually become more evil, and those on a trajectory toward good tend to grow in beauty, wisdom, and compassion. When one makes a conscious choice to change direction, if the change is toward good, then that angel is assisted in cleansing. There are teams and committees that specialize in this. Oh, there are exceptions—angels whose improvement is slow. You met one of those, the self-righteous one who answered the door. Some angels, like humans, tend to hold onto an erroneous idea or trait with clenched fists for a very long time."

"Interesting. And what do you know of the realm where human souls go? Where my mother likely is? You see, Eriel, I am a half-breed. My father was an angel and my mother a human. I was born just before the great flood and have existed on the Earth ever since."

Eriel regarded him thoughtfully again. "A half-breed, you say? Well, I do know something of the place where she likely resides. I have never actually been inside this place, though I do have acquaintances privy to that realm. I have worked with groups from within on one project or another, but human afterlife is different from that of angels—angels, as you know, do not really have an afterlife, but a continuing life of service. At least, that is the norm from my experience. Please stop me if this is information you already know."

"No, please continue. I have merely pieced together what I have seen of reality, but never before had an opportunity such as this to speak with an angel and learn. Few angels have ever before willingly spoken with me. Please continue and do not think any information too small to share. What is the chief mission of angels?"

Eriel laughed. "The chief mission of angels—is that not the question we have all tried to answer for eons of time? I must admit I do not know the answer. All I can say is that angels tend to work with others above and below them in rank, and possibly up or down a couple of levels, but rarely do we zoom up to communicate with the archangels—certainly not on a whim."

"Have you ever met another half-breed? And do you know our ultimate fate?"

"Unfortunately, I have never had the privilege before this day. Neither do I know what you can expect in the future or how you might get invited into one realm or the other. This is a puzzle for me, as well. Hmmm, not totally human, nor totally angel—that is a tough one."

Eriel looked at Aaan with such deep and sincere sympathy that Aaan had an urge to beg him to become his guardian angel. He really liked this angel.

Aaan told Eriel about the stones and was shocked to see the old angel snap to attention so ardently that for an instant his eyes glinted. This did not last long and soon he seemed to shake something off and compose himself.

Then Eriel put his palms up and said, "Please forgive me for my lust for power. And take this as a warning. Angels can be fiercely loyal, but can always at any moment be tempted, just like people. And guard your own heart from temptation. You have used a power that beings throughout the ages would have killed many times over to obtain. I am sure in your readings you have come across the old saying that, 'power corrupts and absolute power corrupts absolutely.' Well, I do disagree with the 'absolutely.' I would say almost always, because there are some who can and do resist. Some were martyrs, some common folk never becoming known as heroes among men, but crowned with honor far above any place I have ever been invited. And there is the lamb, but he was never an angel." His eyes glowed upon making this observation.

"My advice to you, son, is to go back, leave the stones alone, and finish anything you have left undone. You will know what that entails. As for how to get back into your original state, I cannot give you any further advice, other than to use all the tools you have—this includes spiritual gifts, intellect, ideas from other great minds, and, chiefly, connecting to the great love and allowing it to flow through you to others. I will commit to seek information that might help you in your dilemma, but no promises."

"That is more than I could have hoped. I am forever in your debt."

Eriel was deep in thought for a moment before continuing haltingly, "I do have an idea ... and a few promising connections ... "

Aaan waited excitedly to hear more, but Eriel abruptly changed the subject by saying, "And now, I think it is getting close to five p.m. Eastern Daylight Savings Time and I wish to resume reading my book."

Aaan was spellbound by the wise old seer's knowledge of his own affairs. He had not mentioned that he needed to be back to the lab by 5:10 nor anything about Eastern Daylight Savings Time.

The two exchanged a hearty handshake; then Aaan found himself pulled into a warm embrace. He felt such love emanating from this being that he felt oddly strengthened and refreshed. "Thank you, Eriel. I will never forget you and your kindness."

The grizzly old angel smiled. "No thanks necessary. Just go and save Danaak and Zaak. And of course, take good care of Anya. I will make sure to send a word of love up to your mother from you as well."

Aaan's eyes widened. Once again shocked by the words he was hearing, he opened his mouth to speak, but Eriel was gone, leaving only an ever-expanding mist.

Aaan's thoughts turned toward the lab. He hoped he wasn't too late for Erik. He flowed toward the golden beam on which he had traveled earlier. In no perceivable time he was zooming back to Earth, again with planets and stars going by so fast it gave the impression of a golden tunnel.

He focused his thoughts on the lab and arrived there in just moments. Looking at the clock, it read 4:55. Good. He was here on time. But the lab was unoccupied. This was not a good sign. He decided to wait and see if Erik showed up within an hour. If not, he would have to assume Roy had lied to Erik about bringing him back. Then he would have to employ all his resources.

While he waited, he decided to try using the STAG controls on himself, though in his present state he knew chances were slim he could make it work. He went to the safe and could see the controls inside. His hand could reach inside but went right through them. This was no good.

Eventually, he gave up, left the lab, and went to find Erik and see what he could learn. Perhaps he would visit Roy as well.

He found Erik at the hospital, visiting his mother. Sonia was there with him. Aaan learned from their conversation that his mother was being released within the hour. *Ah, so this may be why he did not show up in the lab—he was needed at the hospital.* But Aaan knew this was wishful thinking. If Erik knew Roy had failed to bring him back, he would have found a way to have either himself or someone else at the lab zap him back to his normal state.

Aaan decided to visit Roy to see what he could learn. Roy was at his apartment, apparently getting ready to go out. He was whistling to himself, in a good mood. *Must have a date,*

Aaan scoffed, and tried hard to suppress his own feeling of self-righteousness at the obvious hypocrisy. After all, Aaan reasoned, it had been self-righteousness and fear that led Roy to entrap Aaan away from his own loved one. Aaan could see where seeds of hatred could take hold and exerted an effort to force them out. The best he could do at this point was to simply observe.

Aaan saw Roy towel the last of the white foam from his freshly shaven face as a knock sounded at his door. Roy looked puzzled but nonetheless sauntered calmly to the door and opened it widely without hesitation. Upon seeing the visitor, his lively mood became serious and he seemed to be trying to close the door on an unwelcome guest, his body positioned in such a way as to block entrance. "Lorenzo, I—I certainly wasn't expecting you. Look, I'm on my way out and—"

"Si prega amico," came an almost whispered, pleading voice. "Please, Roy. I need your help. You have to believe me. I am not with them. I am clean. Look at my eyes."

Roy hesitated a moment, looking into the man's eyes, and then reluctantly relaxed and opened the door. "Okay, sorry. It's just that I couldn't really see any good reason for you to return here, unless you are after the stones again."

"I know, I know." The slender man sidestepped into the room, keeping his back to the wall, fretfully twisting a cap in his hands. "It is my brother. Antonio. He's just a kid. Only fourteen and they've got him. Those ... *diavoli*. They prey on the young and weak." Aaan perceived venom in the declaration.

Roy seemed impatient and reluctant to get involved. "Look, Lorenzo, I have to meet someone and I'm going to be late if I don't leave now. I feel sorry for you. I'm glad you're still clean. I wouldn't wish that horrible fate on anyone, but I don't see what any of this has to do with me."

"Roy ... he's here."

"What?" Roy's voice was fearful and angry.

"Yes. My possessed kid brother is here. And not alone."

"What the hell? But we sent the stones back. I thought they knew that. Let them go up against the Vatican and leave us alone." He seemed to be on the verge of hysteria.

"Roy, they know you didn't give every bit of the stones back. I don't know how you or that *professore* did it but, the word on the street is that you *mantenuto una scrota*, er ... held back, stashed some bits from the stones."

"The STAG controls," Roy stopped trying to evict Lorenzo, and turned, crestfallen, into the room. He motioned Lorenzo to a seat. "Tell me everything you know. I'll see what I can do for your brother."

Lorenzo seemed somewhat relieved and humbly nodded, saying, "*Grazie,*" as he shuffled to the seat.

"Whiskey? Rum?" Roy rose and walked to a sideboard with crystal decanters and glasses and began turning over two glasses to an upright position.

"No, thank you. I need to keep my wits about me to stay alive right now. Once they learn I have informed you ... " He shrugged sadly and slowly shook his head.

Aaan thought Roy looked worried. He poured himself some whiskey and downed it. Then he replaced the glass and sat back down. He and Lorenzo talked for only a few minutes. There was not much to learn other than the fact that two men and Lorenzo's kid brother, all possessed, were here, aiming to find any remnants of the stones that had been retained by Professor Hamilton and his research group. They would stop at nothing.

Lorenzo added, "And you know firsthand how evil this group can be. The leader, they say, is the very devil from Hell. Though I don't know if they are right about that. It seems to me more likely that he is indeed a powerful demon, but perhaps not the most powerful one. You know Roy ... I do not think any of them are more powerful than the good power. The power that saved you and me. I will never fear evil again. I wanted to warn you because, yes, they are a dangerous group. They should be taken seriously. And they are very dangerous to one they have possessed—you know, their property."

Roy seemed to be speechless.

Lorenzo wiped away a tear streaming down his own cheek. "But Roy, do not fear. Good will prevail. *Dio è in carica.*"

He stood to go. Roy walked him to the door, still seemingly at a loss for words. Lorenzo gave him a bear hug, saying, "Be safe, my friend," and left.

Roy seemed in shock. His earlier joviality was totally gone. Like a robot, he flipped off the lights and also left. Aaan followed.

Aaan stayed with Roy while he picked up Xenia and drove to dinner. Aaan observed that he seemed kind and affectionate to Xenia; she, in turn, seemed genuinely fond of Roy. Aaan listened to see if he could get any information that might help predict Roy's next move, but Roy mentioned nothing to Xenia about either purposefully trapping Aaan in a transformed state or Lorenzo's warning. In fact, Roy seemed somewhat withdrawn during dinner. Once they determined they would go to a movie, Aaan decided further surveillance of Roy tonight would be fruitless.

He next found Erik at his parents' house. He and Red were doing the dishes, chatting companionably as they worked. They were being flirtatious, mostly in the form of jokes and splashes. Aaan enjoyed watching the young couple in love, but it made him think of Anya and he sighed.

After finishing the dishes, Aaan watched Erik and Red go see if Viggo or Minah, both in bed, needed anything else that evening. They offered several times to stay in case either needed help during the night. Viggo rolled his eyes and Aaan thought for a moment that he would say something rude to Erik, but he refrained and thanked him but urged the two young lovers to go out and enjoy their Saturday night. They conceded and drove away.

Aaan rode along and they pulled into the parking lot for the Maryland overlook at Great Falls National Park. They got out, and, holding hands, walked to the overlook.

Aaan tried to strike up a conversation with their guardian angels hovering overhead, but was shushed. The angels seemed a little nervous around the churning water and Aaan knew it was not worth the bother to try and get anything out of them while they were on duty. So, he contented himself with cruising behind the couple and their angels and listening to their conversation to see if he could learn anything that might help. He felt a little odd doing this, but he really needed to do all he could to figure out how to get back.

After a few minutes he had some success. Erik asked Red about Annie's return flight. Red said it was three days away; Annie would return to Dulles around ten o'clock Tuesday night. "I'm anxious for her to bring Aaan back," Erik said. Aaan felt a momentary shock. So, this confirmed that Erik did not know Aaan was still transformed.

Aaan heard Erik's voice become excited as he told Red about cracking the riddle of how to transform Aaan. "Well, it was more Aaan than me. Or, I guess you could say it was our minds working together in sync. Aaan said that Annie made some comment about Aaan's angel and human aspects cancelling each other out, and then I think we both realized at the same moment that this was what was happening with the STAG controls."

He saw Erik pause a moment as they passed another couple coming from the opposite direction. Erik and Red nodded to them. Once out of earshot, Erik continued, now speaking loudly because they were nearing the falls and the sound of the cascading water threatened to drown out their conversation. "You see, we have always used the particles from the first two stones together in the same laser beam and we simply added the third, but something was getting cancelled."

"Ah, you mean like an acid and a base neutralizing each other?" Red seemed to be fascinated with the conversation.

"Precisely, Watson," Erik said with an exaggerated British accent.

Red smiled.

Erik continued, "So, know what we did?"

"Don't tell me. You separated the stone particles and used separate laser beams?"

"By Jove, you've got it, Watson!"

Red beamed and Erik continued. "We triangulated. I arranged three STAG controls in a circle, with Aaan in the middle, each aimed at a point in the middle of his trunk, and turned on the laser, using one stone in each STAG control. And he disappeared."

"Oh, my gosh. He was transformed? Erik—that's wonderful. Was that today? I know he was excited about possibly finding his mom that way." Red was obviously ecstatic at the good news. Aaan smiled.

Erik's brow furrowed as he said, "Well, that's the thing. It was actually last night and he was due back half an hour later. I had everything ready to zap him back to normal and was, as you might expect, quite anxious to hear the details of his experience, when I got the call."

"Oh, yes, the horrible call no one ever wants to get." She used an animated voice, "'I'm sorry, sir, but there has been an accident.'"

"Exactly."

"So, I don't understand, what did you do?"

"Well, luckily, Roy was working in the lab and I showed him the array of STAG controls and what to do. He agreed to do it at the appointed time and I rushed off to the hospital."

"Lucky that Roy was there. What did he say?"

"Well, that's the other thing. I haven't actually gotten to talk to him about it and find out what Aaan said about the transformation. We exchanged text messages and he said Aaan came back just fine ... um, or something like that, but I didn't get any details. And since I've been stuck at the hospital most of the time since, I haven't been back to the lab. I assume Roy told him about my parents' accident. In fact, I was a little surprised he didn't stop by to check on them before going back to Anya, but he was probably anxious to tell her all about the success. I missed our rendezvous time today, and feel a little bad for not at least popping over and leaving him a note."

"Oh, I'm sure he understands. After all, he's an angel. He probably knows exactly what's going on. He may even have had a hand in making sure they didn't get hurt worse. No, I guess he'd have been transformed at that time, though I don't know if that would prevent his assisting anyone. Guess we'll find out soon enough."

"Yep, I guess we will."

"Though, what I don't understand is why he needed all three stones. I mean, one works on quarks, one on electrons, and one on whatever angels are made of—right?"

"Right."

"And while transformed, Aaan's pure angel, isn't he? I mean, he doesn't have a human body with quarks and electrons, right?"

"Yeah, as usual, we're on precisely the same page. I've wondered the same thing, especially since I've had time to think in the hospital waiting room. But I guess he isn't completely angel, even when he doesn't have a human body. Or at least, he doesn't think he is. So, all I've come up with is that I still have a lot of research to do—evidently there's something in the human soul part of him. And that matter or energy is affected by at least one of the other two stones."

"All I know is that when you say you need to do a lot of research on Aaan, you'd better tread lightly with Annie and not take her beau away too much or you're liable to 'draw back a nub,' as Mom would say."

Erik smiled and the two strolled on, conversing in a lighter vein. The rest of their conversation was difficult to hear because of the churning water under the bridge to the Olmsted Island overlook.

Aaan knew now that Roy lied about his return, so there would be no plan B with Erik showing up each night to triangulate the STAG controls. But Erik would be in the lab tomorrow to do more research. Aaan could try communicating with him.

If that didn't work, he had no choice but to wait until Erik realized he was absent and perhaps he might try reactivating the controls again. He would have to be ready to position himself at the locus when—or if—that happened.

He hung around for a while longer until he realized they were not going to broach the topic again tonight. He decided to see if he might find any helpful information about the stones in Alistair's study.

He popped over there, but was frustrated to find all the information was inaccessible to him. No book lay open so that he could read, and try as he might, he could not move the volumes. Similarly, the computer was off—not that he would be able to press any buttons, anyway. Of course, pressing a button seemed more likely to be something he could master in this state than lifting a book.

Eventually, he gave up for the night. Anya would awaken soon, likely within the hour, and he wanted to go back to check on her. As much as he longed to see her, this filled him with sadness because it emphasized the gulf between their worlds. He would, again, not be able to communicate with her to let her know he was okay and had not left her alone. But at least he could try, he thought, as he began to teleport to Anya.

The instant he saw her, however, his mind exploded. *"Noooooooooooo!"* He was totally unprepared for what he saw. Anya slept peacefully, but inside her form was another presence other than her beautiful essence. Aaan started to leap onto the demon and rip it out, but felt his arms pinned back by iron grips on both sides. He struggled in his anger but two beings held him firm.

Finally, realizing that struggling was useless, he stopped. He looked first to the left, where his arm was being gripped by an evil presence, the likes of which he had never beheld. The creature resembled the devils of legend. It had a snake-like face, with a flicking forked tongue, and yellow irises with pupil slits running side to side like a goat with horns, and bright red skin. It was naked, its lower half coiled in a snake-like stance. Its pointed teeth gleamed brightly between puffy red lips drawn back in a broad, self-satisfied grin.

He looked to his right and was even more taken aback, if that were possible. He saw, of all things, a face he recognized. In another scene, he would have leapt with joy. If only he hadn't seen the hateful sneer on the face of his father. His emotions were in turmoil.

The snake-like being roared with laughter, watching Aaan react to the fact that his own father was involved. Aaan snapped his head back toward the devil. "What have you done to Anya?" he growled through a clenched jaw.

"Now calm down, baby boy." The words came out with a hissing sound, likely due to the structure of the forked tongue. "My, how I love a family reunion. And if you will look closely, the demon possessing your dear one is none other than your dear, long-lost brother, Zaak. Say hi to your brother, Zaak."

Aaan felt a humiliated loathing rise deep within his breast. Then he heard a deep, hoarse whispery sound come from Anya's sleeping lips. "Hello, Aaan."

"Zaak, what have you done?" Aaan wailed.

The devil was obviously enjoying his reaction and cackled at this outburst. "It's very simple, Aaan. Your father, your brother, and I would like to arrange a little deal. In exchange for getting your little girlfriend back unharmed—well, alive, anyway—" here he stopped to snicker "—we would like to have those stones, please. And from the looks of you, it appears you have been enjoying them yourself. Tsk, tsk, tsk, you naughty boy," he said in a sing-song rhythm.

Aaan looked toward his father. "Father? Is this true?"

"Aaan, I ... " His father seemed to soften somewhat but then snapped back into character. "Yes. We need those stones or at least the fragments. I want to find your mother and I want to find and punish those involved in taking her away from me." Billowing hatred increased with each word, masking the earlier hint of tenderness.

The mocking slithery voice chimed in, "But do not despair, we are not impatient. We will give you one full week. But I do love a game, and so, please indulge me. It goes like this: Your little girlfriend will be compelled to do one outlandish deed— by outlandish, I mean harmful—each day until you bring us the stones. Simple. And each deed will be ... something fun, I think. Hmmm, perhaps a few piercings, tattoos, and assorted body mutilations. Then a little prostitution—that's always a favorite.

And you know, hospitals always need donated organs—I am sure she has a few extra."

Aaan strained in fury against the vise-like grips on his arms. The demon seemed to gain strength from Aaan's fury. He beamed with delight. "My friend, by the end of the week, she will wish she were dead, and you will, too—that is, unless you are cruel like me." His voice sounded like a screaming wheeze as he stopped talking to laugh again. The sound was infuriating to Aaan.

The demon continued, "And then, one week from today, if I do not have those stones in my greedy little hands, she will cast herself to her death in one form or another, perhaps from an overpass—although ... I would really like for it to be by fire. Yes."

Here the snake-like demon stopped and smiled, shaking his head as if seeing humor in some old memory. "My, how my old friend Baal and I used to have fun with fire. I can still hear those crackly sounds and, oh, the screams." He giggled with delight again in the squeaky wheeze.

He now addressed Daanak. "You remember him, don't you? Oh, Baal wasn't his real name, of course, but that was what we called him for a time. Wonder where he is now? When I get the stones, perhaps I will find him again—what fun." He giggled again and his red lips skewed to one side in concentration. "Hmmm, but a bonfire may be difficult to find since it is summer." Then, snapping back to his former grinning self, he said, "But do not worry—I will find *something* fun." He laughed heartily, obviously delighting in his perceived cleverness.

Aaan looked to his father to see if he supported this plan. "Father?" Aaan gazed intently into his father's eyes.

His father looked away. "Just get the stone fragment, son," he said with seemingly forced detachment.

CHAPTER 8

Annie Comes Home

TUESDAY, JULY 15

Red was beginning to get a little annoyed at the number of cars still parked in the hourly lot at the airport at ten o'clock on a Tuesday night. She'd waited until the last minute to drive out to Dulles Airport to pick up Annie. Her plane was probably landing now and Red would have to make a mad dash to make sure she was in place when Annie came into sight. She sensed Annie needed her and wanted to make sure Annie knew she was important to her, which wouldn't be conveyed if she slouched in late.

Red knew she'd been preoccupied with Erik for the past year, but hadn't Annie been preoccupied with Aaan, too? Red couldn't believe she'd be moving out in just a few weeks to begin her college career. Georgetown wasn't far away and she knew she could still see her sister any time she pleased, but she also expected she'd become preoccupied with new friends, new studies, her new life. It was inevitable.

And Erik would be there in her new life, too. She allowed her mind to begin going down a thought-chain, thinking of how she'd wanted to get an apartment with him but knew her parents would have a cow. It had hurt her feelings a little that he had urged her to stay in the dorm, saying that he wanted her to have the full college experience. That still prickled a little. But that was something she'd have to deal with another time. It took some effort to break the thought-chain, but right now, she needed to think about Annie.

Her worry stemmed from a phone call she'd received from Carrie that morning. It had been reverberating in her head all day and she didn't know what to make of it. She'd known Carrie for many years, but this was the first time she'd received a phone call from her. Carrie had always been Annie's friend and kind of part of the woodwork to Red; Carrie had never really ventured to communicate with anyone in Red's family except Annie — they were two peas in a pod. This had made her urgent phone call even more disturbing.

What were Carrie's exact words? Red replayed the entire conversation over in her head as she walked to the luggage pick-up. She'd noticed a curious text message on her iPhone that morning from an unknown number. *Red, this is Carrie. Please call me soon as you get up. I'm worried about Annie! :-(*

She hadn't registered the message at first. She'd been thinking it was funny that Carrie put a nose on her frowny face. She made a mental note to mention to Annie that she might want to warn her that a nose wasn't cool. Then she realized what the message said, and even though it was a pain to call before she was fully awake, she decided to just do what Carrie had asked—call as soon as she got up.

Carrie had answered on the first ring, which had alarmed Red a little—she must have been waiting for Red's call. "Carrie, it's Red. What's up? Your note sounded serious."

"Yeah, I know. Red, I didn't know what to do and so decided to call you. It's Annie. Something's wrong."

"Wrong? How? Is she sick?"

"No, I don't think so. It's more, well—mental. I mean, I think something happened when we were in Transylvania."

"Transylvania, huh? She sleeping all day? You find chicken feathers in her bed?" Red had tried to laugh it off, wondering if Carrie was being a worrywart. She knew Annie could be hard to figure at times. But she'd immediately felt bad for making light of this when she heard the panic in Carrie's voice.

"I know this sounds strange. But you've got to believe me. See, we went to this costume ball in our hotel when we were in Transylvania. You know, one of those touristy things where you dress up like a vampire, kinda like LARP-ing. But not really organized role-play. Anyway, there was this Dracula character that Annie was dancing with and this creepy Diavol guy that kept hanging around me. So I left and went to bed to get away from him, but Annie stayed because she liked her Dracula guy. Oh, Red, I think that was a big mistake. I should've stayed with Annie." Red was alarmed to hear Carrie's voice break a little here.

"What did Annie say? Did this guy do something?"

"That's just it. She didn't *say* anything. It was like, one minute she was squealing about him in the bathroom during the dance, but then the next day or any day after that, she didn't mention him at all. And I couldn't get anything out of her about it. But it was like her personality changed, like she became some kind of badass."

"Wait, back to the night of the ball. What time did she come back?"

"I don't know. I was asleep."

"Do you think she stayed out all night with him? Do you think he raped her or something? Drugged her?" Panic began to rise inside Red.

"I don't think it went that far. I mean, I think Annie would've told me if something like that'd happened. But ... " Red heard Carrie hesitate and blow out an exasperated breath of air. "Well, she was drinking champagne. I mean, it is legal here as long as an adult gives it to you, and maybe I should've said something, but she seemed to be having fun. Oh, maybe I'm making too much of this. Maybe she's just mad at me for leaving the dance early, but she was different the next day. She was not herself. I asked her to talk to me until I was blue in the face, but she blew me off and said I worry too much."

Red considered this. "That actually sounds like something Annie would do. She blows me off all the time. You know, Carrie, maybe she's just changed since the last time you two were together."

"But she told me some weird stuff, too. Though come to think of it, that was before the dance."

"Like what?"

"Promise you won't tell her I told you?" Carrie sighed. "She told me a really bizarre story about smoking something and then seeing an angel in a cave. And she tried to tell me it was tobacco she'd smoked. Like, come on, Red, I'm not that naïve."

Red laughed inwardly, greatly relieved. So this was the crux of the matter. Annie had tried to confide in Carrie and Carrie hadn't believed her story as reality and determined Annie had either mental or drug issues.

Red was ready to dismiss Carrie's worries, when Carrie added something else. "And then there were the piercings."

"Piercings? Don't tell me Annie got a belly-button ring?" Red couldn't picture it.

"Yes. And others, too, on her face. At least, she got one on her eyebrow one day while she was here and my parents are a little freaked out about what your parents will say. She just disappeared one morning and came back with a little gold ring in her eyebrow. She told my parents that your mom had said it was okay, but I didn't believe her. And one of the few times she talked with me was to show me her new belly button ring and tell me she was going to get more done after my parents dropped her off at the airport," Carrie said. "I tried to talk her out of it because I know your parents will be mad, but she just laughed and said I worry too much. She said that a lot."

Carrie had asked Red to see what she thought of Annie's behavior and keep her posted. Red assured her that whatever had happened with Annie wasn't her fault; Annie was very independent and made her own decisions. She promised to follow up and let Carrie know what she thought of Annie's behavior, but she suspected that Annie was fine—more likely Carrie was the one with issues, having an anxiety attack or something.

But she was admittedly a little worried as she walked to the baggage claim. *Poor Annie.* Those stones had certainly complicated both their lives. The "ghost" Red had discovered turned out to be a real person, resulting in a fairytale romance for her, but Annie hadn't been so lucky. Her "ghost" had turned out to be a real apparition, and as sweet as he seemed, who really knew exactly what he was? She couldn't see how Annie's story could end happily ever after. She was determined to be a good big sister and find out if Carrie was just overreacting or if Annie really was becoming mental.

As she approached the carrousel for Annie's flight, she saw people were beginning to gather there. The flight must have unloaded.

Red scanned the crowd but didn't see Annie. People were still walking toward the carrousel, and so Red leaned against a column and waited. After ten minutes or so, the stragglers seemed to be all in and the luggage was coming out onto the conveyer belt, getting snatched up by travelers. Red was starting to worry a little—where was she? She then saw Annie's favorite old cheetah-patterned, rolling duffle bag move around the carousel and a hand reach out to take it. Red's eyes followed the hand to see a skinny teen in dark glasses even though it must be ten-thirty by now, her hair stuffed into a backwards baseball cap. *Annie?*

Red approached the sulking form. " 'Sup?" Annie said.

"Annie?" Red stood speechless for a moment. This had to be Annie, but she wouldn't have recognized her. She'd gone totally Goth. White-grey makeup, black lips, several eyebrow piercings, and a nose ring. "Annie, Mom and Dad are going to kill you for getting all those piercings. Um, doesn't that one on your lip hurt when you eat?"

A long, black fingernail reached up and flipped the nose ring. "You worry too much." Then, without another word, she began walking toward the door, pulling her rolling duffle.

Red trotted to catch up. "Annie, you don't know where the car is."

"Whatever," Annie said carelessly, continuing to walk toward the hourly lot.

Red sped up and walked alongside Annie, who seemed to know the way. "So? How was Bucharest?" Okay, so Annie really *was* acting strange. Carrie may have been on to something.

"What? Oh. Fine." Annie kept walking toward the car, not bothering to look at Red.

Red walked alongside in silence, temporarily speechless. They walked straight to the car and Red could've sworn Annie was the leader. Red was so perturbed by Annie's behavior and piercings that she wasn't really paying attention where they were walking, but there was Dad's Volvo, canoe rack and all.

"Annie, how did you know where I parked?" Red was feeling a hint of hysteria.

"Don't be stupid," was all the response she got from Annie.

Red pressed the button to unlock the doors. Annie walked to the back door and shoved in her luggage. Annie then plopped down in the passenger seat and slouched, her knees resting on the bottom of the dashboard.

Red got in and waited a moment. "Annie, I'm not going anywhere until you buckle." Annie could be as rude as she liked, but she needed to know Red wasn't playing along.

Without a word, Annie reached across and buckled the belt over her. Red was a little taken by the speed with which she did this—like a movie on fast-forward. Then Annie just sat there, staring ahead.

Once out on the open road, she tried again. "Okay, Annie— dish. What the hell happened in Bucharest? You let Transylvania go to your head? Why the piercings? You know Mom and Dad's rule—not 'til we're eighteen."

"You ask too many questions. Got the piercings 'cause I wanted to. Laws were different there. Minors can get piercings without permission. I didn't see a reason not to."

"What, in some back alley? Did they even use alcohol?" Red was getting annoyed at her younger sister's reckless attitude.

"Whatever," was the sullen response.

"Did something happen to you? Annie, you can tell me anything." Red felt her throat catch on the last sentence. She was really beginning to get scared for her sister.

"Are you about to cry?" Annie cackled cruelly at her show of emotion.

"Annie, what's wrong with you? Did that creepy guy do something to you? That Dracula guy? I figured Aaan would protect you. Where is he? Did he come back with you?"

"How do *you* know about the Dracula guy?" Annie's face suddenly turned toward Red in a direct, menacing stare, or at least that seemed to be the gist, though her eyes weren't visible behind the dark lenses.

Red wasn't used to Annie being belligerent like this and felt herself taken aback. "I talked with Carrie. Don't be mad. She was worried about you and said she wished she hadn't left you with a strange guy. Don't worry—no parents know any of it. So, was that guy Aaan? Or did you really dance all night with a stranger?"

"You're stupid. And nosy. And so is Carrie." At this, Annie faced forward once more, *incommunicado*.

Red gave up for the moment, needing to focus on her route to make sure she didn't miss the exit to the Beltway. But after a few minutes she felt her spunk rekindle and decided to try a different strategy. "Annie, I'm so sorry I've been preoccupied with Erik this past year. I know we've grown apart, but hey, you're my little sister. My best friend. I love you. Please, I'm moving to Georgetown in just a few weeks and will be out of your hair. But while I'm here, can't we be close again?" Tears trickled down her cheeks.

Annie seemed to be unperturbed by Red's dismay. But after a few minutes, Red felt a flicker of hope when Annie finally sighed and opened up briefly before shutting down again. "Look, Red. I'm okay. Aaan was the Dracula guy that night, and yes, he's here with me. This is just something I have to do. Just don't worry about it. I'm okay—just don't ask too many questions."

"Okay, I—I guess. But don't do anything else stupid, like more piercings. I still say that Mom and Dad are going to ground you 'til you're thirty."

"Whatever." Annie said once again, and it was like the curtain fell once more. Red wasn't able to engage her in further conversation as she drove.

At the ramp to the Beltway, Red made a snap decision to swing by the lab. It was roughly ten miles out of the way, but at this time of night the traffic would be light. She knew Erik would be working and wanted to get his take on Annie's strange behavior.

"Hey, Red, you missed your exit," Annie said without much animation.

"Yeah, I wanted to surprise you and swing by the university. I mean, I'll be living there on campus in a few weeks and you might want to come by sometimes to visit."

"Whatever."

Red was able to park on a side street near the old science building that housed the lab. "That's the building with Uncle Alistair's lab. Erik's there now and I thought you might like to see it."

"Nah, I'll just wait here in the car." Annie slouched down further in the seat and seemed to be napping.

Unwilling to take no for an answer, and having significantly more strength than Annie, Red marched around the car, opened the passenger door, and yanked Annie out of the car by the hand. "Hey, what the—" Annie spat.

"Annie, I'm not taking no for an answer. I've driven about ten miles out of the way to share my new life with you and you're going to see it, *comprende*?"

"Fine." Annie brushed Red's hand off hers and straightened.

Red pressed the button to lock the car, making sure they both heard the beeping sound so Annie would know she was locked out and had no choice but to follow Red. Red led the way up the walkway to the wide steps before the grand entryway. Annie balked here, stepping backwards as if she had seen a ghost.

"Annie, c'mon. It's just in here. What's wrong?"

"Red, I can't go in there." Annie seemed horrified all of a sudden and began to tremble as she slowly backed away.

"Annie." Red reached out and embraced her. "It's okay. It's okay."

"Red, I don't know what it is, but I feel like I'd be somehow damned if I go in there." Annie cringed pitifully, her trembling intensified.

Red tried to look Annie in the eyes through the dark glasses. "Annie, what is it?"

For an instant Annie looked like she was waking up from a bad dream. "Red, help me," she whispered.

Red knew her sister well enough to know that Annie wasn't bluffing. "Hey, no problem. You don't have to go in there tonight. It was a stupid idea anyway. And Annie, I am here to help with whatever you need, okay?"

For the first time since Annie had returned, a faint smile formed on her lips and she hugged her back. Red closed her eyes and savored the moment, not sure what was going on but knowing she wouldn't let her sister go through whatever it was alone.

"Hey, listen, know what we're close to?" Red said, hoping to pull Annie out of her dark mood.

"Um, the parking lot?" Annie seemed to be picking up the surly attitude again.

"Georgetown Cupcake, silly." This was Annie's favorite treat, as close to fail-proof as anything she could think of.

To Red's dismay, all Annie said was, "Whatever." Red knew something was terribly wrong. This wasn't Annie.

Red thought a minute and decided she really wanted a second opinion on Annie's behavior before her parents saw the piercings. She had some vague notion of an intervention to get Annie to remove at least some of the piercings before they went home and she got into trouble. Erik was good with weird, while her parents probably wouldn't be in this case. She was pretty sure he was in the lab and tried texting him to see. She didn't get an immediate response but he didn't always answer right away when he was immersed in his lab work. She'd pop up and check.

"Annie, if you don't want to go in the lab that's okay. But do you mind if I pop up and see if Erik wants to go get cupcakes with us? I'm pretty sure he's still here. You could wait on that bench—do you mind?"

"Whatever."

"Okay, wait here and I'll be right back. I promise." Red bounded up the steps two at a time. No one else was in the hallway. She was encouraged to see that the light was on in the lab and the door stood open, but was immediately disappointed to see Roy but not Erik.

"Oh, hey Roy."

"Hi, Red. Looking for Erik?"

"Yep. He still here?" she asked doubtfully.

"Sorry. He just left about fifteen minutes ago. I think he said something about swinging by his parents' house to help with something before going home. I don't think he's coming back tonight."

Red glanced up at the clock. It was already a little past eleven. "Oh, right. Guess it's later than I realized."

"Yeah, it's getting late even for grad students. You need a ride or anything?" Red thought Roy seemed a little uncomfortable offering this. It wasn't surprising, given all that had transpired between them when he was possessed. But she knew he meant well, and this offer was in a very different context than anything he'd said to her when he was possessed.

Wanting to put him at ease, she tried to sound nonchalant, but her words came out a little rushed. "No, I got my car, but that's really sweet of you to offer. I was just driving by and decided on a whim to see if Erik wanted to get a cupcake."

"Well, good luck. Most places are closed, I think."

"Yeah, like I said, it was just a whim. No biggie." Red shrugged her shoulders awkwardly as she began to step backward toward the door. "See ya."

Red started to feel a little uneasy at having left Annie outside, given her strange behavior, and was hoping to see her calmly sitting on the bench as she swung open the heavy door to the outside. But she saw immediately that the bench was empty.

"Damn it, Annie," she said with gritted teeth as alarm washed over her. She quickly grew frantic, realizing Annie was nowhere to be seen. She looked in all directions in the open area in front of the lab and saw many of the buildings nearby had darkened windows. A few students seemed to be walking toward a building that was still well lit and Red thought about checking that building in case Annie had decided to go exploring. But she would first check the parking lot to see if she'd gone back to the car.

She trotted down a walkway until she could make out the canoe racks jutting up from her dad's Volvo. Her heart fell when she realized Annie was not with the car. She bounded back up some steps and felt sweat trickle down her back as she hurried toward the lighted building. But upon passing an outdoor stairwell going down to a basement level, she heard voices. *Annie?*

She was startled to see a couple making out in the stairwell. But something was off about the scene. It appeared that the guy was trying to pull away and the girl was forcibly kissing him on the lips, her hands holding his face to hers. She was horrified to see that the girl looked like Annie.

"Annie!" she shouted.

Annie looked up smirking, then pushed the stunned guy away. She sashayed away and disappeared through a nearby door into the building.

"What the hell?" the guy said as he tried to regain his balance. He gazed toward the door where Annie had disappeared and called after her, "Um, hey, you don't have to leave."

"Sorry 'bout that—sorority thing," Red said lamely as she ran past him and through the door, following Annie.

But as she entered the dimly lit hallway, she saw a door on the opposite end closing. *How'd she do that?* Annie seemed to be moving at incredible speed.

She sprinted toward the door and swung it open to reveal another outdoor stairwell going up to the main courtyard. She bounded up those steps. Once again, no Annie.

She was now fully frantic. She ran back to the open area in front of the lab and checked out each walkway leaving the area. She peered as far ahead in each direction as she could see, hoping to catch a movement that would give away which direction Annie had gone in.

Only one other person was in sight, a guy walking across the open area. Red walked swiftly toward him, trying to not scare him by running.

But he did seem startled to see her approaching him, so she tried to smile calmly.

"Hey, um, hi. Did you see a girl just now? She'd have been coming from that direction." She pointed hopefully from the direction she'd last seen Annie.

He pulled an earbud from his ear and said, "Sorry, didn't catch all of that. You're looking for a girl?"

"Yeah, just now. Did you see anyone?"

"No, sorry. But I was kinda into my music."

"Okay, thanks anyway."

She looked around again. She had to pick one direction to search, and decided to sprint down a walkway opposite to the direction where the guy had come from since he would've seen her. It ended in a parking lot, and seeing no sign of Annie, she ran back to the open area and tried another, and another. Nothing.

She stopped to catch her breath and think. It felt like a lot of time had passed, though in reality, it couldn't have been more than fifteen or twenty minutes. Could it? She looked at her phone. Almost half an hour. Her heart sank.

She thought about calling her parents or the police. But no—Annie had just flown by herself from Europe, she could take care of herself. She didn't think Annie was likely in physical danger and she didn't want her to get in trouble. But boy, was she acting strange—even for her.

Red tried to think. Where would Annie go? The obvious answer came to her. To the lighted building she'd seen at first. She was pretty sure it was a student center and students studying late would be hanging out there, drinking coffee from vending machines. She sprinted toward the building.

She slowed to a walk as she entered an area with comfortable reading chairs and a few card tables. And there was Annie—playing cards with three guys, who were each staring intently at their own cards.

As Red approached, she saw one of the guys throw down his cards in exasperation and push back his chair. "Damn, how do you do that?" the guy asked.

Annie didn't answer, merely shrugged and raked a pile of bills toward herself.

"Annie. What the heck are you doing?" Red tried to keep the anger out of her voice for fear Annie would bolt again.

"'Sup, Red," Annie said, not looking up.

"What's *up?* It's after eleven-freaking-thirty. We gotta go home."

One of the guys eyed Red with a pleading look. "Please take her. She's taking all our money."

Another guy retorted, "Hey, speak for yourself. I wanna win mine back. And I want her to show me how she does it."

Red interjected, directing her comment to Annie, "Annie, we really, really gotta go—now."

"Fine," Annie said, as if there were nothing unusual going on. She rose and grabbed a handful of bills, leaving most of them still on the table, and stuffed them in her pocket.

As Annie began to walk past her toward the door, Red grabbed hold of her shirt. "Hey, not so fast. I'm not letting go of you 'til we're in the car."

CHAPTER 9

Oh Annie

Red hardly slept at all that night—she was worried sick about Annie. What had happened on her trip? And where the heck was Aaan? As soon as they got home, Annie had gone straight to bed despite Red's pleas for a talk. When asked about Aaan, Annie had merely shrugged and said that he was "around." *Big help, that.* Red wanted to talk to him. He'd know what was up with Annie. Had they had some type of lovers' quarrel and he'd left? That seemed unlikely. But who knew? Maybe it had something to do with his transformation. She needed to sit Annie down and drag the whole story out of her.

Red finally gave up tossing and turning when she heard a robin begin his morning song. *Kinda late in the season, isn't it, fellow?* Then, from somewhere in the backyard, she heard a crow caw. That *was* unusual for early morning. She thought of Moon and wondered how he was doing. She made a mental note to take a walk on the towpath this morning and look for him to say hi to him and to his mate, maybe see if there were any berries or nuts around she could put out for them. She wondered if he had baby birds right now. She made another mental note to google crows to see their annual timeline for offspring rearing.

She steered her focus back to Annie. She thought it likely that either the creep at the dance had made moves on her, or that she was angry at Aaan for some reason. Then it occurred to her—what would Annie have been doing, dancing with a stranger at the ball and then kissing another strange guy last night? Red knew her sister too well; she was head-over-heels in love with Aaan. Was she getting frustrated with him because he wasn't a real person she could go on a date with? Red knew all too well how that felt, remembering when Erik was an ethereal being.

Red's imagination ran rampant. She concocted a pretty convincing scenario of Annie getting frustrated for not having anyone to dance with, picking out this Dracula dude and dancing with him to make Aaan jealous. That had to be it. Aaan had gotten jealous and gone back to his cave. That would also explain why he hadn't made contact with Erik. Perhaps he'd washed his hands of the lot of them.

Red had almost convinced herself she had this thing figured out when a sickening thought crept into the back of her mind. *Then why couldn't Annie go into the lab? Was it because of the blessing the priests had recited, the one that was intended to keep out evil spirits?* Aaan had no trouble entering the lab after the blessing—of course, no one suspected him of being evil. In reality, she'd kind of poo-pooed the whole ritual. She liked the idea of those rituals and formal prayers—there was something deep and ancient about them—but logically she didn't know how effective they were. An obvious answer to Annie's behavior lurked in the back of her mind that could no longer be suppressed—Annie might be possessed by a demon. That would explain why she'd been unable to enter the lab. Red sprang out of bed, wanting to escape the idea, and, slipping on shorts and a T-shirt, went downstairs to make a cup of coffee.

As it turned out, coffee didn't help much. Red had never really liked coffee, though she had to admit the vanilla soy creamer her mom was hooked on really was tasty. She was just too restless. She went to the window to see if she could see any birds. She heard several, but the foliage was too dense now that it was mid-summer to actually see the little things. She had a fleeting thought that she'd like to take ornithology next spring.

Her mind returned to Annie. *Oh, this is ridiculous. I'm going to go wake Annie. I don't care how early it is.*

But Annie wasn't in her bed. And what's more, the bed didn't appear to have been slept in. Red hoped against hope to find Annie asleep on a couch in one of the other rooms—she often fell asleep in front of the downstairs television, but this wasn't the case. She checked the closets, under beds, behind doors—Annie was known to be quite a prankster. Nothing.

She went back to Annie's room to see if she could pick up any clues. Annie's rolling duffle was still plopped on the floor where she'd left it, unpacked. She checked the clothes hamper. Empty. Annie had apparently not changed clothes and must be wearing the same ones she had on last night. She didn't see Annie's small, black leather daypack/purse that held her wallet. She must've taken that.

Cell phone. Ah. She rushed into her own bedroom and almost pulled the recharging cord from the wall in her haste to unhook it from her own phone. She selected Annie's name on her speed-dial and waited as it rang. *Please*, Red thought, closing her eyes.

On the forth ring, relief swept over her as her sister's familiar voice said, "'Sup?"

Red felt hysterical. "Where are you?"

"Out. Why?"

Red could've rung her neck if she had her hands on her. "Annie, do you know what time it is?"

"Not really. Red, did you call to complain?" Annie's attitude was so detached that Red was having difficulty figuring out how to respond.

"Annie, have you been out all night? I mean ... " Red was beginning to fear that Annie would just hang up and she had to think quickly. "I, uh, had hoped that we could go to the mall together this morning. I haven't seen you much lately and was just surprised you weren't in your room."

"Oh, okay."

"Okay, what? Are you going to come home now? Want me to pick you up somewhere?" Red could feel sweat starting to trickle down her spine. *Please say yes,* she begged silently.

"Um, well. I gotta do something now but then we can meet up later."

"Do what? Maybe I could drive you wherever you need to go."

"Nah, I'm almost there. I have to make a donation. Listen, Red, I'll call you later." The phone went dead.

Shit. Okay, Red, think. She knew she should go wake up her parents and tell them. They'd already been in bed last night when she returned home with Annie and hadn't even seen the piercings. She knew they'd freak out. Yes, they were determined to allow her and her sister to have as much independence as possible and make their own mistakes; they certainly didn't spy on them, like some parents. She'd always been happy about that, but now she wasn't so sure. Maybe Annie *needed* a parent to spy on her. But if Red told them, she knew Annie would be really pissed and so wouldn't be as likely to confide in her.

She decided her best course of action would be to call Erik and get help, but also cover for Annie for the time being.

She could tell Erik had obviously been asleep from the lazy way he answered. "You know, Red, your voice is always welcome to my ears, but perhaps sometimes it's a little more welcome than others, like ... an hour or two from now."

"Yeah, sorry. But Erik, I need your help."

Erik's voice was suddenly very different. "Red, what is it?"

She told him everything that had transpired with Annie, starting with the strange phone call from Carrie and ending with the conversation she and Annie had had a few minutes ago.

"Red, stay put. I'll pick you up."

"No, I'll meet you somewhere. I don't want to waste time."

"I don't know, Red. We're going to have to play this by ear. It might be better if we stuck together."

"Okay, but hurry."

"I'm on my way."

Red felt bad lying to her parents and so left a note in the kitchen with just enough information to get by without actually lying: *We're out for the morning, catch you later!* She signed it with a smiley face. Her mom was a sucker for smiley faces. Hopefully, her parents would assume the "we" included Annie.

She went out front to wait for Erik, which didn't take very long. He'd obviously been speeding. She got in and they shot away from the curb.

"Do you know how to track a powered-down cell phone? I tried to locate Annie's but looks like she powered it down." Red said breathlessly.

"I think I can do it on one of the computers in the library." He looked at his watch. "But the library doesn't open for an hour and fifteen minutes. I think we should first go see Roy and ask him exactly what Aaan said when he brought him back from being transformed. I think there may be a connection. If I have to, I'll beat the truth out of him." Red saw Erik's jaw clench. She thought this was a reasonable idea. Perhaps Aaan had said something that might clue them in.

Roy had obviously been sleeping, because Erik had to knock loudly for what seemed like at least five minutes. In the meantime, Red kept dialing his apartment phone and cell phone alternately, while knocking on the windows. Eventually, a tousle-headed Roy opened the door.

On seeing the expressions on Red's and Erik's faces, a look of resignation crept over his face. He seemed to make a decision. He invited them in and told them everything, confessing that he'd never let Aaan transform back. "We have to get to the lab," Erik gasped. As he and Red rushed to the door, Roy called after him, "Watch out for those three from the cult. They're here somewhere and will likely be coming for you."

It was still early and traffic wasn't in full rush-hour mode yet, but it was getting close. It ended up taking almost an hour to get to the lab. Neither spoke more than a few words and Red thought this was because neither wanted to admit the obvious: Annie was possessed by a demon. Aaan hadn't been there to protect Annie, the cult was in the picture again, Annie couldn't enter the lab, her personality was barely recognizable ... it all added up.

There was no way Red could slow to a walk as they ran up the hill to the lab—she had far too much adrenaline. Red saw Erik's fingers fumble with the locks to the main door as well as to the lab, but they were finally in the lab. Wasting no time, Erik went to the safe, took out three STAG controls, and positioned them in a circle pointing inward. He said aloud, "Aaan, I'm very sorry for Roy's behavior. If you're here, I'm going to activate the triangulation right now, so please position yourself." He turned on all three controls and waited. Nothing happened.

Disappointment washed over Red as she realized Aaan could be anywhere right now. "What was the plan if he couldn't make it back in time? Same as usual? Every ten minutes for an hour and the same time each day for a week?" Red asked, her brow furrowed as she tried to think through what to do next.

"Exactly He was supposed to be back here at 5:10 every night if I didn't transform him. But since I didn't show up at that time on Saturday, Sunday, Monday, or Tuesday, he may have given up. All we can do now is return at 5:10 tonight and give it a try."

Red checked the clock. It was only eight in the morning. "Erik, that's nine hours away. We've got to do something sooner than that. Anything could happen to Annie. What about the library? When did you say it opened? Maybe we could find Annie's cell phone location now. I've been checking on my phone and her phone's still powered down."

"The library opens at eight."

They rushed to the library, sprinting once again. They bounded up the stairs just as the front doors were being unlocked. They each nodded to the middle-aged lady dressed in a suit who had unlocked the doors. She nodded back, saying, "That's what I like to see, young people excited about higher learning."

Erik made a beeline for a computer, Red hot on his heels. His fingers typed rapidly and Red saw various screens come and go. "Okay, what's her number?"

Red recited Annie's cell number to him as he typed it in.

Red had to struggle to remain patient as a series of typing and pausing ensued. Then: "Got it," he whispered, and hit a button initiating a buzzing sound from a nearby printer, which proceeded to spit out a page. Erik snatched it, then turned off the computer. "Let's go."

They jumped into Erik's car and sped away. Red studied the page. Annie's most recent call had been from Red's cell phone at 6:42 that morning. Red couldn't believe her eyes. Annie's location during that call had been on Tuckerman Lane, near Cabin John Shopping Center—that was only about a mile from their home.

Relief washed over Red. That meant Annie could've walked there, and made it less likely that she had been kidnapped by one of the cult members. Red sighed as she thought of the three possessed men Roy had warned them about. "Erik, Annie's at Cabin John. I hope this means she just went exploring and didn't meet up with those three creeps who are after the stones."

"Yeah. My thoughts exactly."

Red noticed Erik was driving as fast as the now-heavy traffic allowed, but that wasn't fast enough for her. "So, let's make plans."

"Yeah, good idea."

In a few minutes she felt better having at least the beginnings of a plan. They'd pull into a secluded part of the parking lot behind Cabin John Shopping Center and Red would zap Erik to the invisible ghost transformation. He'd search the area from overhead and ghost in and out of each shop. Red, meanwhile, would search the shopping center on foot and man her cell phone in case Annie called or turned her phone back on so Red's frantic text messages could go through.

As they pulled into the lot, a flock of crows cawed in the trees behind the shopping center. It reminded Red of the birds from that morning. "What's up with crows today? I heard them squawking this morning, too—I don't usually hear them call in the wee hours like robins. Is this their mating season or something?"

Erik was distracted. "What?"

"Oh, it was nothing, really, just wondering why the crows are so active today."

He started. "Crows—you said they were chattering this morning? Sonia—that's awesome." He excitedly took Red's face between his hands and planted a loud smacking kiss on her lips.

"Wow. I'll have to observe birds more often."

"No. Don't you see? It's *Moon*. He knows about demons. I had him watch Roy sometimes. He was trying to tell us that a demon was around this morning when you heard him. That was likely when Annie was walking away from your house. The fact that he's still here is a very good sign. He's keeping an eye on the demon that's possessing her."

"Or on the three possessed men," Red pointed out, suddenly looking at Erik with renewed panic. He seemed to mirror her concern. She quickly reached for the STAG control, ready to transform him. He took a moment to strip so his clothes wouldn't be ruined—no time to think about his leather thong; he'd have to do this *au naturale*.

Once he was away, Red got out of the car and walked toward the drug store. It seemed likely that Annie might be there browsing makeup, maybe buying some more black lipstick. Red tried to call Annie's cell again—still dead. She checked the time; just after nine.

She went into the drug store, but a scan of each aisle revealed no Annie. She spotted a woman she recognized at the makeup counter, though she didn't know her name. "Good morning," she said, trying to sound chipper.

"Good morning. Nice to see you again," the sharply-dressed woman responded. "What can I help you with today? We're having a two-for-one on nail polish." She swept her hand to gesture toward a nail polish display.

"Hmmm. I'll look at it later. Right now I'm looking for my sister. Do you remember her? Annie? Skinny Goth kid?"

"Oh, yes. I mean, I remember her, but haven't seen her. But I just came on about half an hour ago. Sorry."

"No problem," Red tried to smile. She scanned the grocery store next. She thought it was more likely that Annie would be at the donut shop, but wanted to be efficient and scan the stores as she came to them. She didn't bother with the ones that she didn't think Annie would go into, like the veterinary clinic or the hair salon. But there was no Annie in the grocery store, ice cream shop, smoothie place, or donut shop. Red was disappointed and anxious.

She looked at her watch. It was almost nine-thirty. She decided to head back to the car to see if Erik might be waiting for her there. In their haste to begin the search, they hadn't arranged a time to meet up to zap him back to normal. But really, it didn't matter now that Erik and she were well practiced in communicating via his whispery voice from the transformed state. She knew how to listen for it and look for signs that he wanted to be transformed back to normal.

She walked to the back parking lot toward Erik's car. Luckily no one was even close to that corner of the lot and definitely not within earshot. "Erik. You here?" She waited a moment or two but didn't hear a whisper or see anything move to indicate his presence. She checked her cell phone again— nothing new.

She leaned against the car exasperated, trying to think through what Annie might be up to. What had her exact words been? *Something like,* I've gotta do something. *What the heck would she have to do the moment she got back from Bucharest? Think, Red, think!* She knew there had been something else, but it wouldn't come to mind. She leaned her head back and closed her eyes, listening to the bird songs.

The bird songs. Where were the crows? Suddenly, she was frantic again. Had Annie left the shopping center? Why weren't the crows here now? And where the heck was Erik? She decided to risk irritating other shoppers and used the car horn to do an SOS signal, hoping Erik would understand the signal. She gave three sets of three short blasts on the horn. She didn't have long to wait before she heard Erik's whispery, "I'm here, Sonia!"

She quickly pointed the STAG control and was about to zap him back when she stopped and thought better of doing it in the open. "Guess we'd better do this in the car," she said.

Once they were both in the car, she zapped the driver's seat side, and there was Erik.

He quickly pulled on the shorts he'd left carelessly on the driver's floorboard. "What's up? Why the panic?" he asked urgently.

"Erik, the crows are gone. Doesn't that mean that Annie's probably gone, too?"

Erik nodded his comprehension. "Not necessarily. I did get to communicate with Moon and he and his flock, gang—well, technically they're called a 'murder' but I hate that name—anyway, they *were* following the three men, not Annie. Get this—those three men were prowling outside your house early this morning. Moon said they tried to break into Annie's room through her window. And when they left—she was *not* with them." He emphasized the word *not*, perhaps recognizing the panic rising in Red's eyes.

157

Erik continued, "Anyway, I guess she'd already gone. I don't know if she knew they were coming for her or what she was thinking exactly, but the best I can make out from Moon, the men have been driving around the neighborhood ever since. The crows have kept an eye on them. They're watching out for the neighborhood—nice, huh?"

Red chuckled slightly, despite her bleak mood. "Moon— gotta love him."

"Yes, Moon's a good friend."

"Now what? Want to split up? One of us could follow the crows while the other keeps looking around here for Annie."

Erik blew out a long breath. "Let's think about this. We know Annie is, or was, here. We know the three men don't have her. We know Aaan's still transformed." He hit his fist on the dashboard out of frustration. "I just wish I knew where he was."

Red suddenly snapped up her face to look him in the eyes excitedly. "Erik, that's it. He's got to be here. Don't you see? If Annie's here, he's here, too—he always hangs out around her. He wasn't in the lab because he's *here*."

"Okay," Erik said slowly, obviously thinking it through. "But if he's with her, why does he allow the demon to stay in her?'

Red felt sick, thinking of a demon in Annie. She said sadly, "I don't know, Erik. Maybe something keeps him from having the power to rip the thing out of her. But mark my words, he's somewhere near Annie. Unless he's being held elsewhere," she added, the thought making her panic rise again.

"Okay, I guess you're right. It's worth a try." He took three STAG controls and placed them in a circular format in the backseat. "Aaan, if you can hear me, please sit in the backseat and I'll zap you back."

He flipped a switch on each control and looked at Red. She met his eyes, then fixed her gaze on the locus of the triangulation. She gasped as she saw Aaan materialize. "Aaan! You're back! Do you know where Annie is?"

Aaan opened his eyes and sighed with obvious relief. "Thank you. I feared I would never make it back." He turned to look at Red and answered, "I know Anya is nearby, though not exactly where. You see—" he hesitated a moment as if dreading the words that must come, and then said with obvious misery, "Anya is possessed and has two other demons guarding her to keep me away. They say that she will do a harmful thing to herself each day until they get the stones. And ... if they do not have the stones by Sunday, Anya will kill herself."

Red gasped and slapped her hand over her mouth in disbelief.

Erik nodded, obviously trying to stay positive and give hope to Red and Aaan. "Look ... we can do this. It's only Wednesday. We've got four days—although I guess we should say three, because we don't know what time this deadline is on Sunday. Aaan, do you know her location? Can't you just think of her and teleport to where she is?"

Aaan shook his head. "No, with two powerful demons defending that space, whenever I do that, I get bounced back

159

and always end up further away, rather than closer to her. I have been searching for her, just as you have been. In fact, I have been frantically going from you to your home, to her friends' homes around the neighborhood, watching those three possessed men snooping around, to Roy's and back to you again ... I was drawn by your SOS signal and hoped against hope you would make an offer to transform me back before the appointed time this evening—and you did. Thank you again for that. So, why do you think she is here?"

Red quickly explained about the cell phone call. "She said that she had something she had to do and I ... can't ... no, wait. I remember now. She said she had to *donate* something."

Aaan's reaction startled her. "Oh *no*. Are you sure?" His mouth hung open and then he said, "We have to find her immediately. The demon told me he would have her donate an organ."

Red looked at Erik again, feeling panic, and saw he, too, was open-mouthed and speechless.

Tears began to stream from Red's eyes. "We've got to find her. We should call the police!" she said hysterically, her voice beginning to sound more like a scream. She grabbed her cell phone to dial 9-1-1, then gasped. She had a voicemail from Annie. Red's typing thumb felt clumsy in her haste, but she managed to bring up the message and listen. She heard Annie's unhurried voice say, "Sorry, Red, phone died. Home now. Going to bed."

Red burst into relieved tears. "She's at home," she cried and laughed simultaneously.

Erik whipped the car in a tight circle and Red heard tires squeal as they left the lot. Luckily no policeman saw him speed, and no pedestrians were in the way. "Uh, Erik, I think you can slow down now before you kill someone. Just sayin'."

"Sorry," Erik said.

She patted the hand resting on the gearshift. He looked briefly at her and smiled. "Uh, eyes on the road," she said.

They laughed, and Red felt lightened with relief, though she knew this was far from over.

It was going on eleven when they pulled into the driveway of the mansion. The downstairs seemed unoccupied and Red figured her parents had both gone to work. She checked for the note she'd left on the table and it was gone. That was good—it'd been received. She took the stairs two at a time and then took long strides down the upstairs hallway to Annie's room. The door was pulled almost closed but not fastened. She eased it open a few inches, and relief washed over her. There was Annie, in the flesh. Her face looked peaceful, buried in her pillow, sound asleep. But her hair, Red realized—it was gone. Not totally gone, but very, very short. It looked cute, almost pixie-like, but she'd never before heard Annie mention an intention to have her hair cut short.

She tiptoed into the room to get a closer look at her face, to reassure herself that Annie was okay, and bent down to plant a brief kiss on top of her head. She saw a ghostly image of Aaan move into the room and sit down in a chair nearby, his head in his hands.

This must be hard for him, seeing the demon and being *helpless to do anything,* Red thought. He didn't look up as she tiptoed out and went downstairs to talk to Erik.

She was surprised to hear voices as she descended the stairs. Her parents must not have gone to work after all. She hoped this didn't mean she'd have to explain everything to them right now. She sighed. Guess it had to be done sooner or later.

The voices were coming from the library. Funny—only Uncle Alistair ever really hung out in there. *Uncle Alistair!*

She dashed into the library and saw Uncle Alistair's face light up when he saw her. She rushed into a huge bear hug from him. Then she turned and hugged her new aunt, who kissed her excitedly on both cheeks. Red awkwardly followed suit, unused to so much kissing. But oh, was it great to see them. Her eyes threatened to tear up, a combination of the morning's frustrations, fear for the future, and joy at having the voice of reason back amongst them.

She saw on Erik's face the same relief and quickly found an empty armchair to listen to her uncle's account of recent events. Their appearance just when things were getting weird with Annie had been no coincidence. It turned out that he and her aunt had been hanging around their home in a transformed state recently to help keep watch just in case. They had enjoyed their honeymoon for a few weeks, Uncle Alistair said, but then decided to use their unusual circumstance to gather information on the enemy, as well as guard and protect their loved ones. Red knew they had meant well, but had to bite her tongue to keep from stating the obvious— their oversight of Annie had fallen short of successful; after all, she'd been possessed.

Her uncle's next words, however, echoed her feelings and she felt his sincere gaze directly on her. "I know what you're thinking—that we dropped the ball and allowed Annie to become possessed on our watch."

Red couldn't help but blush a little. It was as though they'd read her mind. She saw her uncle and aunt exchange a look and she was a little shocked at how little panic they seemed to exhibit. He took his wife's hand companionably and resumed, "There's some truth to that. However, I think you will find that the demon in Annie isn't really as bad as you might assume. You may not know this, but I had this house blessed when the lab was blessed. So any angel or spirit that is truly on the path to destruction—the evil path—cannot enter. Since Annie came here last night, and is here now, the demon inside her cannot be truly evil."

"But Uncle Alistair," Red was totally confused now. "That's not the case. Annie *couldn't* go into the lab last night."

"I suspect that was play-acting on the part of the demon," Uncle Alistair said, rubbing his chin. "It seems that the demon in Annie is none other than Aaan's brother, Zaak."

Both Red and Erik gasped.

"Yes, I know, it seems incredible. The best I can decipher, Zaak has been hanging around his father for centuries, maybe ages, watching out for him and trying to draw him back to the good side. He pretends to be a demon so he can stay close to his father. I suspect some of the evil has rubbed off on him—his essence is murky, though not nearly as much as his father's. You know the old saying about lying down with snakes and getting bitten."

Red saw Erik's brow furrow deeply in heavy concentration. "Then he has made a grand statement by coming here. He has effectively blown his cover. But why?"

Uncle Alistair sighed and shook his head. "I guess we'll have to ask him."

He looked Merlin-esque, Red thought, as he looked around the room at each person in turn before venturing, "How about it? Anyone for a good old-fashioned exorcism?"

Before anyone could respond, a scream tore through house, an earthy, growling sound, like an angry great jungle cat. *Annie!* Red was up the stairs in a blur before anyone else could register what was going on. She was closely followed by Erik and then the older couple.

She burst into Annie's room in time to see her sister struggling to rip herself out of Aaan's grasp to fly at another ethereal being that looked very much like Aaan. The other being was backing away, his hands up in a defensive position.

Annie was screeching like a banshee. "What the hell did you do to my hair, you pervert?"

"Anya, please, he might hurt you, please, calm down!" Aaan pleaded, still holding her by the elbows as she tried to kick and scratch in the general direction of Zaak.

"I'll calm down when this pervert tells me why the hell he made me cut all my hair off! And what's this on my face? What the—" She ran her fingers over the piercings on her face.

"The piercings are okay, I guess, but I want my hair back." She growled the last sentence.

Red flung herself at Annie, catching her in an embrace intended to both comfort and hold her back. "Annie, it's me. Calm down. You're okay. Aaan is here and so is Uncle Alistair. We're going to get to the bottom of this. But please calm down so we can discuss this rationally."

"He made me kiss some strange guy, Red! *I* was the one being rapey! What if I caught something?"

Red hugged Annie as hard as she could, until eventually she felt Annie stop struggling. She stood, still panting, apparently too angry to hug her back. Her eyes still glared into Zaak, who seemed to be just beginning to drop his defensive stance.

"Zaak, I think you have some explaining to do." Red heard calmness in Aaan's voice, though she sensed a deep threat there, too.

Zaak had the grace to look sheepish.

Aaan continued, "Zaak, please explain to me why you possessed the girl I love."

At this public proclamation, Red saw that Annie finally tore her eyes away from Zaak. Her anger seemed to turn to wonder as she looked adoringly at Aaan for a moment, then her face hardened again as she turned back to Zaak. She gave a huff and spat through gritted teeth, "Okay, Zaak, my sister and I are a team, and unless you want to see some major demon butt-kicking with you on the receiving end, you'd better start dishing. *Now.*"

PART TWO

The Battle

Quote from <u>The Lord of the Rings</u>: "What of the dawn?" they jeered ... "None knows what the new day shall bring him," said Aragorn.[2]

CHAPTER 10

The Council

A nnie felt confused and angry. Ever since that night in the howling Transylvanian wind when she'd agreed to help Aaan, everything had felt like a dream. She remembered feeling wicked and mischievous while she was getting facial piercings … at the time, she'd wondered why she wasn't worried, but then, she was only dreaming, so it hadn't mattered.

Then, she was kind of aware of Red picking her up at the airport, but the only clear memory she had was the panicky feeling she'd had when Red tried to take her into the lab, as though there would be doom and destruction if she crossed the threshold of that building. It had felt like her brain was boiling. And she was dimly aware that she'd kissed a strange guy.

And then her hair was gone, and her sister and Aaan were telling her she'd been … *possessed*? She'd needed to lash out and had flown at Zaak, who had caused it all, kicking and scratching.

But now—Aaan was saying he loved her ... Red held her back, and Annie gasped to catch her breath. It was all too much. She couldn't process it all right now.

Uncle Alistair stepped forward and took charge of the situation, saying, "Under the circumstances, I think it would be best for everyone to withdraw into my study. We will meet around the table to hopefully keep each of us from kicking, scratching, or grasping another's throat as we discuss this situation rationally. I am sure Zaak has much to share."

Annie took Aaan's hand and led the way, her adrenaline making her steps feel like angry stomps as they went into the study. She had a bone to pick. Red and Erik followed behind them, then her Uncle Alistair, who escorted Zaak, keeping him within easy reach. Annie noted the absurdity of a human trying to be a physical guard for an ethereal being such as Zaak. Behind her uncle came Aunt Zsofia, who made sure everyone had a chair and retrieved two more from another room before sitting herself down to the civilized discussion.

Uncle Alistair stood at the head of the table and cleared his throat. He briefly introduced each person, then turned to Zaak and said, "Now it's your turn to explain yourself. The floor is yours."

Annie was shocked to see Zaak politely rise to a standing position. He began, "It is an honor to meet you, Professor

Hamilton, Mrs. Hamilton." He bowed to each in turn. "And your fine family, Miss Greene." He nodded to Annie.

Annie shunned him with a look, and he continued, nodding at Red and Erik, and then turned to his brother. "And Aaan, I cannot tell you how wonderful it has been to see you again after all these ages."

Aaan eyed him cautiously and nodded slightly, suggesting that the sentiment was not mutual.

Zaak sat back down. "And now, to explain." He looked around the room as he spoke, though chiefly addressing Alistair and Aaan. "When our father began his descent into the darkness, I followed, hoping to keep him from going down that path. I tried everything I could think of to bring him back into the light, and there were times when I thought he was on his way back. But over the years, I have been reincarnated many times." He looked at Aaan, who nodded understandingly. "You too, brother?"

"Yes, many times. And perhaps one day you and I can trade stories, but for now, please continue." Annie thought Aaan was beginning to show a hint of softening toward his brother.

Zaak nodded. "I think Aaan loved our mother best and I our father. Over the ages, I have had one obsession—bringing our father back to the good side. I think in this way my brother and I are alike—he has been obsessed with joining our mother, and I with bringing our father back. I am sure this trait is partially due to us being half-angels, needing to have an assignment. Perhaps, also, for Aaan and me, we are like children of divorced parents, always dreaming of reuniting the family so we may live happily ever after. Or children of war, who never really move past it." Annie saw Aunt Zsofia pull up a lacey handkerchief to dab a tear.

"I have often intervened when he was on a destructive course. Especially when he planned to harm others. Both for the sake of the victim, and for his sake, to avoid later regret. Oh, I know many times he suspected this, but he has retained enough good to play along just to keep me close. There really still is some good in him."

Annie saw him look at Aaan, who seemed to be drinking in every word and looking quite affected now. Zaak went on, "As an aside, I should say here, as I have been obsessed with saving our father, he has been obsessed for at least a thousand years with obtaining the stones. He has an idea he can access some place or places in the high realm with the Angel Stone that would give him access to our mother, or at least information about where she is and how he might get there."

He continued, "But in his evil, twisted state, and especially now that he has teamed up with Satan himself—" Here several gasps were heard around the room. Zaak quickly raised a hand, "No, no, sorry. The demon is not actually known to be Satan; that is just a nickname I use for him sometimes. In fact, he refuses to tell us his name. Some of the ancient ones fear that knowledge of a name affords some degree of power over the named." He made a flippant gesture at this.

He continued, "He is very old, and, I think fairly, high ... or low ... as demons go. And, I think, very dangerous." He paused to look around the room. Annie noted all eyes were intently watching him.

He addressed Aaan directly. "Last winter, when our father saw you, Aaan, he became obsessed even more with the stones. The thought that you might have access to the stones was so very exciting to him. I think he thought he, you, and I could team up to go find our mother. One big, happy family."

His face darkened. "Unfortunately, so did his obnoxious friend. I have long wondered why our father associates with him—I have come to the conclusion he is somehow trapped in some evil deal the two of them made long ago. Whether he is *actually* trapped by him, or just thinks he is, I do not know. But he doesn't seem to like this character. Who could?" He shuddered visibly.

Annie cringed as Zaak said, "This ancient fiend is very cruel. He delights in cruelty. This whole thing with tricking Anya into inviting demon possession was his idea. The idea was to gain control over you, Aaan, so you would obtain the stones for them, and he could have fun in the process."

Zaak now looked at Aaan with an almost pleading expression. "You have to believe me, brother. The only reason I possessed your loved one—" Annie heard Aaan growl under his breath "—was to keep someone else from doing it. This demon has hoards of minions to do his bidding. Like the ones who possessed your friend Roy, and his friend, Lorenzo. They were not as nice as me, believe me. And that goes for those possessing the three men from Italy who are lurking around as we speak, looking for you, only kept at bay by the incanted blessing performed here recently. But that won't last much longer, I fear."

Annie was still angry and couldn't help but blurt out, "If you're so nice, why did you make me cut my hair? And kiss that creep?"

Zaak looked at her now and said, "I am very sorry about that. And the piercings, too, but the plan was that you would do something self-destructive each day. I had to play along or my cover would be blown. I couldn't do that until I got you in a safe place. The original plan was for you to donate an organ."

Annie gasped as she realized how insignificant the loss of a few inches of hair was in comparison. "Oh ... " was all she could muster.

Zaak looked alternately at Annie and Aaan. "I tried to think of actions that would *look* self-destructive, but would not leave permanent damage. Like piercings, rather than tattoos. Like donating hair, rather than a kidney. I had promised to have you donate something from your body to convince them to let me be your possessor. And I couldn't really go back on my promise. It gets really ... complicated when we try to do that."

He looked at Aaan, who nodded emphatically.

"So, I thought of hair. And the stranger she kissed did not have any serious diseases—I can tell when someone is diseased. But I wasn't sure what I was going to do next, so I have to say I am very glad to get Annie safely here. I mean, she was here last night, but Aaan wasn't. I could see the professor watching her, but didn't know if that was enough. Then, when I realized we were in a safe zone and Aaan was here as well, and that Father and the others were held at bay for now, I decided it was time to emerge. Well, that and the fact I didn't have Father to keep my brother at bay."

Here Zaak ventured the first slight smile Annie had seen from him. She realized, like his brother, he was handsome.

Then he flashed a full dazzling smile at her and said good-naturedly, "So, Anya, am I forgiven for the piercings and haircut?"

Annie felt her face relax into a mischievous smile and said, "Okay, as long as you can talk my parents into letting me keep the piercings." She looked to Uncle Alistair for support.

She was disappointed to see that her uncle had an eyebrow raised and was shaking his head. She decided to drop it.

Aaan then began, with feeling in his voice, "It seems, brother, I owe you an apology as well as a world of gratitude."

Annie felt warmed as the two brothers stood and embraced, slapping each other heartily on the back in some ancient form of friendship hug. Like many things Aaan did, it was recognizable as a forerunner of modern mannerisms. The two brothers seemed to be identical in their mannerisms as well as similar in their physical appearance.

Annie said, "Thanks for saving me, but don't go tricking me again, okay?"

"Agreed." Zaak reached for her hand and implanted a most gallant kiss on it.

"And I probably gained five pounds from all the donuts I ate before the haircut," Annie said, sighing.

"Yes, sorry about that, too, but it seemed like the safest place for you to stay. After all, those three men were looking for you. I had to move you around quite a bit to avoid them. But I saw they had just checked the donut shop and so we ducked in. I didn't think they would be back for a while."

"That's okay, actually, they were really nummy. But next time, make it Georgetown Cupcake, okay?" Annie heard Red laugh.

Erik spoke up now, this time addressing Alistair. "So, what's our plan for dealing with the three men? And the two demons. I guess that's actually three men and at least five demons."

Just then, Annie was surprised by the sound of doorbell chimes. Uncle Alistair, in his commanding air, simply stated, "Guests, we have a visitor. Let's take a break and reconvene in half an hour."

As they herded down the stairs, Uncle Alistair in the lead, Annie felt Zaak sidle up to her and ask, "So, who is this Nyah I saw in your thoughts? She is quite a fascinating woman."

Aaan interjected good-naturedly, "Anya, protect your friend. My brother has been known to be quite smooth with the ladies, in at least one of his incarnations."

Annie rolled her eyes and smiled at the thought of Nyah and Zaak together. "Listen, Aaan, Nyah can take care of herself. Your arrogant brother may have just met his match."

Zaak played along, taking on the appearance of a Shakespearean tragedian and wailing a quote Annie recognized from <u>Hamlet,</u> " 'Tis bitter cold and I am sick at heart."

Aaan nudged Zaak, who continued. "Alas, dear brother, thou dost cut me to the quick. For, I have endured many hardships at the hands of unscrupulous wretches when in the form of a maiden since those deliciously reckless days." His arm was thrown up onto his brow. "And now, am I not wretched and misunderstood?"

"Zaak, stick to Shakespeare. The freeform soliloquy was a bit much," Aaan said, taking Annie's hand and drawing her away from Zaak, who still maintained a wilting tragedian expression.

Annie loved holding Aaan's hand and smiled at him. She thought it was cute hearing the brothers bicker like any set of siblings, and couldn't help but smile inwardly at how her impression of Aaan's brother was changing. She had to admit he had charm.

"Those two certainly are entertaining," Red said as she caught up to Annie, seeming to enjoy the lightened mood as well.

"Yes, they certainly are." Erik smiled beside her. Annie saw him gently put his arm across Red's shoulders and give her a small squeeze.

CHAPTER 11

Gathering Forces

Downstairs, Annie learned the visitors were Roy, Xenia, Rachel, and Daniel. Roy had confessed all to Xenia, who'd called on Rachel and Daniel for support. The group had decided to come right away to the Hamilton mansion to see what kind of damage control was needed.

Annie felt a nudge and Red whispered, "Annie, shouldn't we feed them something or at least offer coffee?"

The homey thought felt good, though her stomach rolled at the idea of more donuts. "Maybe just coffee?"

"You've been through a lot," Red said. "Why don't I put together a quick brunch of cheese, toast, and salad? Those are probably the only things we have enough of that are quick. That won't take two of us and you can rest. But do you know what angels eat? Or *if* they do?"

Annie noticed that Aaan and Zaak were talking together near the stairs and decided to ask. "I'll find out," she told Red.

She was delighted at the way Aaan's face lit up as she approached. She couldn't take her eyes off of him and felt their gaze was packed with meaning now that he'd said he loved her. Her heart pounded as she approached.

He held out a hand to her. As she gave him her hand, he raised it to his lips. She almost forgot what she had been going to ask him. "Red's getting some food and coffee out for everyone and I wondered if you wanted to eat something. I mean, I know you don't usually ..."

"What do you mean, don't usually eat?" interjected Zaak, obviously still in a playful mood. "I am starved. I require angel food cake. Right, brother?"

"Do not pay him any heed, Anya. We could eat a morsel to be polite if that would please you."

Annie found this adorable and couldn't help but giggle. "That is very gracious of you. Yes, I would like for you to eat some of Dad's stinky Gruyere cheese."

Zaak raised an eyebrow. "Pardon, but I thought we were getting prepared for battle. Are you sure you want us to give our location away so readily?"

Annie laughed. She was amazed at how light and playful this was after the anger she'd felt toward Zaak just a while ago. Now that she understood his motives, she started noticing so many similarities between the brothers, and felt she would very much like to be his friend. They both seemed like such great guys and she didn't feel at all odd anymore for giving her heart so fully to Aaan. She felt a little sorry that Zaak didn't have anyone. He was good, she realized; so good he had spent centuries trying to help his father.

Aaan interrupted her thoughts by squeezing her hand. She turned to look into his face and wished so much that they were alone so she could kiss him. She didn't care if he was afraid of the consequences of their love. At this moment, she would have done it anyway.

She realized Zaak was addressing her and forced her attention toward him. "Um, what did you say? Sorry."

Zaak laughed knowingly. "I was just asking to be excused while the humans are having lunch and I expect my brother could also use a rest. We need to rest in our ethereal forms. The manifestations we have presented this morning have been draining."

"Regretfully, what my brother says is true," Aaan said. "But know that I will not leave your side. You will not be able to see me until the meeting reconvenes but I can always reappear if you need me."

Annie felt touched by his politeness and consideration. "No, of course. That's fine. I just need to check in with Red and I might take a nap myself. I mean, I know you're not going to be napping, but just the same. Please rest in whatever way you need. Both of you. Goodness knows what this day will bring and we'll need our strength."

Aaan smiled and nodded and the two vanished.

Annie smiled, knowing Aaan was still nearby and really liking that feeling.

She went to check on Red and found her in the kitchen with everything apparently under control.

On seeing her approach, Red said with mock bossiness, "Hey, I thought I told you to rest. Now scram."

"Everything good here, then? I just wanted to check. Wow, looks like you've cleaned out the fridge."

"Not to worry. I was clearheaded enough to text Mom and ask her to pick up a few things. I told her it was because Uncle Alistair and Aunt Zsofia had returned. I conveniently didn't mention the others—that would've required too much explanation for a text message."

"Yeah, thanks for thinking of that. Oh, yeah, and the angels don't need any food, though Zaak did angle for some angel food cake."

Red laughed, "He seems really nice. Or maybe *good's* a better word for an angel. Got a lot of personality, too—or would that be angel-ality?"

"Okay, the angel jokes have started, so I'm outta here."

Annie passed the library and noticed that the rest of the group was gathered there. Most seemed to be listening to Uncle Alistair. Roy caught her eye and gave her a regretful smile and Annie quickly looked away, unsure what was up with that. She went to her room to lie down for a few minutes.

Half an hour later, Red called her back downstairs. The council had reconvened in the dining room, probably because the group had grown—Aaan and Zaak had reappeared. She reseated herself next to Aaan, thinking how different she felt now than when they'd convened earlier.

Annie listened as Uncle Alistair welcomed the newcomers, gave a brief overview of the morning's discussion, and took an opportunity to urge the utmost secrecy. He acknowledged that all present knew some of the mysteries surrounding the stones and used the three possessed men as an example of the type of consequence that occurred when knowledge of the stones was leaked. So far, they'd only had to battle a few members of a cult, but things could get much more dangerous if, for example, a corrupt foreign government got in on the act.

Everyone at the table agreed to secrecy, with the exception that Erik asked for permission to confer with his parents since they were also immersed in the whole business. This was generally agreed.

Next, Annie had a similar request for involving Nyah, as did Red for Tatyana. This was also agreed, though on a need-to-know basis only.

Uncle Alistair ended that part of the discussion by stating, "The least said, the better. However, when additional help is needed, we do need a list of those who can be trusted and thus may be called upon. I would say at this point, this includes, in addition to those present, the Wolfeningens, Nyah, Tatyana, Ms. Oglethorpe, Reverend Joan Carly, and the team of priests who helped in the exorcism of Roy and Lorenzo. And I'm afraid in the hours ahead, in battling this cult, I will need *carte blanche* to confer with experts in the field who can be trusted."

Annie saw nods of approval all around the room.

Xenia, Rachel, and Daniel were obviously awed to be in the presence of two ethereal beings. They kept glancing at them and seemed to be trying not to stare.

Annie sensed Aaan and Zaak were expending a lot of effort to appear human and they mostly succeeded, though Annie did notice an occasional glow from one or the other. Aaan seemed to have this problem more than Zaak; she thought this was probably because his aura was likely much brighter at present. Annie had to nudge him occasionally to remind him to tone it down.

She noticed Roy looked penitent and wondered again what was up with him. Maybe since he'd been possessed he didn't like any kind of ethereal being—from what she'd seen of him, it seemed to fit. She wondered about that since she was pretty sure he was studying theology or something similar.

Her uncle moved the meeting forward. "Now we need to move on to the real reason for this meeting. We need a plan."

Before he could say more, Roy stood, his hands twisting the bottom of his shirt in an expression of submissiveness. "Professor Hamilton, before we go further, I feel the need to speak ... if that's okay."

Uncle Alistair nodded. "Briefly, please," he said and seated himself.

Roy now looked at Aaan and began, "Aaan, I would like to ask your forgiveness for my betrayal of you in not bringing you back as I'd promised."

Here Roy looked at Erik. "And Erik, I would also like to ask your forgiveness. I—I thought I was doing the right thing ... protecting someone else from the horror of demon possession. I didn't trust any ethereal beings at that time, but I see now that I was wrong. If there's anything I can do to make it up to you, Aaan, I will." Here he sat down.

Aaan answered his look and nodded, a signal that he was forgiven. Annie was a little surprised at this. So it had been *Roy* who'd messed things up and gotten Aaan stuck in a transformed state? She felt angry with him. Wasn't it also partly his fault she'd been possessed? Not that it ended up turning out so badly, but still ... She looked at Aaan again and was impressed with his tranquility.

She noticed Erik didn't look at Roy, though—obviously he was still miffed that Roy would betray his trust after all he'd done to rescue Roy from his possession. This would take time, Annie thought. She sided more with Erik; she wasn't ready to forgive and forget yet, either.

Uncle Alistair stood. "Thank you, Mr. Oglethorpe. I am sure all will be well, but please realize there are always consequences for our actions, so even though you are forgiven, you'll be expected to make amends as needed."

Roy looked relieved at the public pardon and seemed to be grateful for the opportunity to make amends. "Absolutely," he responded. Annie saw Xenia pat his hand in support as it rested on the table.

Uncle Alistair continued. "As I was saying, we need a plan. The scenario is this—a cult is after the stones. This cult consists of the father of our friends, Aaan and Zaak, another powerful demon, and at present, at least three possessed men, probably others. We no longer have the stones, but I do have five STAG controls that contain powder from these stones. I think our goal here is two-fold—to decide what to do with the STAG controls, and determine how to defend ourselves from the cult. I now open the floor for suggestions." Alistair sat down and leaned back with a grave air, as if beckoning serious ideas to be drawn forth from the minds of those present.

Aaan went first. He stood and began, "Friends, I have an idea. Our father, Daanak, formed this cult and has been the leader for many centuries. This other powerful demon is a fairly recent addition to the cult, I believe, but I will ask my brother to speak to that. My suggestion is this: I would like to step up to my family obligations and assist my brother in trying to turn our father from his evil path—a type of family intervention, if you will."

Annie saw the brothers exchange a warm glance before Aaan continued, "Our father needs to move past his obsession with our mother. So, perhaps we should assist him by allowing him to use the power of the Angel Stone."

A hush filled the room. She knew this was what the cult was after and to just give in and let them have it was opposite from what she would have guessed he would say. She looked at Uncle Alistair for his reaction and was surprised to see he seemed to be considering Aaan's suggestion. He was nodding his head slowly, almost imperceptibly.

Aaan continued, "I do not know where it would take him. I know it transformed me into a reality deeper in the angel realm than I usually occupy. With him, perhaps it would take him deeper still, since he is pure angel. My proposal is for us to offer to help him transform, but be very clear this will be on the condition that we use the STAG control on him. He at no time will have possession of the STAG control, and he must recant evil before we transform him, because we do not know what the consequences would be of interjecting evil into an unknown place in the angel realm. I think with him gone, the cult will disband. We may also need to do something about the other demon—any ideas, brother?"

Zaak stood next. "Thank you, brother. I have waited long centuries to have you join with me in persuading our father to change his path. I do believe we can accomplish this if we stick together." Then his face became grave. "However, the other demon is another matter. When I teasingly called him 'Satan,' there was a reason I gave him that nickname. He is very simplistic in his evil—somewhat like a child. He delights in the power he feels when he actively causes suffering, or does anything against someone's will. I do not think he is particularly interested in the stones—oh, maybe he has an idea that he could cause problems in the angel realm, but I think his chief interest in the stones is simply that he has been feeding off our father's anger and misery for almost seventy years, since the second World War ended. I think taunting our father is his game much more than acquiring the stones. If we got Father away from him and Father recanted evil—I am not certain, but I believe this demon would lose interest and leave. Who knows, perhaps he would be *compelled* to leave. It would take something like exorcising him from Father, even though I believe that term is usually reserved for human-demon interactions."

Uncle Alistair was obviously very excited by this idea. He now stood. "Gentlemen, this is indeed fascinating. So, the idea would be to get Daanak away from the other demon, convince him to recant evil in exchange for ... no, let's not make it a bribe—that might backfire. We will simply state that we are willing to help him gain access to whatever place in the angel realm the stones will take him, but that we are only willing to send one pure of heart deep into the angel realm. Then, once we have gained his trust and recantation, we might be able to simply order the other demon away. Is that an accurate summary?" Alistair stroked his beard and looked from Aaan to Zaak and back again.

Aaan said, "I think that is an accurate summary of the ideas so far." Zaak nodded in agreement. Annie noted the meeting seemed very formal but it was somehow fitting for this group.

But then Red changed it up a little by saying somewhat flippantly in a loud whisper to Erik, "It's too bad we're not at the Vatican so Aaan and Zaak could talk to their father without the evil demon being able to enter—of course, I guess their father couldn't enter, either."

Alistair cleared his throat and began to say, "Dearest niece, no side-bar conversations. Please share your ideas—your thoughts are valuable to us."

Red blushed. "Oh, sorry, I was just saying it'd be nice if the family intervention could take place in the Vatican so that the Satan character couldn't interfere."

Alistair's face lit up. "Child, that is brilliant."

Erik looked puzzled. "With all due respect, sir, the Vatican—"

Alistair cut him off, "No, no, not the actual Vatican. Don't you see? The National Cathedral. It's only about two miles from the lab as the crow flies."

At the mention of a crow, Buddy, who had been asleep under the table, ran to the window and barked two short barks, his tail curled over his back. Annie watched Red quietly stand and walk to the window to see what Buddy was barking at.

"What is it, Sonia?" asked Uncle Alistair.

"I don't know," she said, peering out the window. "But something on the small footpath that runs down to the towpath certainly has Moon and his friends excited."

Alistair looked at Erik. "What do you think, Son?"

"My thoughts exactly," Erik replied. "Red, I need you to transform me." Without explaining what he was up to, he handed Red a STAG control and pulled her into the next room.

Red was back in her seat in moments. Rachel, Daniel, and Xenia seemed shocked, though Annie noted the others didn't seem to think it odd at all.

After Erik's curious disappearance, the meeting continued. Eventually, they decided they'd lure Daanak to the lab by telling him Aaan and Zaak had now joined forces and knew where the STAG controls were hidden.

Annie offered to have Aaan possess her and try to make Daanak believe it was Zaak, but both Alistair and Aaan said absolutely not.

"Besides," Red added, "you aren't going to be able to leave your room for a month when Mom and Dad see those piercings."

Annie rolled her eyes and sank into her chair, feeling frustrated and a little concerned about what Red had said. Everything had happened so fast she hadn't really had time to sweat over her parents' reaction, but Red was probably right.

Red asked, "Uncle Alistair, something I have always wondered is, why didn't the demons in Roy just go inside the safe and use the stones? I mean, I know they couldn't remove them, but couldn't they go into the safe? They can go through walls."

This caught Annie's attention. She heard Uncle Alistair laugh briefly before responding with, "Very astute, niece. There is a very good reason for that, and one we don't have time for me to give you in full, but it has to do, I think, with a very sincere and powerful incantation or blessing that must have been performed on the safe in bygone days. That safe must have held some very important artifacts or writings. It seems impenetrable by both mankind and demon-kind without a key."

Annie saw Red look at the clock and then quickly excuse herself, disappearing out the door and returning momentarily with Erik.

"So, Erik, what did you learn?" Alistair asked.

"It was indeed Moon," he said, explaining who Moon was to the others. Annie saw Erik's birder-friends faces light up with keen interest. Erik hesitated a moment, allowing their questions to die down, and then continued. "But what I learned is that Moon saw three demon-possessed men walking around behind the house and down the path to the towpath—just as Red had guessed. The men weren't able to enter the house, but seemed pretty determined and will likely eventually find a way. Um, that last part wasn't Moon's thoughts, but my own commentary. Moon and his group will keep an eye on them and make noise when they come close to the house."

Erik's birding friends were obviously impressed by this and the meeting threatened to get sidetracked by the accelerating chatter, mostly involving recent studies on avian intelligence, until Uncle Alistair stepped in. "So, friends, this confirms it's imperative to move the action away from this house to the lab with the intent of luring it to the cathedral. And it's imperative we move quickly. My nephew and niece will be returning home from work in about two hours and I'm sure they're in danger of getting waylaid by those three goons if they try to enter the house—as anyone would be right now. I'm sure the cult members will be trying to capture a hostage to force us out. None of you are expecting a visitor here, right?" He looked around the room at each face.

Several checked their cell phones for messages. Annie gasped when she saw a text message from Nyah. "Nyah texted me to say she's stopping by on her way home from work!"

"What time does she get off work?" Erik asked urgently.

"I don't know." Annie felt a touch hysterical.

"Text her back and say you'll meet her at the mall," Erik demanded.

"The mall? Erik, she's on her bike. She doesn't have her driver's license yet." Annie felt frustrated.

"Well, tell her *something*. Just make sure she doesn't come here. Meantime, I'll pop out and keep an eye on the place." Red nodded and they both slipped out of the room again.

Annie quickly texted Nyah. WAIT! DON'T COME HERE. I'LL EXPLAIN LATER.

"Professor Hamilton, if I might make an observation," Aaan said. "Other spiritual enclaves, or sanctuaries, do exist that are closer than either the lab or the National Cathedral. There are at least two fairly strong synagogues and a few temples of various types that would exclude the entrance of a demon. Would it not be best to go to the nearest sanctuary?"

"Hmmm." Alistair stroked his beard. "You have a point. We may indeed need to use one of these sanctuaries, but let's aim for the cathedral. I have acquaintances there I could certainly call upon for assistance, and I know of a special room that is kept just for working with the possessed—one that allows their entry but at the same time, seems to limit their abilities. I, by no means, am trying to say only those who proclaim any certain set of beliefs are right and others wrong, but I am more familiar with some. Also, we need to act here with the utmost speed and having made recent contact with friends at the cathedral in the arrangement of our wedding—" he exchanged a loving glance with Zsofia, "—I would like to make an executive decision to shoot for the cathedral."

Aaan nodded his assent.

Uncle Alistair added, "I do think the idea put forth earlier to lure Daanak to the lab first is sound. He would be suspicious if we asked him to come straight to the cathedral. He will not be able to go into the lab, however, and so, naturally, the brothers can broach the topic of his recanting so he can enter. Then, once the first breech in his evil armor has been made, he can be told the only way he can possibly be transformed by the Angel Stone is within the cathedral by a team of priests. Once he agrees to this, we must be ready to escort him from the lab to the cathedral—this will likely be the most difficult and dangerous part of the plan. However, I think it is a sound plan. Agreed?"

There was unanimous agreement and her uncle asked, "Any questions at this time?"

Annie felt puzzled. "Uncle Alistair, I don't understand. If going from the lab to the cathedral is the most dangerous part, why does this need to be done? I mean, can't the angels just materialize at the cathedral?"

She looked at Aaan for help in understanding the necessity of this part of the plan and added, "I know Aaan could pop back and forth between here and Hungary in a split second. I'm sure Daanak can do that, too. I don't understand."

She saw Aaan exchange a look with Alistair and both nodded. Aaan then rose to explain. "You see, dear one, although you are correct in suggesting our father could just pop over to the cathedral, there is a concern with this method of transport. We think he would be vulnerable to interception by the more powerful demon, or devil or ... whatever he is, who I am sure is watching his every move. Once he has made even the tiniest step toward breaking whatever deal or promise he has entered into with this *shetani*, the villain will likely turn on our father and attack him with everything available. Father will need to be under the protection of sanctuary every millisecond until the transformation is complete."

While some further discussion ensued, Red popped out and returned with Erik. The plan was explained to him and further details were added. The group disbanded to man their assigned stations just after four o'clock.

The plan was for Alistair to ride with Roy, Xenia, Rachel, and Daniel. They would leave for the lab right away in an effort to beat rush-hour traffic. They would take three of the STAG controls, leaving one with Erik. Uncle Alistair would use his cell phone to arrange for someone to receive the STAG controls at the cathedral. They would go first to the lab to retrieve the other one from the safe. They would transport the lot of them to the cathedral—this would take care of all STAG controls except one, which Erik and Red would retain for their own part of the plan, which involved enlisting help from a make-shift animal brigade.

All except Aunt Zsofia would converge on the lab to help with the escort of Daanak from the lab to the cathedral. She would stay behind at the mansion to explain the situation to Annie's mom and dad.

Annie liked the role Erik and Red would play. Red would keep a STAG control and use it to transform Erik, who would use his well-practiced skill in communicating with the animals to inform Buddy, the cats, and Moon to be on the lookout for the possessed men and to alert the humans to any attempts to break into the mansion or take a hostage. Erik and Red would also attempt to enlist aid from animals in the area of the cathedral, chiefly birds, to keep watch.

When all but Aunt Zsofia, Annie, and the brothers had left, Annie got on her computer to prepare maps of the route they would use from the lab to the cathedral to text to the cell phones of all those involved. Aaan stayed close to her, and Zaak stayed close to Aaan.

Annie knew Aaan and Zaak needed some time to plan, since they were at the core of the intervention. But she also wanted to hear about what Aaan had seen when he was transformed. There was little time and she had work to do. Still, there were seconds here and there while waiting for websites to load, and Aaan was able to tell her in bits and snatches an overview of his experience in seeing the angel realm and meeting Eriel. This intrigued her and she felt he had tapped into something important. She regretted each time she had to refocus on the computer screen to keep moving forward with her assignment. She wanted more time to hear about it. Zaak seemed interested in Aaan's experience, too, but the two of them spent most of that time planning how they would approach Daanak.

After a few minutes, Annie was almost done with the maps. She was so attentive to the computer screen that although she heard a commotion from the crows in the yard, it didn't register as an SOS signal until she heard a crow squawk as if in pain. She looked at Aaan and saw the same alarm in his face that she felt and realized something was wrong outside.

At that next instant she heard a frantic call from Aunt Zsofia downstairs, "Annie! Come quick!"

Annie and the brothers rushed downstairs to find the elderly lady trembling and on the verge of hysteria. It took a few moments to calm her down to get a coherent account. Annie suspected all her fears from the war reoccurred whenever she felt threatened and this exacerbated her panic.

Eventually, they were able to ascertain that she'd heard a commotion in front of the mansion and had peeked out a window in time to see a teenage girl being thrown into the back of a van by three men, who quickly raced away. And they had a gun, Zsofia said. She'd seen another man shooting into the trees — there must've been a silencer because she couldn't hear the shots.

"They must have Nyah! Aaan, we have to do something," Annie begged, feeling frantic.

"No, you stay here, I will find her," Zaak quickly stated and was gone.

Annie hurried out the front door to see if she could find any clues. She found two bicycles cast aside at the entrance of their driveway. She tried to calm herself to think. Two people. She recognized the metallic purple frame of one, but where had she seen that? She closed her eyes for a moment. *Tatyana*. This was Tatyana's bike. The other was also a girl's bike, but she didn't recognize it. She rushed back inside to text Red.

Aaan was tending to Aunt Zsofia, who was now seated and sipping a glass of water. Aaan was seated on a nearby chair pulled up close and the two were conversing. When he saw Annie, he quickly communicated that the girl Aunt Zsofia had seen was very short, with dark skin and long black hair.

"Uma. That's Red's friend, Uma. They must've bicycled over to drop in on Red. Oh my gosh, this is bad." Annie frantically pulled her phone from her pocket.

She typed a few strokes and then exclaimed, "Oh shoot. Nyah's on her way over, too. I told her not to come, but she said she was worried about me because I haven't called her since I've been back." Annie could tell her voice betrayed her tears, which were on the verge of gushing.

"Anya, you need to calm down. It will be okay," Aaan soothed. "We are a team. Remember that good always wins in the end. It has to. Evil does not exist on its own, it is just perverted good. It lacks substance."

"What?" Annie was upset and couldn't quite get what he was saying, though she thought it was sweet that he was trying so hard.

"Never mind, just trust your friends will be all right."

Just then, Zaak re-appeared. "It wasn't Nyah," he said. He seemed oddly relieved. "It was two of your sister's friends, whom I recognize, but don't know their names."

"Tatyana and Uma," Annie said distractedly as she continued to text. "Red's freaking out. Those are her two best friends. I'm afraid she'll do something stupid." Annie paused. "Wait a minute. I just had a thought. Danaak and the freaky devil dude don't know that I'm not possessed with Zaak, right? I mean, this house is a sanctuary, so they couldn't get close enough to see that Zaak isn't possessing me anymore, or to hear all the talk about Zaak not being evil after all, right?"

Aaan and Zaak nodded.

"And they're probably looking for me, right?"

Aaan and Zaak both looked perplexed. Aaan spoke, "Anya, what are you suggesting?"

Annie was excited now. "Okay, guys, here it is. We have to do something quick, right? So, Zaak'll jump back in and we'll go and distract them. They'll certainly allow us into their group.

Um, or, better yet, Aaan could possess me—you two look a lot alike, you know."

Now Aaan's voice rose almost hysterically. "No, Anya! What reason could they possibly be telling themselves for why Zaak could enter this sanctuary but they could not? Isn't that a giveaway that he's not evil? In other words, his cover already has been blown. And, second, yes, they can tell us apart. We have assumed the manifestations of the way we each looked in our first incarnation. That's how we identify ourselves, how we see ourselves as humans. And yes, there was a very strong family resemblance. But they see our essences, and remember, those are quite different. I mean, I suppose that Zaak could have done some repenting, and he will likely have to before he can enter the lab—won't you?"

"Well, actually not," Zaak replied sheepishly, "I was play-acting, as Alistair suggested, when I pretended we couldn't enter the lab. They have long known my essence is not as murky as one might expect, but I guess they think I will always be loyal to Father. Still, I have become accustomed to some bad habits and have been straying further from the fold for quite some time. I think some serious repentance and redirection may be in order."

Aaan interrupted here. "Regardless, third—you may recall, dear Anya, the council said no to that idea. It was deemed too dangerous." He gave heavy emphasis to the last phrase.

Annie's controlled her voice so it began on a deceptively calm note. "But, dear Aaan," her calm voice rose progressively, "that was before Red's friends got kidnapped. If you think for one instant I'm going to wait until my parents get home and ground me, you have another think coming. After all, this is mostly my fault. *I'm going to help out*." She felt she'd made her point clear with the extra emphasis she'd given to the last sentence.

"Anya, please calm down. How could any of this possibly be your fault? You were a victim of a sham." Here, he paused to eye his brother, making it clear that obviously not everything had been totally forgiven. Zaak lowered his eyes.

"Sham, spam. Whatever, but I'm not going to sit here and allow my sister and her friends to fight evil while I'm safely locked in my room. And what about Nyah? She's on her way over, too—that is, unless she gets kidnapped on the way. I'm going to help one way or another and you can't stop me."

Despite Aunt Zsofia's attempts to calm her by patting her shoulders, Annie didn't feel at all calm. She stood and began to walk toward the stairs to prepare for departure.

Aaan apparently was unaccustomed to seeing a woman be so defiant. He seemed to back down, saying, "Okay, Anya. Perhaps you have a point. If you are bent on joining the battle, Zaak and I will do our best to protect you?"

He looked at Zaak, who nodded his assent. "I think Zaak should pretend to possess you so hopefully we can convince them that the Anya-Zaak combination is still one of them. I will stay nearby to keep watch, agreed?"

Annie and Zaak both nodded.

Annie felt relieved to have an action item. "I want to either find the three men and offer to exchange myself for the hostages, or go to the lab and wait outside for them to find me. Either way, once your father and the demon show up, the two of you can talk to him." She paused. "Can either of you drive a car?"

"First, exchanging you is Not. Going. To. Happen," said Aaan. "Remember, we want to draw the action to the lab. Plus, I think the three men may be highly unpredictable. If you are going to join the action, it should be with the group—we stick together, okay?"

Aaan was being demanding now, and it was Annie's turn to back down. "Okay," she responded, pleased with the decision.

"And second, yes, I can drive, but prefer to have the freedom to move about in case we get waylaid. So, let's try to hook up with your sister and Erik," said Aaan. "Now, may I use your cell phone, please?"

CHAPTER 12

Intervention

Annie watched from a window as Viggo and Minah, with Minah at the wheel, pulled up in front of the mansion to pick up herself and her entourage of half-angels. The group drove south on the Clara Barton Parkway, along the Potomac River, to meet up with Red and Erik. Red texted Annie to say they were now on Roosevelt Island, a national park near Georgetown. Their business there was finished and they were heading onto the Georgetown campus. Erik had given instructions about where to park, and despite rush hour, they made fairly good time because most of the traffic was traveling out of, rather than into, the district.

Annie and a very handsome manifestation of Aaan were seated in the backseat. So as not to freak out Erik's parents, nothing was said about Zaak, who Annie knew was comfortably ensconced inside her, but this time, he allowed her mind to enjoy its usual freedom, unlike the dreamlike state he had used on her to fool the others the last time.

Aaan, using Annie's cell phone, finally reached Uncle Alistair. Annie was relieved to hear that he had arranged everything with his contacts at the cathedral and was now waiting with Roy and his three friends inside the lab. They were to contact him when they entered the campus so he could meet them downstairs, with Annie and Zaak pretending to be unable to enter the building. Luckily, as this was the summer semester, no evening classes were held on Wednesday nights in the old science building, so he expected only a few dedicated graduate students and cleaning staff would be present.

Annie was relieved to see Erik's car parked in a nearby space as they parked. Out stepped Red and Erik, who walked briskly to join them, Erik still buttoning his shirt after his earlier transformation.

Red came straightaway to Annie and embraced her, neither sister stating the obvious—they were going into unknown danger and this could be the last time they saw each other alive. Annie squeezed her sister hard, but knowing the time was critical, didn't linger. Then they clasped hands in a fierce show of solidarity.

Annie saw that Erik was doing the same with his parents. She knew his dad had been through a lot and his resolve seemed to have hardened into steel. Erik thanked them for bringing Annie and Aaan and suggested they go home, but the suggestion seemed to reach deaf ears. Annie felt curiously strengthened from the fierce determination he saw in Erik's father's eyes. His mother seemed to echo that resolve as she hugged each girl and then her son.

Aaan gave Annie a very long hug and Annie didn't want to let go. She'd just today learned that her beloved Aaan also loved her. Now, who knew what would happen?

Annie saw Erik and Red exchange a long kiss. Annie felt like they were a group of warriors as they all turned soberly and began walking toward the front of the science building, each holding the hand of a loved one.

As they approached the fountain adorning the hilltop in front of the building, Uncle Alistair emerged and walked toward them. Roy, Xenia, Rachel, and Daniel had apparently either stayed behind in the lab or went ahead to the cathedral.

Red's phone buzzed with a text message. "Mom and Dad are on their way and are bringing their tandem bike in case the traffic gets bad and they need to ditch the car," she told the group.

Alistair nodded to Red and began to speak. "Dear friends, we will each now be called upon to stand firm for what is right no matter what we must sacrifice. The cult must not get the STAG controls. No one on this planet, or perhaps even in other realms, would be safe again. And we must protect each other and anyone else in the picture this day, from this evil group. You each know the part you must play here. I shall not reiterate your roles for fear of being overheard. Just know that good trumps evil every time. As I have learned of late from our friend Aaan, evil doesn't exist on its own, but is merely per-verted good, and thus, we need not fear evil itself, but we must only be cautious of its specific acts—those can produce frank danger. So, let's divide and conquer." The last sentence was spoken with such a commanding voice that all cheered, their fists raised in readiness for war, Annie felt it was the same as countless others had done since time immemorial.

As if on cue, two well-dressed men walked toward them. Aaan whispered to the group that he recognized them as man-ifestations of his father and the demon.

Annie thought one demon's manifestation was very sim-ilar to that of Alistair, a somewhat wizened, though pridefully erect, graybeard. The other, the one that must be Daanak, was a strikingly handsome, middle-aged man with a chiseled face and golden ponytail. Annie was amazed at his beauty and won-dered if this was the way he'd looked originally when Aaan and Zaak's mother fell in love with him.

As the men approached, the graybeard seemed to be in charge, holding up a hand to halt their progress when they were a couple of feet away from Uncle Alistair.

"Greetings, Alistair Hamilton. I am delighted to make your acquaintance. I have long admired your work from afar." Here he grinned widely, showing glistening and somewhat un-natu-rally pointed teeth. Annie felt sick.

The graybeard continued, "My name is ... oh, never mind that for now. And I think you are somewhat acquainted with my colleague, Daanak?"

Daanak and Alistair nodded to each other.

He continued, "I think you know what I want and I am sure we can come to a mutually satisfactory agreement. Like, for example, let's see ... not asking your niece to jump from a window, or something similar for those two dear, sweet girls my friends are entertaining. If you give me what I want, perhaps I will ask my friends not to push the smallest girl into traffic in the next few minutes."

Red gasped and Annie saw Erik steady her from behind by squeezing her shoulders. He whispered something into her ear and she nodded.

Two female students walked briskly toward them, daypacks slung across one shoulder. They seemed to be deeply engaged in conversation; though they did each glance toward the unexpected gathering, they kept walking and luckily did not turn into the old science building.

The graybeard began again, "Perhaps we should step inside one of these fine buildings to conduct our business in private." Uncle Alistair began to respond, but the graybeard cut him off. "What have we here?"

Annie looked around to see her mom and dad approaching from the parking lot, wearing bicycle helmets.

The graybeard now seemed totally distracted from his original thought and unable to resist toying with them. "Ah, Dr. Greene. So glad you can join us," he said, with a snake-like hiss. "I have followed your work for the past few years, though I have not always been happy with it."

He approached Annie's mom, wagging a finger in a no-no gesture. "Yes, I have seen your name pop up quite a few times as a proponent of this new push for *humane* animal testing. You and your colleagues don't seem to realize just how boring that would be." Here he laughed heartily as he turned to pace back to the center.

Annie noticed that Red and Erik took advantage of his turned back. With the slightest of movements, Erik disappeared. Neither the graybeard nor Daanak seemed to notice.

As the graybeard paced, he mockingly made sounds of animals screaming in pain, which obviously affected her mom, who tensed as if she'd launch herself at him. He continued, "You see, since the Nazis were defeated, I was getting quite bored," he said, pretending to fake-cry at this. "Until I began convincing a few key scientists that whole animal testing was a must for any dedicated scientist who wanted to ... get this ... *protect human health and save the environment.*" Here he paused to guffaw maniacally. "Isn't that wonderful? I love it when I can twist a passion for something so good and make it mandatory that something diabolical must be done to ensure the good thing. It was a brilliant ploy because I win either way, you see."

And then his face suddenly became enraged. "Until the likes of you began whining about how this isn't necessary and inventing other methods to gather the information. Well, know this, Dr. Greene." Here his eyes bored into hers. "It simply will not work. I will make sure of that. There is way too much pleasure in all that suffering for me to just drop it. You naïve little tart," he hissed through his pointed teeth.

Annie saw her mom brace herself defiantly as he continued, "It won't work. The strong will always torture the weak. And I will see that it continues. Any progress you make in your *in-vitro* and *in-silico* methods will only anger me and I will take my vengeance on the factory farms and slaughterhouses. Do I make myself clear?" As he spoke, he seemed to approach Annie's mom without walking, but more gliding eerily toward her.

As his face approached hers, she stood her ground and as soon as he was close enough, she spat in his face.

Both Annie and Red gasped and Annie feared for her mother.

But rather than retaliate, he simply turned and laughed maniacally again, actually throwing his head back in a huge guffaw.

Once he stopped laughing, he began again. Annie noted that Daanak stood by, looking resigned, as if he'd seen this display countless times before.

Now he drifted toward her dad. "And the bicycling statistician. Trying to help solve the world's problems with mathematics, evaluating feeding programs and medical interventions in poverty-stricken areas. Just like your uncle, aren't you? Both trying to help the poor. Didn't your messiah even say the poor will be with you always? You know, I cannot actually take credit for the poor. That springs from the deeds of others like myself, as well as, I must say, the selfish choices of your kind.

But back to today's fun, let's see. Now that I have the parents of my little puppet, I can have some real fun."

"Young Anya—or Annie, as you are called," he said, turning toward her. Her heart pounded. "I would like for you to do one outlandish thing every half hour until your uncle gives the stones to me, or those gadgets that contain them."

His spider-like fingers drummed on his cheek as he considered. Then, his face brightening as though pleased by a thought, he said, "We will begin by mooning everyone—here and now, in front of anyone who walks by, and especially your parents. Simon says 'Moon them.' " He commenced again the maniacal laugh.

Annie heard her mom scream and saw her dad hold her back. Annie wasn't sure what her parents knew about her supposedly being possessed by an evil demon. Aunt Zsofia might or might not have mentioned that little detail. She decided she'd better begin acting.

She stared straight ahead, trying to envision herself a mindless automaton and walked a couple of steps forward, swinging her hips as if about to do a strip tease.

She heard Red make an audible gasp and tense, likely making an effort to brace herself for whatever Annie would have to do to convince them that Zaak was on board.

Annie turned her back to them, bent over, did a quick waggle, and bounced back up again, simultaneously pulling her shorts down and back up in an instant, glad for an elastic waistband. Luckily, at the same moment, a huge bird flew by just behind her in a flash of gold.

Annie stood staring straight ahead again. She eyed the others as well as she could without actually looking at them. She thought no one seemed certain of what they'd just seen—they were looking from one to another. Aaan's jaw jutted forward defiantly and his brows were angry, but he also looked puzzled. She was pretty sure of one thing—no one had seen her moon.

The graybeard was obviously enraged. "What? You damnable eagles! You will pay. And you, Zaak—" here he began to pace in front of Annie.

Annie felt like stepping back but stood her ground. She was amazed at how calm she felt and then decided that Zaak must be doing something inside her to calm her. She noticed that Uncle Alistair seemed to be suppressing a smile.

Then the graybeard stopped just in front of her and rudely knocked on the top of her head with his knuckles. "You in there? Anyone home? I expect much better obedience than this, you moron. Is this your best attempt at cruelty, donating hair? Indeed. How lame can one get? I did *not* say to donate hair." His voice was rising in anger and he continued shouting, switching to some ancient language Annie didn't understand.

Annie could tell from her peripheral vision that everyone seemed to be bracing now that his ire was riled. But before any further action could occur, there was the sound of a phone ringing.

Daanak reached inside his immaculately tailored jacket and pulled out a cell phone. "Sir, it's the kid. He's ready with the first girl," he said.

"Excellent. Now the fun begins," the demon said, clapping his hands together like an excited child, momentarily seeming to forget about Annie. She thought she saw her uncle and Aaan brace at this.

The graybeard walked toward Alistair. "You see, Professor Hamilton, your denial of my request for the stones has consequences. My young friend has one of your niece's friends beside a heavily used section of road and is poised to push her into oncoming traffic. And the best part?" He stopped again to giggle to himself and then clap. "The best part is we get to watch."

Here he held up the phone for first Alistair and then the others. The screen showed a clearly terrified Uma, blindfolded, standing beside a road. Whoever was holding the phone panned the area and Annie thought it showed a familiar stretch of road. Annie heard her mom exclaim rather loudly, "It's close by, at the entrance to Clara Barton from M Street!"

Annie hoped Erik heard this in time to save Uma.

As she and the others watched the tiny screen helplessly, time seemed to stand still. She felt sick watching the continual stream of traffic; and sicker when the camera panning back to Uma. Uma's wrists, tied behind her, were grasped by another young man and she was shoved forward. She screamed in terror. Annie heard Red gasp and felt her own eyes tear up.

The demon laughed. "That was just to taunt you. Okay, Alistair, your time is up."

He spoke into the phone. "Go ahead, push her. And Antonio, you go, too." He held one hand in front of his mouth as if to indicate that he knew he was being naughty, and with a sickening snicker, he added, "Did you hear me, Antonio? Stay with her and make sure the two of you land squarely in front of an oncoming automobile." He laughed now with evil hysteria.

"*Noooo!*" Annie heard Red scream and the others gasp in disbelief. The video was hard to follow because of the small size of the screen, but it appeared someone was pushing Uma forward, push-dragging her into the road from a bank that dropped down onto the blind curve.

The video went blurry. It looked like another form entered the picture, then they heard screams and screeching tires.

Red was obviously horrified as she clutched Annie's hand. Tears were streaming down her cheeks. Annie tried hard to stay in character and play her role as one possessed.

"Now, you fool. Scan over so we can see the carnage." The demon had such eerie excitement as his hands flailed about. Annie was sickened by his reaction almost as much as by the horror of the scene.

The video panned over to show the bloody face of Lorenzo. A young man was bending over him, crying and shouting his name. The video panned up and caught a shot of Uma running up the road, attempting to escape.

"She's okay," Red squealed.

"After her, you idiots," shouted the demon. Daanak still stood by, appearing bored.

The screen showed some confusing scenes of large golden birds swooping down and attacking Lorenzo's brother, then coming for whoever held the phone. There was a scream, and the video went dark.

"Aaaarrrrrrrhhhhh!" the demon wailed almost as if in agony. "Why can no one obey me? Those three will pay."

Annie saw that a student had begun to walk up the sidewalk toward the building entrance, but witnessing the screams and shouts, he apparently thought better and turned back the way he came. Annie wondered if he suspected this to be a drama club or fraternity hazing activity.

Uncle Alistair seemed to purposefully seize this moment to interject. "Pardon me, sir, but did not you suggest you wished for a private audience with me? I think the young man we just saw is likely calling the campus police as we speak."

"What?" The demon, evidently still smarting from the failed attempt to kill Uma, seemed to be thinking very hard, his tongue licking his lips in snake-like flicking movements. Eventually, he snapped his head around to look at Uncle Alistair and then seemed to think of something that made his mood change. "Oh, yes. A private audience. I would like that very much."

He looked toward the lab, but likely remembering that it was not a place he could enter, at least not comfortably, looked toward another nearby building that seemed to be empty now. "There."

Uncle Alistair could've won an Oscar for his performance. He looked longingly at the building housing his lab and then huffed out some air, pressed his lips together, and said sourly, "Very well."

The demon again showed his child-like excitement at winning the game and began to prance, almost skip, toward the building.

Annie saw Daanak roll his eyes and then look toward Aaan. Both seemed intent on waiting until the two were out of sight to venture any communication.

"What kind of birds were those?" Annie whispered to Red as they waited.

"Golden eagles." Red had a mischievous glint in her eyes. "I'll explain later."

"You," Daanak admonished Annie and Red. "Do you have something to share with the group?"

"No," they said in unison and she saw Red look nonchalantly skyward.

She saw Uncle Alistair cast a glance back to the others and nod to Aaan as he and the demon stepped through the doorway into the building.

Annie watched Aaan slowly advance toward his father. "Father, I have something I wish to say to you."

"Yes, Aaan. Please say anything you like, but also realize that I am committed to this action and have given up my free will to do otherwise." He looked saddened, but also somewhat like a cornered wild animal.

At that moment, Annie almost lost her balance as she felt her body jerk and her hair move slightly. She felt Red grasp her by the shoulders and steady her. At the next instant, the manifested human form of Zaak appeared.

"Zaak, what are you doing? You need to get back to your post—didn't you see he is already angered?"

"Father, I have a confession to make. I have never been truly evil."

Zaak spoke cautiously as he steadily advanced toward his father. "I have stayed with you to watch out for you. I have pretended to share your hatred for those who took my mother— but I am happy for her. She is no doubt in a wonderful place doing fascinating things. And I have looked for long years for an opportunity to save you from your destructive course, so you, too, can be happy. And now I have found it. I have found it in a plan that my dear brother and I have concocted. Please, I beg you: listen to us."

Daanak looked down to the ground in seeming confusion and then slowly back to Zaak. "You are telling me you have lied to me? Your own father? You have betrayed me? You are going to stand in my way of getting the stones? Son, I have waited for ages of time to find a way to enter the land where my dear Ila abides. And the two of you, my own sons, are going to betray me? To stop me from achieving my goal?"

Now Aaan stepped forward to clasp his brother's shoulder. "Father, no, it is not like that. Please, listen to our plan. We will use the power of the stones on *you*. We will not give the controls to the evil one for his evil work, but we will rescue you from him. Just, please, we do not have much time. Come into this building with us and we will take you to a place where there will be others to help you."

Daanak looked mistrustful. "What you are saying does not make sense. Why not transform me now if you have the stones? You know I cannot enter that building—it is possessed of an incompatible energy—no evil may enter and I have gone down that road for a long time. Is this some trick?" He looked from one to the other suspiciously. To Zaak, he said, "Son, all these years that we were together, you are telling me you did not enjoy the evil?"

"Father, this is exactly what I am telling you. I had to train myself to learn to laugh at some of the cruelty so I would not be discovered. My essence is not nearly so clear as Aaan's, but if you will look, it is not nearly so murky as yours, either."

Daanak acknowledged this.

Zaak went on, "I have been in constant fear since you joined forces with that snake-like demon, that devil." He gestured toward the building where the two had entered only moments before.

His father said, "Son, please do not guile him. Let us show respect for all angels, even if they do not seem to deserve it."

"Yeah, yeah," Zaak continued. "Remember all those times that you agreed to 'encourage' soldiers to be heartless and businesslike in their killing of the enemy? I went behind you and made sure each and every one saw a member of the enemy that reminded him or her of a little sister, or mother, or brother or grandfather. And when you did anything to desecrate a holy place, I went behind you and fixed it or cleaned it, at least those times I knew of such a desecration."

His father was now hanging his head, "Son ... I ... "

Aaan picked up the attempt. "Father, as you know, Zaak was always your favorite and I our mother's. But I have also spent ages searching for her. I have never been able to really love a woman as a man should in any of my lives because no other woman has ever been her equal—well, at least not until recently." He glanced at Annie and she felt her eyes fill with tears.

Aaan seemed to sense he had little time and refocused on his father. "But Father, in all my searching, though I have never found a way to her, exactly, I have learned much toward that end. I have learned that if we all seek joy and love, we will naturally end in the same place. And it is never too late to turn from evil to good. Please, Father, come into the lab. Quickly, to get away from the ancient one before he returns."

"Father," picked up Zaak again, "Please try to see yourself in our memories. You were once golden. A force for good. A protector, a peacekeeper. Now, you are the one you would have destroyed then. Please, please come back to us."

"Zaak is right, Father. I, too, remember you as you were. You were beautiful. Terrible. Good. I could hardly look upon you. And that is the angel our dear mother loved. Not who you are now. If I could hold a spiritual mirror so you could see who you have become, you would not wish to find our dear mother. She would recoil from you."

Daanak seemed unable to look at his sons, his eyes now closed, his face contorted in pain.

He tried to speak, "But, son ... even if I could change direction, I cannot enter that structure. As it keeps him out, it also keeps me out. And Zaak, as well."

"No, Father, I can enter. I just pretended I could not to keep from blowing my cover."

"And *you* may enter, too if you take even a tiny step toward good, by renouncing evil." Aaan said forcefully.

Daanak seemed to be in shock, unable to comprehend the enormity of this statement. "I could enter a sanctuary—even I? But you do not know what you are saying. You do not know the things I have done in my hate and grief."

Zaak fell upon his neck at this moment and wept. "I do know, Father, and—" he looked up into his father's eyes "—it doesn't matter. All can be healed. The gift of redemption is for all, and all you have to do is choose ... good."

It was Aaan's turn. "Yes, Father, all you have to do is take a step forward. To cut the ties that bind you to hatred. To cut off the offending hand. Let go of the evil. Step into the light."

Daanak looked skyward and in that instant, the iciness inside him seemed to break apart. He laughed uncontrollably, not an evil laugh, but a joyful laugh, Annie thought.

Finally, after what seemed like eons, he got control of his emotions enough to ask, "Well, what are we waiting for?"

Both Zaak and Aaan hugged him and the rest likely would have done so had Viggo, who had been quietly watchful, not announced, "Quick, they're coming back."

Zaak and Aaan lost no time in carrying their father, using ghostlike, flowing movements but avoiding an instant materialization, into the foyer just inside the doors, though he began to moan in discomfort.

Uncle Alistair evidently saw what was happening because he began to try to distract the demon, but to no avail—the demon had obviously seen them enter the building. "What is going on?" the demon demanded.

"Oh, don't bother with them. Did not we agree the deal would be between just you and me? Let's go get the stones," she heard her uncle say in an effort to buy time.

"Alistair Hamilton, if this is a trick ... " the demon hissed and stopped abruptly, looking at the sky with alarm.

The sky had become noticeably blackened. Annie and the others were hurriedly following Daanak and his sons, but she looked up as she ran and saw hundreds of crows, several great blue herons, and bald eagles circling overhead. The flock began to swoop down and attack the demon.

Annie tried to see what was happening. It looked like the birds were winning. She thought she could see many bloody lacerations appear on his face and arms. Then he switched forms into some kind of misty ethereal form she could barely make out.

The diversion only lasted a few seconds, but it was enough. Uncle Alistair took the opportunity to rush into the old science building. Inside the door, they were just in time to hear Daanak proclaim with a thundering voice, each word an obvious struggle to get out, "I, Daanak ... renounce ... evil ... and choose ... good ... this day ... and forever! " Then he straightened and Annie thought he looked more regal than before. His glow grew markedly brighter as he said something in another language that Annie assumed to be Latin. He was shockingly beautiful, she thought.

"And I, Zaak, also renounce evil and ask for redemption," Zaak spoke the words so fast they blurred together. He also straightened to stand taller and glowed a little brighter, but the transition was not nearly as great as that of his father.

"This way!" Uncle Alistair motioned them quickly up the stairs and into the lab.

CHAPTER 13

The Sound of Distant Thunder

O nce in the lab, everyone seemed to take a moment to breathe before preparing for the next leg of the battle.

Annie heard Red check to see if Erik was nearby, ready to be transformed back to normal. "Erik," she said, and seemed to be trying to project her voice throughout the lab but not shout loud enough for anyone else to hear in any of the nearby labs. "You here?" She waited a moment and then said, "If you're here, stand right here and I'll zap you."

A moment later she pressed a button and he appeared. Red squealed with delight. The two embraced.

Annie and others gathered around Erik to hear his news. He excitedly told the group that Uma, along with Tatyana, who had also been there, had been rescued by motorists with cell phones. They were en route to the police station to file charges against the three possessed cult members. In his excitement, he also announced it had been golden eagles from Roosevelt Island that had attacked the three men, allowing the girls to get away. A cheer went up.

He continued with a much more somber note. Lorenzo had probably been killed saving the lives of Uma and his brother by shoving them out of the path of an oncoming car. Erik hadn't been able to tell for sure, but his body had looked so bloody and contorted Erik was certain even if he lived, he'd likely be severely maimed. An ambulance had arrived. Erik hadn't stayed to learn the outcome.

Annie thought Uncle Alistair looked worried after hearing this account. He confided, "You know our laws don't exempt those possessed by demons. They will be held accountable for their actions, even if they were not acting of their own power. I suspect Lorenzo's brother will be caught and charged with kidnapping and attempted murder in the least, and his brother will have died trying to save him only to have him rot in an American prison. This is a loose end I intend to tidy up." He rubbed his beard thoughtfully and said, mostly to himself, "It wouldn't do for those three to be interrogated and reveal what they know of the stones. And I'm sure our friend the demon will make sure they don't speak of the stones."

Then looking up to the group, he said, "We need to find those men before the police do and take them to the cathedral for an exorcism. They won't last ten minutes in prison. Erik?"

Erik looked pleased to be of service. "I'm on it, boss."

"Oh, and Erik, good job sending the birds to attack the demon. Clever." Alistair took a moment to smile.

"Well, I couldn't have done it without Red's help." He gave her a huge smile. Annie suspected that despite their success, Red would likely be dismayed at being relegated to the role of assistant—all she'd done so far was drive and zap Erik. If Annie knew her sister, her fighting spirit longed to be in the center of the fray.

Annie was dealing with similar feelings herself and decided to take action. "Uncle Alistair, I think Red and I should transform and help escort Daanak." She heard her mom gasp at this.

Uncle Alistair quickly raised a calming hand toward her mother. "Actually, that isn't a bad idea." Then, directly addressing her mom, he added, "Kaye, the girls would actually be safer in the transformed state." Her mom looked somewhat confused but nodded.

To Annie, he said, "You do recall, don't you, that metal objects disintegrate under this transformation? Thus, I am afraid your piercings would disappear." He had just a hint of a humor in his voice as he raised one eyebrow and awaited her response.

She didn't respond right away, seriously weighing the two options and purposefully not looking at her mom or dad. Then she looked at Aaan, who was engaged in conversation with his father. He glanced over and their eyes met. He smiled and her heart thumped. She straightened her back and proclaimed,

"It doesn't matter. I'll be in a better position to help Aaan and Zaak take their father to the cathedral. That's more important."

"Very well," declared Uncle Alistair.

Red hugged Annie, squeezing her shoulders from the side in a huge, crushing sister hug. Annie felt content to share the same fate as her sister, no matter what this day would bring.

"What about us?" asked Roy. "Should we be trans-formed as well?"

Annie saw Uncle Alistair consider for a moment. "Actually, Roy, the four of you are needed as sentries along the way, equipped with cell phones. A critical part of this mission is constant communication between the members of our group and the priests at the cathedral. And the same goes for you Kaye, Yates, Viggo, and Minah, although—" He paused, then addressed Annie's dad. "We may need to use your bicycle to transport Daanak since it's peak rush hour by now."

Annie saw her dad nod.

Her uncle walked over to the window and peered out below. "What the dickens?"

The others joined him at the window and saw a slender female form drop her bicycle at the foot of the stairs and race up, taking them two at a time, obviously on a serious quest.

"Anyone you know?" asked Viggo.

"Not in the least ... unless—no, it can't be." Uncle Alistair laughed delightedly as the door to the lab burst open. The female figure removed her bicycle helmet and only her uncle and mom seemed to recognize the tiny woman.

Alistair advanced gallantly, took her hand, and bowed. "Bishop Hannah. Words cannot express my gratitude for your coming here today. I certainly didn't expect this."

She nodded in acknowledgement. "Thank you, Alistair. But I wouldn't have missed this for anything."

Her face glowed with a natural high energy. "Reverend Joan has kept me informed of your struggles since we exorcised the demons from those two men some time ago." She looked around the room and nodded in recognition at Roy, who nodded in response. "I see only one here today. Did we lose the other?"

"Yes, and no," replied Uncle Alistair somberly. "Not to the enemy, but he was injured, and likely killed, in a heroic rescue of a teenage girl and his own younger brother."

"I see." The bishop looked thoughtful and then plowed on. "And today, I've been informed you may need to have an escort for a fallen, and lately redeemed, angel under attack by demonic forces. I came both to help with the escort and to fill you in on recent progress from the cathedral front."

"Please, do sit for a moment and rest. You have clearly exerted yourself." Uncle Alistair motioned to a chair.

"No time, but I'd really appreciate it if someone refilled my water bottle while we talk briefly."

Annie saw Erik's mom step forward. "Please allow me. I've barely contributed thus far and am anxious to help."

The bishop smiled her thanks and handed a bicycle bottle to Erik's mom.

The bishop wasted no time in conveying the new information. She looked around the room and her gaze lingered on the manifested forms of Daanak, Aaan, and Zaak. Then, she straightened and announced, "I am sure all present here today realize this battle isn't with flesh and blood, but with spiritual forces. These spiritual forces can harm you, but only with permission from above, or from yourselves. As you know, they can only possess you if you give them permission, and this will likely be one of the attempts of the enemy on the road to the cathedral, so you will all need to be on your guard against this. Don't fall for any deceit. Don't allow any being access to your inner self. Is that clear?" She looked around. Annie nodded and everyone else seemed to do likewise.

She continued, "Unfortunately, others along our path today may allow access to the dark forces. This will provide the means for the enemy to physically harm you. So we need to be prepared for attacks in any form, but since we have the advantage of surprise, hopefully, the time will be too short for the acquisition of any weapons of consequence. So, be prepared to defend yourself against fists, rocks, sticks, and—" she seemed to pause for emphasis, "automobiles."

Everyone nodded again.

"My team is attempting to amass spiritually enlightened and sincere souls to line our path to offer prayers to combat these spiritual forces, but on such short notice, no one yet knows how successful this tactic will be. Serendipitously, this day, July sixteenth, happens to be the recognized anniversary for the destruction of the second Jerusalem temple in 70 AD. So, it is a fitting occasion to have a parade for peace and protection from evil—a prayer walk. Some of this was already in the works, but the program has been seriously stepped up. We will walk from Georgetown University to the cathedral and will be joined by people from diverse faiths on the prayer walk. As bishop, I will lead the parade on my bicycle, as many are accustomed to seeing in my ministry. I will ask the one I'm escorting to ride with me, perhaps in the ethereal form, so we can both ride on one bike, staying in close physical proximity since I carry certain blessings of the church and the prayers of many."

Annie saw her look at Daanak and bow. "I am honored to be your escort. Will your sons accompany us?" She looked first at Aaan, then Zaak.

Daanak now spoke, "No, the honor is mine. I thank you for this rescue, but please, I beg you not to place yourself at risk for one such as I. My sons and I could, perhaps, stay here for a time and continue to ask for forgiveness until such a time as we feel all is well, and then battle the demon without risking the safety of any of you lovely people."

Uncle Alistair spoke up. "Daanak, I, too, am honored to be acquainted with one who is, indeed, an angel. And I am grateful, as I'm sure are all here today, for your decision. As one who was recently hindered from entering this building due to the incanted blessings that were spoken here, you are, I'm sure, keenly aware of the vast number of prayers and blessings spoken daily in and for the cathedral and how much more impregnable that fortress will be."

Daanak nodded and said, "Yes, you speak the truth. Perhaps some of my hesitation is a feeling of sheer unworthiness of entering such a place. But this place is sufficient, is it not? Perhaps you could transform me here. That way, you would no longer be at risk."

Uncle Alistair said, with an air of finality, "Daanak, it is far too risky to use the power of the Angel Stone here now that we know what it can do and given that we are under attack by evil forces. If we tried to transform you, the demon might force his way inside and position himself to be transformed with you too quickly for us to stop. We couldn't take that risk. We have taken all but one of the devices to the cathedral to await your arrival and will do the transformation there."

Annie noticed Red and Erik involuntarily glance at each other, seeming to regret this obvious betrayal of the location of the only STAG control outside of the cathedral to one who was so practiced in reading human behavior.

She sensed that Daanak knew right away all he had to do was take the STAG control from Red and he could transform himself. Others seemed to realize this, too. A silence fell and a palpable tension filled the lab. Annie felt good and evil hanging in the balance for an instant.

Then Aaan broke the tension by slowly approaching his father. "Father, if you zap yourself with only one of those devices, Zaak and I cannot come with you. Because we are both human and angel, we need three of those devices to be transformed. Please, Father, wait for us. And listen to reason. Wait until we get into the better sanctuary."

Slowly, Daanak's eyes moved from Red to his sons, and the moment of temptation seemed to pass. He lowered his head. "Please, forgive me, I am weak. I will go with you."

Annie felt everyone in the room breathe a sigh of relief.

Erik's mom stopped twisting the bishop's water bottle in her hands, smiled embarrassedly, and handed the bottle to the bishop.

As if this were a signal, the bishop looked at the wall clock and said, "The parade is scheduled to begin in ten minutes, at two o'clock. We'll be pressed to get to the starting point at Reservoir Road and 37th Street on time. Are we ready?"

Annie heard her dad speak up for the first time. "Excuse me, Bishop, but my wife and I rode here on a tandem bike and I would be honored to use my experience as a randonneur to power your ride to the cathedral. I'm sure Kaye wouldn't object to riding your bike and allowing you to ride with me so you can focus on guarding the ... um, angel. That is, if you don't mind riding with an atheist."

Annie's mom shot him a look at his hesitation over the word "angel." "Still?" she asked incredulously.

Annie saw her dad shrug.

"I thank you for your kind and useful offer and accept it," the bishop said. "One much greater than I once said, 'you have not chosen me, but I have chosen you.' All gifts are good and your gift of strong legs will serve our purpose well."

Annie saw her dad smile. He seemed to be grateful for a chance to help.

The bishop opened her mouth to speak but once again was interrupted, this time by Red. "Um, excuse me, please, Bishop Hannah. Annie and I were planning on helping Erik from the ghost transformation, but I'm thinking now that I need to be my normal self and use my tae kwon do skills to help defend you in case of mob attack. I'm a black belt."

"Excellent. I'm happy to use your gift of fighting acumen to help guard the way," the bishop said graciously.

Annie knew she must have shown her disappointment because Red glanced at her and quickly added, "And Annie and I work as a team. She can be ethereal and keep a watch for trouble. I can ride your bike to keep pace with you and be there if someone attacks."

Annie liked the sound of that plan and to make Red feel better about altering their plan, high-fived with her.

"Sounds like a plan," the bishop said, nodding. "Now, are we ready to roll?"

"I think we are ready," said Alistair, whose words were partially drowned by applause from the group. "Annie, could you please text your maps to the bishop? She can give you her number. These maps show other sanctuaries along the way we can use as needed. This is in case any are unknown to you."

The bishop nodded and Uncle Alistair added, "Those to be posted as sentries need to assume their posts as soon as possible." Here he pulled up a map on his cell and indicated their posts at each location.

After Annie texted the bishop, Red and Erik quickly helped her find a leather covering from a box they kept in the storeroom for just such a purpose during their research.

Daanak, Aaan, and Zaak disappeared into their ethereal forms.

Annie ducked just out of sight into a closet and quickly changed into the awkward leather piece, making sure it covered the important parts, and came back out to see Erik and her uncle wearing similar leather pieces.

She saw Red zap first Erik, and then Uncle Alistair, then finally turn to her. They exchanged a meaningful smile and Annie said, "Be careful, Red."

"Don't worry 'bout me."

She felt a snap and then saw the bishop's glowing essence exiting the door with Daanak hovering just over her, flanked by Aaan and Zaak on either side and followed by Erik and Uncle Alistair.

Aaan turned to look at her and smile. He looked like a warrior, his face set with a determination she had never seen before. She saw him mouth the words, "I love you."

She had a thought and called after him, "Aaan, remember the angel, Eriel—he might be able to help if you get in trouble. And I love you, too."

He nodded, smiled, and was out the door. She got in step behind her uncle, feeling the ancient thrill of an upcoming battle.

CHAPTER 14

Flanking an Angel

Red followed her dad on the bishop's bicycle as the troop left the campus and progressed north on 37th Street. Her dad led the procession in the front position of the tandem, the bishop on the second seat. A crowd grew behind her on foot, unable to keep up with the bicycles.

Other participants were also waiting, stationed along the way. She knew the most important participants in the procession, however, were not visible and were not even vaguely suspected by the crowd.

At first, the progress seemed eerily uneventful, although an occasional motorist shouted something ugly and a couple of times a lone person assumed a threatening position, but seemed to lose interest as the troop drew nearer. Red found this eerie and wondered if the ethereal contingent was doing something to combat the threats.

As Red peddled, she noted several groups of people standing on the sides of the road to cheer them on. Some were chanting. Especially obvious was one group of Orthodox Jews, who were bobbing back and forth, beards swaying as they chanted. Their presence did not surprise Red because of the Jerusalem Temple theme. But the diversity of groups did surprise Red and she knew a lot of work must have gone into eliciting all this participation. It was hard to tell the religion of some of the groups—most were dressed in typical American style, though a few were obviously from diverse cultures, some wearing robes or saris, some with headwear—Red saw yarmulkes, habits, turbans, and veils, along with several shaven heads. Some were colorful, some somber. Some sang, some chanted. One group harmonized in a bluegrass *a capella* version of an old spiritual hymn that Red recognized as one her Mamaw sang while working in her garden. Another small group was loudly belting out the "Hallelujah Chorus." Red was in awe of the energy she felt from the crowd and suspected others in her group must feel the same way.

Red peddled hard to keep up with her dad's seasoned cycling legs. She was impressed with his pace even with the extra weight of the bishop, though maybe that was giving him too much credit since the bishop didn't appear to weigh much more than a hundred pounds. And the bishop was probably peddling, too, though Red could see she seemed to be spending most of her efforts waving and interacting with the crowd; her dad's idea had been a good one, she thought.

She tried hard to keep her senses keen and to focus on looking for trouble now that the crowd had become thick. She looked for the sentries positioned along the way and was pretty sure she spotted Daniel and Rachel. She felt somewhat strengthened by their presence.

She heard Annie's whispery voice alert her to look to the right, where a group of rough-looking men in torn jeans were eyeing the bishop with obvious menace. Her heart thumped and she started to accelerate her peddling to try and move up beside the bishop so as to come between her and the threat. One of the men began to step forward, but to Red's surprise, he put his hand up as if to shield his eyes from brightness, and then stepped back. By the time Red was parallel to the spot where the gang had been, they were nowhere in sight.

A similar event happened again with the same result. A threatening group approached, this time shouting insults directed at the bishop. But then they seemed to recoil and had disappeared into the crowd by the time the bishop and her dad got to that spot.

Then Annie directed her to look at a shiny black sports car approaching from one of the side streets. It seemed to be maneuvering toward the bishop. Her heart pounded but she knew what she had to do. She knew what Red Sonja would do!

Red pumped her pedals to position herself between the car and the bishop. She knew her tae kwon do skills wouldn't help, but duty called nonetheless.

She heard the driver gun the engine and braced herself for the impact. Others must have seen the threat because she heard screams from the crowd. But the impact didn't come. The hood of the car thudded to a stop at the end of the side street before it could even come close, and she rolled on through, passing the car without being touched.

She could hear the car grinding to try and restart but it was too late — she, her dad, and the bishop were safely past.

She saw that her dad didn't look back, but she ventured a glance at the bishop, who was now beside her. The bishop looked pale but mouthed a clear, "Thank you," to Red.

Red smiled and fell back into place behind her.

The crowd had grown so large that traffic had all but slowed to a stop. Red knew from the map the situation might get more complicated; soon they'd have to cross Massachusetts Avenue, a major route through the city. It was too early for rush hour, but it was a workday, so Red wasn't sure how bad it would be.

As they approached Massachusetts, though, she was glad to see someone had obviously alerted the police — a team of traffic cops was there to usher them safely across.

As she was peddling across the intersection, she heard Annie excitedly tell her to look to her right. She saw a group of supporters, mostly elderly and very vocal, singing a familiar old spiritual while they swayed and clapped. "Take my hand, precious Lord ... " they sang. She looked closely and recognized Annie's friend, Nyah.

She smiled, catching Nyah's eye. Nyah waved. Red had never before felt such a profound sense of love and community support.

Then, she felt warmed to see her Aunt Zsofia and Roy's mother with Nyah. They must've driven down together. She felt a pang of pity for her new aunt—the poor lady had already been through so much in this life. But as she rode past her, she heard her call, "That's the way, Red, stand fast against evil. Never back down."

She caught Aunt Zsofia's eye and her aunt raised a fist in the air. Red returned the gesture of solidarity and was once again filled with determination; she felt reenergized.

As the cathedral came into view, Red saw why their journey had been so easy. Most of the forces the demon could amass were gathered in front of the cathedral, blocking the way. Her heart sank. The crowd was huge and angry. This gathering between them and the cathedral looked impenetrable.

"Go to hell, you liberal heathens," she heard a woman scream at them.

Some carried sticks, and much to her horror, she saw at least three armed police officers in the crowd, assigned there to preserve order and eyeing the bishop's approach with threatening body language. One, presumably the highest ranking, held up a hand in the universal 'halt' signal.

Red had a terrible thought as she eyed the guns on their hips. Surely they wouldn't risk shooting the bishop? Even if they didn't, she didn't think they'd hesitate to shoot the animals Erik enlisted to help. She spoke aloud into the air, unsure if Erik could hear her, but she had to try. "Erik, don't use the birds! There are men with guns and I don't think they'd hesitate to shoot them. Heck, I'm not sure if they'd hesitate to shoot us." She felt a shiver.

Her dad and the bishop stopped the tandem and Red pulled up beside them.

"Dad, maybe we should head to one of those other sanctuaries Annie mapped for us," Red said. She had to say this too loudly for comfort but loud enough to be heard over the din of the crowd.

"You may be right, Red. There's one only a few blocks up that way." He pointed.

"Not just yet. Hold on a minute," the bishop said. She dismounted and walked cautiously toward the police officer, who still had his hand raised.

As if they expected her to draw a gun at any moment, the other two moved their hands toward their pistols.

The bishop stopped a few feet from the line of people.

The crowd was rowdy and several shouted, making conversation practically impossible. "Go back, go back, go back ... " a few chanted.

"Baby killers," a well-dressed man shouted, obviously seething in anger.

"Women haters," a chubby, matronly woman shouted.

"Thieves wasting our tax dollars," a youthful male voice shouted from somewhere.

There was no rhyme or reason. It seemed anything that angered the accusers was fair game—they were throwing out random accusations, some contradicting others. This *had* to be something demonic, Red thought.

Red stood and watched, holding her bike, mesmerized, then decided to lay it down so she could respond more quickly if the crowd rushed the bishop. Moving slowly, so as not to perturb anyone, she began to ease forward, trying to get in position to flank the bishop. She knew the bishop had an ethereal flank, but it couldn't hurt to have a black belt nearby.

The bishop made an attempt to communicate with the police officer that seemed to be the leader. Red marveled at how well her voice carried from such a small form. "Good evening, sir. I am Bishop Hannah Zingly from the National Cathedral. My friends and I wish to proceed through the crowd and into the building."

"I'll bet you would." He seemed to eye her with seething hatred. It seemed personalized toward her. "A bishop, huh? In whose church? The church of the devil?" he spat. "*My* friends and I would like to see some ID."

His two comrades shouted, "Yeah," with raised fists. A few others nearby who had overheard the exchange echoed the support.

The bishop, rather than cower, raised her chin a fraction of an inch. She pulled a card from a small fanny pack worn around her waist and handed it to the man.

He snatched it from her rudely, barely glanced at it, then handed it to one of the other policemen beside him. "Well, little lady, I'm going to have to arrest you for disturbing the peace."

Chapter 15

Call 911-Angel

Annie thought this march to the cathedral would have been grand fun if people she loved hadn't been so vulnerable down below. It was always surreal to see all the essences around when she was in the ghost transformation. She'd seen Aaan's ethereal form before, of course, and though it could certainly never be old hat for her, she had known what to expect from his essence. Zaak's essence was also not a surprise to her; he looked a lot like a slightly murky version of Aaan, though he couldn't match Aaan's heart-throbbing attractiveness.

But Daanak was a different story. She hadn't been prepared for his appearance. Daanak, viewed from a ghost transformation, was stunning. But like a faded painting, his beauty was only a hazy replica of what it had likely once been. He looked different now than when she'd glimpsed him last year, more magnificent; his glow was still murky, but more fiery than before.

And he was *big*. Bigger than Aaan and Zaak, though something about his shimmering form made her think he controlled his size and could change at will, becoming more or less diffused. He was quite a bit bigger than the guardian angels she'd seen. Bigger, in fact, than any being she'd ever seen—well, maybe not bigger than a whale but she'd never actually seen one in person. Aaan and Zaak were probably close to nine feet tall in their ethereal forms; Daanak was close to fifteen feet tall, though height was not an exact thing in this form because they didn't really have feet, just something like flowing fabric where their feet would have been.

She didn't have much time to observe, though, because Red, her dad, and the bishop were in constant danger and she had to be vigilant to make sure and let Red know when danger approached. And danger was definitely all around. Many people in the crowd below were possessed with horrid orange things, like the ones Red had described seeing in Roy when he was possessed. They seemed to be jumping out of some people and into others, obviously trying to get closer to their troop, like a hideous leapfrog game.

Other orange, remora-like shapes were hovering around Daanak, trying to get closer but continuously repelled, as though a force field surrounded their troop.

Periodically, she had to shout to Red to watch out for a car or group of people. But she was pretty sure that by now there really was some type of force field around them, because when they were approached, the threatening person often either changed direction or lost his or her demon and seemed to be confused.

A few times, she saw either Aaan or Zaak position themselves to do something like a mind meld and the occupying demon was forced out of the person and the host was left seemingly confused.

Eventually, they neared the cathedral and she was glad it was close. But the enemy forces seemed to be growing as they approached.

She heard her uncle groan and looked to see an ethereal barricade between them and the cathedral. A crowd of people several persons thick formed a wall between them and the entrance to the cathedral. All the people there seemed to be possessed by the orange forms. And the air was filled with yet more of them.

And what was just as alarming was that the people had begun to fight each other. She got an impression of rampant anger and rage, probably meant for the bishop and her entourage, but spilling over so the mob fought amongst itself. Her heart raced as she saw a few with broken bottles, one with a gun, and one with a baseball bat walk in the direction of the bishop.

She heard a maniacal, witchy laugh that sounded like the demon that had accosted them outside the lab earlier and looked ahead to see the scariest thing she'd ever seen floating toward them. It was the same size as Daanak and looked like some medieval painting of Satan crossed with a snake. It was red and had a snake's face; its tongue flicked in and out. Its lower half coiled like a snake. But its eyes were the most disturbing things—they were glowing yellow slits.

She felt panic rise and looked to her uncle for guidance. She saw that he and Aaan were talking urgently, though she couldn't hear what they were saying. Aaan seemed to be gesturing emphatically and Uncle Alistair drinking in what he was saying.

Then she caught a movement out of the corner of her eye and saw a huge flock of birds, much like the ones who'd attached the demon earlier, flying straight for the snake-like demon. Several things went through her mind. First was relief that help had come, but this was followed by dismay at the knowledge that birds likely wouldn't be able to harm the demon in his current ethereal state. Still, she saw him look furiously at the birds and his witchy laughter turned to shouts of rage.

"You pesky beasts will pay," she heard him screech, and he was blocked from view by a vortex of swirling birds. Their cries drowned out his shouts so she couldn't make out what else he was saying, but it didn't sound like English anymore. He was still approaching the cathedral, but not as fast, and the birds seemed to be effectively blocking his view.

Then she saw that Zaak and Daanak had taken the opportunity of the demon's distraction to join in the conversation with Uncle Alistair and Aaan.

She dared not leave Red to go close enough to hear. She watched helplessly, wishing she could hear what they were saying.

She looked back down and was shocked to see the bishop dismount her bike and walk toward a possessed policeman. This couldn't be good. She was just about to warn Red that the bishop needed to get away from the policeman when a brilliant glow coming from the direction of the angels caught her attention.

The glow was too intense to look directly at it, but eventually it seemed to tone down. She tried again to look and saw the most beautiful glowing form she could imagine floating near Aaan and apparently conversing with him. She was awed both at its form and at Aaan's bravery to be interacting with it.

Zaak and Daanak were approaching the glowing form as well but Uncle Alistair seemed to be having the same difficulty as Annie in looking directly at it. He put one hand up in front of his eyes, as though shielding himself from the extreme brightness.

She felt curiously peaceful despite the mayhem below and the approaching demon. She was pretty sure the peaceful feeling was emanating from the glowing form. She guessed it was some type of angel.

She was relieved when Aaan approached her. "Aaan, what's going on?" she asked urgently.

"Anya, please do not fear. I would like for you to meet my friend, Eriel. I met him in the angel realm."

She heard a beautiful voice that sounded more like falling water than a voice. "Greetings, dear Anya. Please do not fear me. I will not come closer."

"H-hello." Annie felt overwhelmed between the visual stimulation and the adrenaline that was coursing through her veins. She couldn't think of anything else to say.

"Anya, there is no time to waste. But I need to tell you what Eriel has told us. You see, dear one, he can transport us to a place in the angel realm where he can help our father."

"But we don't have three STAG controls."

"He doesn't need them—at least, if we give him permission to bring us with him. It seems he could have done this at any time if he had known it was needed. He will help our father and he can even deal with the snake-like demon if we transform him first. We will need one STAG control for that. The transformation will make him incapable of breaking away by sending him to a place deep in the angel realm, where he will be received by powerful angels. So, Eriel is here to save the day. We invited him and here he is—a miracle. And I have you to thank for suggesting I ask him for help."

"Oh, Aaan, that's wonderful." Annie felt like a huge weight was being lifted and wanted to hug Aaan. She looked at him, ready to rejoice, but saw something else in his face. She waited.

He continued, "Anya, my visit to the angel realm allowed Eriel to see that half-angels really do exist and are in need of help. He said he might be able to help us as well as our father."

243

Here Annie saw him pause a moment and seem to pick his words.

"Anya, our father can go without me. Zaak can go and help. If I were to go, I might not be able to return. So I have told him I will stay here with you."

Annie felt like she'd been punched in the gut hearing him say he might not be able to return. But he'd said he'd stay. She wanted to feel relieved. She tried to focus on that.

She looked into his eyes and couldn't tell what he wanted her to say. He just looked at her warmly, as if he were happy with his decision. But try as she might, she didn't feel relief at all, but a sick feeling. It felt so wrong to think of him being stuck forever in a perpetual state of reincarnation, living in a cave between lives. It made her feel like crying, if she could produce tears in this state. She knew she couldn't do that to him.

She braced herself, squeezed her eyes closed, and forced the words from her lips, "No, Aaan, you have to go."

"Anya, I—"

"You have to go. You were never meant to be here forever. You need to finish it. And who knows? Maybe you'll be able to fix things in such a way that will bring you back to me."

"Anya, I love you."

"Aaan, I will always love you."

Annie wanted so desperately to hold him, to cling to him, but she knew she wouldn't be able to let go if she did. As she gazed into his eyes, she couldn't look away. She knew that once she did, she'd suffocate with longing.

She was snapped from the moment by Uncle Alistair's urgent cry, "Annie, here he comes. You need to have Red zap him. No, wait, have her zap me and I'll do it. Now."

Red and her dad! They were in danger. She had to save them. This urgency broke through her grief.

She automatically did what Uncle Alistair told her to do. She leaned down and shouted into Red's ear, "Red, use the zapper. Zap! Zap!"

She watched as if in slow motion but knew Red had heard her. She saw Red zap Uncle Alistair. He transformed back to normal and in one fluid motion, took the STAG control from Red, pointed it at the snake-like demon, and zapped him. The demon disappeared.

Annie quickly looked back at Aaan. He was still smiling at her. She thought it was the most achingly beautiful smile the world had ever seen. She smiled back and stared into his eyes as he, Zaak, Daanak, and Eriel faded from view like a dispersing vapor.

Then anguish swept over her so intensely she didn't think her body could contain the enormous grief. The whole world went dark as she felt herself lose consciousness.

CHAPTER 16

The Barricade

MOMENTS BEFORE

Red was just ready to spring into action to defend the bishop when she distinctly heard Annie scream, "Use the zapper! Zap! Zap!"

Red was totally confused. She watched in horror as one of the steely-eyed policemen grabbed the bishop's upper arm and held her fast, while the other smoothly glided behind her and snapped on handcuffs.

Red fumbled as she pulled out the STAG control and zapped whoever happened to be in front of her. Alistair appeared and quickly took the control from her and with a brief nod of thanks, raised it into the air and pushed a button.

Red looked around. Luckily, the three policemen were too busy with the bishop to see this exchange. Otherwise, they might have thought she was pulling out a gun.

Red decided she'd lost enough time with this distraction and bolted toward the three policemen with the bishop. The crowd began filling in the gap between them, though, and it was impossible to get to the bishop.

One woman with a sign that read, "Save Our Unborn Babies!" was shouting at another woman waving a "Women Have a Right to Choose!" sign. They began to fight with their signs as though they were swords. Red tried to move in a direction away from that activity. Several others were beginning to join the fight with fists, sticks, purses, and various objects they'd grabbed on the spur of the moment.

She inwardly cringed and then braced when she saw a broken bottle flash. Her stomach churned and she feared loss of life might be eminent.

But now the three policemen seemed to slow their efforts and relax their body language. Red tried to seize that opportunity and accelerated her effort to close the distance between them.

She was almost there when she saw them stop and turn.

She realized the deafening roar of the crowd had lessened and people were stopping and looking around, almost as if waking up. Some looked up, some to the side, some looked at the weapons in their hands and either dropped them or seemed embarrassed to see themselves holding them so aggressively. Some quickly pocketed them. What was happening?

As Red neared the policemen and the bishop, she felt a hand on her shoulder. Her adrenaline was on high alert and she reacted automatically—the accoster was immediately lying on the ground in front of her where she'd flattened him after flipping him over her shoulder. By the time she'd realized what she'd done, she was already in a guarded defensive position, ready for further onslaught while eyeing the three uniformed officers at the same time.

A groan went up from the man on the ground and Red ventured a glance at him. She gasped as she recognized her father. "Dad?" she screeched. "Oh my gosh, Dad! Are you all right? I didn't know it was you." She crouched down to help him up, while still keeping the officers in her vision. To her amazement, one of them approached in a friendly manner and reached a hand down to help her father up.

Red looked at the man, her mouth hanging open, not sure what to make of the sudden change of attitude. He tipped his hat to her.

The leader was on his cell phone as she looked up. He said to the other, "Release the bishop. I'm afraid there's been some mistake." He looked embarrassed.

And then to the crowd, the lead officer shouted in a loud commanding voice, "Folks, the show is over. Please clear the area. I repeat, please clear the area. There has been a mistake. Nothing's happening here today."

The third officer unlocked the bishop's handcuffs and spoke to her with a smile on his face as she rubbed her wrists, eyeing him cautiously.

The leader approached the bishop and Red overheard enough to decipher an apology. "I don't know what came over me," he said, accompanied by a puzzled look. He seemed fearful he might be in trouble for his mistreatment of her.

Red got the impression that the bishop knew something about what had just happened and didn't want to prolong the encounter in any way. She spoke calmly and ensured the officers no harm had been done and invited them to attend the many cathedral programs whenever they found time.

As the officers walked away, the leader shouted several times to the crowd, "Move along. Move along."

Red noticed a curious, peaceful feeling had settled over the area as the crowd dispersed. An evening birdsong began as their small troop approached the cathedral. Red laid her bike aside, and didn't feel like worrying with locking it. Their small troop was now down to only three since their myriad supporters, as well as opponents, had disbanded.

Red began to hear many birdcalls and looked around to see a few eagles and a flock of crows settling on trees and spires around the cathedral.

Once inside the massive stone fortress, Red felt surrounded by invisible goodness. She was awestruck and speechless as the bishop escorted her father and her into the special inner room.

The inner room had an ancient altar more intriguing than beautiful, obviously dedicated to an angel theme. Dark wooden chairs circled the periphery, each with woven cushions, embroidered with chubby cherubs in the style of those on valentine cards. Golden candlesticks of winged seraphs guarded either side of a wooden shelf. In the center sat a golden bowl of holy water. A multitude of gold leaf paintings adorned the walls, likely from Medieval times or even earlier. Others looked like something Michelangelo would have painted and Red made a mental note to read up on religious art, maybe even take a class in it next year.

The bishop excused herself, obviously intent on some weighty errand. Her personality and carriage here in her element made her appear majestic despite her slight frame.

A door opened and a stooped, elderly woman shuffled in with a pot of tea. Red thought she must be a volunteer because she carried the unhurried air of one who had no obligations but acted purely out of a desire to do something good. With a shaky hand, she sat the pot of tea on a small table and asked the two if they would prefer mineral water.

After the bicycle sprint, both Red and her dad thanked the lady profusely and answered in the affirmative.

She shuffled back out and in again with two tall and very cold bottles of water as well as two glasses filled with ice. Red had no idea how thirsty she'd been until she saw the frost on the glasses of ice and her throat screamed for relief so much that she had to check herself to move in a politely slow pace and hand a water bottle to her dad before grabbing the other. She shouldn't have bothered with politeness, because she saw that her dad, too, had the lid off and half the bottle engulfed before coming up for air. She did the same and then poured the rest into the ice and enjoyed sipping the cold, pure water and crunching the ice as she browsed the artwork some more, allowing the day's build-up of adrenaline to calm.

After a few minutes, the door reopened and in burst Uncle Alistair and Eric, carrying Annie. Red moved immediately to her side, feeling panicked. "What happened?"

Neither answered. They placed Annie on a chair and she sat, unable to speak, staring ahead as if in shock. No tears formed but her chin quivered.

Her dad dropped to one knee in front of Annie, holding one of her hands and stroking her hair.

Red looked first at her uncle, then Erik. Both had downcast eyes.

Uncle Alistair slowly rose from his position beside Annie and stood. His seventy-odd years really showed now. Red felt like she would suffocate as she realized that the ethereal front of the battle had obviously taken a heavy toll; she wasn't sure she wanted to hear what was coming.

Uncle Alistair straightened and faced them in a way that made Red realize a blow was coming. But it was necessary to hear and she braced herself to listen. She noticed the bishop had slipped back in, along with five other priests, to listen to the account.

Uncle Alistair stood waiting a few more minutes and Red saw others shuffle in. It was the rest of the team—Aunt Zsofia, Nyah, Roy, Xenia, Rachel, Daniel, her mom, Minah, Viggo, Mrs. Oglethorp, and a few others, probably from the cathedral. She saw the kindly volunteer shuffle in and out as well, making sure all were served.

Uncle Alistair seemed to look to the heavens for strength to voice the account. He explained that the ethereal battle had mirrored the earthly one. Good and evil had faced off and, of course, good had won—but not without casualties.

He explained his perception that the demon had instigated the hoards of people into a fit of rage—that the demon could make them think they were right about whatever idea happened to be their pet peeve, and to lash out in anger and hatred.

The team at the cathedral, as well as Reverend Joan and her assistant rector, had fought hard to gather friends from many faiths to stand by and sing, pray, chant, and meditate. As it happened, Reverend John had been leading an interfaith workshop at nearby St. Albans, which had provided much of the variety of people of faith.

He summarized for those who had been elsewhere the events of their journey to the cathedral—the snake-like demon, Erik's bird attack, and finally, Aaan's suggestion of involving Eriel.

"I was at first hesitant because of all the years I'd spent thinking events had gone awry because I'd asked an angel to do something. But that's where Daanak's advice was priceless. He actually came through beautifully in advising Aaan how to respectfully phrase his request to Eriel for help. In brief, Aaan was able to ask this angel for help in way that worked.

"The bottom line is that he came and it was the most amazing thing I have ever seen." Uncle Alistair seemed to stare off into space, almost as if in disbelief of what he was saying, and she thought he seemed to glow as he spoke of it.

After a moment, he continued, "Neither Annie, Erik, nor I could look at him. I know now why the angels always say 'fear not.' It—he—was magnificent. The glow was impossible to look upon. I expect that Daanak will look something like that when he gets fully cleansed. And maybe even Aaan and Zaak ... I ... just ... " Here he stopped again, seeming to want to just be in the moment.

Red thought Uncle Alistair's countenance glowed again. She saw Annie look at his face and her face also seemed to glow a little. Annie's expression seemed to be torn between awe and deep sadness. And then Red began to understand what had happened.

Her uncle finally began to speak again, this time with more emotion. "The angel told Daanak that it was time to go and all he needed to do was ask. He offered that Aaan and Zaak might want to come along as well to assist their father and also to learn. It seemed to be a great opportunity for them. Aaan didn't want to leave Annie, but she urged him to go. She didn't want to hold him back from his opportunity to grow. It was the most selfless thing I've ever witnessed." He had to stop to compose himself.

Red couldn't stand it any longer and jumped onto Annie, holding her and sobbing uncontrollably. Annie's eyes were closed and silent tears flowed, but the hurt seemed too deep for any sounds to come.

All the room was silent except for the sobbing. It seemed to come from everyone.

Red noticed that their mom evidently couldn't hold back any longer and came up behind Annie's chair, wrapping her arms around her daughter and kissing her on top of her head, sobbing all the while.

After a few minutes, Red heard her Uncle Alistair continue. "I guess you've been wondering why the evil seemed to leave. The angel surprised us, well, all except Aaan. The angel told us the power of the Angel Stone could be used on the demon, and this would send him to a place where he and others like him could have a go at helping the demon—yes, even him—heal from evil. He said as long as there was a spark of good that could be fanned to a flame, it sometimes worked. Anyway, it will occupy the demon for a while and also serve to show the demon he really didn't want to take the stones, because they would merely send him back to the angels, which would be the last thing the demon would want if he chose to stay evil. Poetic justice at its best." Red noticed Uncle Alistair ventured to lighten the mood just a bit with a very small laugh.

Uncle Alistair went on, "That was when the sister team saved the day. While the demon approached, Annie had Red zap me back to normal. I knew where he was positioned, and the rest is history. I am told the look on his face when he was zapped was priceless."

Erik nodded and Red saw a slight smile.

"He was gone in a flash," Uncle Alistair beamed, looking at Red and Annie with appreciation. She felt relief that the plan had worked and awed that she'd been part of it.

And then Uncle Alistair's face fell and he proclaimed in a low voice, "But also gone are Daanak, Aaan, and Zaak." The last sentence was obviously hard for her uncle to have to say out of respect for Annie's disappointment. As the implication of his words sunk in, the words of congratulations on everyone's lips for Red and Annie halted abruptly.

All of a sudden, the room felt like a wake. Red realized Annie's love might be lost to her forever. *It's not fair*, she thought. Annie had always been the responsible one—the one who made sure Red got up in the morning; the one who nagged her to do her homework before she'd gotten better control of her ADHD—okay, maybe that had mostly been annoying. But still, Annie was the fairytale princess of the family. She should be getting her heart's desire, not her. Her story had had a happy ending—why couldn't Annie's?

Red wanted to comfort Annie, but felt at a loss for words. The only one in the room who seemed to be so seasoned by grief that she could bear to minister to Annie was their new aunt. Red and the others watched silently as Aunt Zsofia solemnly rose and walked over to Annie. Red moved aside to give her room as she knelt in front of Annie. She clasped both of Annie's hands in her own. Speaking so softly that even in the relatively silent room, her words were barely discernable, Zsofia looked into Annie's eyes. "Dearest Annie, never let anyone tell you that you will never see him again. We will see them. Never ... never give in. *Joy shall be ours*." With that, Annie fell onto her aunt and the dam of pent-up tears broke.

CHAPTER 17

Life Moves On

T he weeks after Aaan disappeared were a blur to Annie. She survived only by going through the motions required each day, with the aid of those who loved her. She'd never realized how much love there was in her family until those first dark days. She'd always considered herself somewhat of a loner, mostly attempting to be a loving child but never really valuing family. Now she knew she only stayed alive because she was being borne on the love of others. She was pretty sure that left alone, she would just sleep and die. She could fully relate to Aaan's sleeping in the cave for decades.

The first few days were absolutely vacant—she was an automaton. She heard others talking around her, but felt almost as if she were still in the transformed state and didn't have to actually connect with anyone. She dressed when Red told her to dress, scratched at her food when her mother asked her to come to the table, sat in front of the computer pretending to do stuff, and lay awake at night pretending to sleep.

Eventually, she discovered a haunting song about being in the arms of an angel and listened to it play over and over again for hours at a time, lying on her back with tears streaming so much her hair got wet all the way around to the back of her head.

One night, she needed to connect with something equally sad and went online. From all her mom's work on animal rights, she got an idea to delve into the worst of the worst pictures of animal suffering. It felt raw. She wondered at all the suffering in the world every day and reasoned that her life was relatively quiet and pain free, and so what did she have to complain about? At that point she began to feel numb. She started looking of pictures of people with terrible maladies and deformities to shock the numbness away so she could at least feel *something*.

She started reading about the aching wonder of existentialism—how can one be comfortable in their skin when there is evil in the world? She read something she had heard her uncle mention once about living in a broken world and knowing you didn't belong. Someday, could she find release from this existence? Yet even while she wished it, she felt ungrateful because she knew there really was much beauty here for her to enjoy.

Yes, there was beauty. But was there hope?

She desperately needed hope. She needed to rise above this existence. She needed to unhook herself from the cruelty of her species. She wanted her soul to be separate so she could soar. She held onto the thread of hope that someday her spirit could soar like it did with Aaan over the falls that day. Maybe she would find him again. She barely dared to hope, but hope was all she had; now that she knew there was more, she could not settle complacently into the mire of hopeless, cruel, earthly existence.

Eventually, she could begin to connect thinly with those around her. She heard others talking of some really great act Erik and his dad had done later on the awful day Aaan went away. It seemed that someone needed to go capture the three possessed men and bring them to the team of priests assembled at the cathedral. The priests had been prepared for a much larger task and were greatly relieved they didn't have to deal with the really powerful demon. Her Uncle Alistair had been adamant that the three possessed cult members be assisted first by exorcism and then helped back to Italy before they could leak information to the police or the press about the stones. His contacts at the Vatican agreed and dropped everything to arrange an escort for them back to Italy.

Erik had offered to capture them using a STAG control to minimize them in the same way he'd rescued his dad and the other prisoners. Viggo, wanting to give something back, had asked to be allowed to assist in the capture, and so Erik and his dad teamed up for the task. They were able to trace their locations via their cell phones, and found they were at a dingy hotel inside the Beltway. After locating them, it wasn't difficult to go there, zap them, place them in a box, and transport them to the cathedral. The whole process had only taken a couple of hours.

Lorenzo's brother had been so touched and horrified by his brother's sacrifice to save him that it hadn't been difficult to convince him to renounce evil and be exorcised of the demon that had been so drastically influencing his emotions and actions. After he was cleansed, he was effective in convincing the other two, who'd been his childhood friends. Then, he and the other two were sent home, with the promise that his brother's body would be sent to Italy. So the Italian cult had a bittersweet ending.

Without Daanak or the snake-like demon involved, her uncle speculated there would be no one to lead the other demonic forces. Once word got out that the stones would only send them to a place in the angel realm where they would be received by very powerful, good angels, any remaining cult members would likely lose interest and the cult would surely dissolve, he said. Uncle Alistair also said Lorenzo's sacrifice had been invaluable in saving not only his brother, but many others as well from a life of evil and misery. Even through her numbness, Annie was glad they'd escaped.

But the only real happiness she seemed capable of experiencing was a kind of peacefulness when she was in the company of a select few. Her favorite human interactions were with her Aunt Zsofia. Annie felt she could shed her automaton persona when her aunt was present and could assume a more mature and serene facet of herself. This part of herself slowly seemed to grow during this time. She thought a lot about Aaan's heart-wrenching losses and she tried to mimic him in better valuing the time she spent with her own loved ones. She started making a point of listening more enthusiastically to Aunt Zsofia's stories of old, and to Uncle Alistair's, too. Before, in what she considered her childhood years, she'd have shunned any time spent with older people. Now she felt like a thirty-year-old version of herself—one that had spent at least a decade in a monastery.

The other being Annie most identified with during those days was Moon. She'd shed tears when she learned his story. He and his gang had heroically made a racket in the nearby trees while Lorenzo's brother and the other two were in the process of kidnapping Uma and Tatyana. Moon hated demons, it seemed. Erik had sworn this wasn't something he'd taught Moon completely—there'd already been recognition within Moon that demons were bad.

Moon, on hearing the girls' screams, had begun dive-bombing the three men and this had angered them. They fired gunshots into the trees. One wounded Moon's wing—but had done much worse to his mate. When the family returned home that evening, Erik had found an injured and distraught Moon on the doorstep, and following him into the wood, had discovered the limp and lifeless body of his mate. Erik had consulted a wildlife rescue group, who'd removed the bullet from Moon and bandaged his wing. Erik also treated Moon for any possible parasites so he could bring him inside the mansion until he could heal. Annie had become his caregiver, fashioning a birdcage on the floor next to her bed with an open door so he could hop in and out at will until his wing healed.

No one except she and her sister knew Erik still had a STAG control that somehow had failed to be among those delivered to the cathedral and then given to the Vatican. He used the ghost transformation to communicate with Moon, learning that Moon had taken the first bullet, trying to fly between the men and his mate. Moon knew he somehow needed to protect his love—crows mate for life. After he fell, she caught a bullet to the heart. Moon didn't have any notion of his mate's body being anything significant now that her spirit was no longer there—Moon had wondered where she had gone. His two beautiful chicks had fledged some weeks before and though he was pleased with their success, he felt lonesome. Annie had grown to feel very protective of Moon and the two bonded irrevocably during those weeks.

In her room alone each night, Annie felt all the animals seemed to sense she needed comfort. Most nights Buddy, Midnight, or Roxy slept in the bed with Annie, with Moon beside her, perched in his cage—sometimes more of these friends than she could comfortably accommodate slept in the bed with her, but she didn't mind, appreciating the sincerity of their affection. Eventually, Moon's wing healed and he was often gone. He'd peck on the window from the outside when he wanted in to sleep in his cage, or on the glass inside when he wanted to go outside for a while. He had the run of the place.

Time marched on. When the time approached for Red's new college adventure to begin, it was both a source of sadness and annoyance for Annie. She knew Red was worried about her and she tried to reassure her she was fine, over and over again.

Annie was dismayed to find that even after Red had their dad's Volvo wagon packed, ready to move into her dorm room at Georgetown, she still insisted she could stay home to keep Annie company. Annie was tired of repeatedly reassuring her and had to shoo her out the door. She knew this was best for Red.

Her sister had tried to angle toward being allowed to rent an apartment with Erik but this hadn't passed the laugh test with their parents. Annie had only been vaguely aware of this argument and knew that Red's feelings had sustained a massive blow when she thought Erik hadn't tried hard enough to convince them. And she knew that at one point, Red had then feared Erik would pop the question so they could have a quickie wedding just to solve the dilemma. Annie knew how Red felt about marriage—as much as she adored Erik, marrying right out of high school just wasn't done these days. This, in turn, had hurt Erik's feelings, as he sensed Red's hesitancy whenever he attempted to come within a mile of the topic. Annie had almost stepped in and asked Red to stay with her and drive to and from Georgetown for her first year, feigning a need to have her older sister nearby just to shut them up. This would have not been optimal—Annie treasured her solitude—but she didn't want Red and Erik to argue.

Finally, Uncle Alistair had saved the day by claiming knowledge that freshmen were required to stay in a dorm for at least one year unless they justified a need to stay elsewhere through an elaborate application process, and he said he was sure the deadline for that had long passed. This seemed to satisfy both Red and Erik, allowing them both to save face. Uncle Alistair had gone so far as to suggest that after all, everyone should spend at least a minimum amount of time in a dorm. That was just part of college life.

So, Red had pulled away with the Volvo fully loaded. Annie had been relieved for Red because she feared Red might've regretted it later if she'd missed part of her college experience, either because she didn't live on campus or because Erik dominated her time. Annie had no doubt that Erik and Red would always be together in some way, this year and beyond—their bond was just too strong. Annie expected they'd see each other every day for now and figure it out as they went.

The time finally came for Annie's new school year as well. Annie was glad to see Nyah on the first day of their junior year. She knew she'd neglected her friend these past few weeks and it felt good to reconnect and get back in a routine. She invited Nyah home with her after school and it was just the balm she needed. She was able to even giggle again, though not with as much abandon as before. Still, it was nice. And Nyah seemed relieved to have her friend back.

Nyah knew the whole story about everything that had happened. Annie didn't know what she'd have done, going back to school without that connection—someone who knew about Aaan, even though they didn't discuss him. Of all the people at school, Nyah would always know what was going on with Annie, and Annie dearly hoped she could be a good friend and support Nyah if a time came that the tables were turned.

CHAPTER 18

New Kid at Churchill

Annie knew she had to somehow deal with life after Aaan.
She didn't know how but she needed to keep going. And
he was her inspiration to keep going. She wiped away a tear,
thinking of all he'd endured. He'd lost so many he loved and
always had to keep existing. She was glad he might now be
able to move forward with whatever the afterlife held for him.
She knew her decision had been the right one for both of them.
Even if they could have managed somehow to be together
during her lifetime, it would have been a selfish thing to wish
on him, asking him to stay in his half-life existence. It would
have meant that when she died, he'd be alone again, sleeping
in his cave until some new owner built a futuristic shopping
mall over it and excavated it to make a parking garage. Then
he would have had to start all over again somewhere else. No,
this was the way it should be. He was somewhere in the ether,

moving forward with his existence. Eriel would help him. And who knew, maybe she'd see him somewhere, someday, in her own afterlife.

This gave her comfort as she went through each day, and she eventually developed resolve—she'd study and devote her life to helping someone or something. She'd have to figure out what exactly that would be later on. Maybe animals, like her mom. Or maybe the poor, like her dad. Or maybe souls, like Reverend Joan and the bishop.

She drew a deep breath. It was now September and she loved leaving her window open at night. She could hear wildlife sounds from the woods below the house and the coolness of the air soothed her. She snuggled into her bed, stroked Roxy's smooth head, and felt peacefully sleepy. As she was drifting off, she thought in the distance she heard a commotion among the crows. She hadn't heard that kind of commotion for some time but for once, she was too tired to think about it, and allowed the soft, cool blanket of a fall night envelope her consciousness.

The next morning as she walked up the driveway on her way to school, she heard Moon call to her from a nearby tree.

"I love you, too, Moon," she called back, smiling to herself. What was up with him?

Walking to school was definitely different this year. For the two previous years, the daily trek had been something of a circus. Red had always been difficult to rouse in the morning and she'd felt it her duty as the non-ADHD sister to fill in for her sister and, in a sense, be the responsible one.

This was a laugh, she realized. Red had, in reality, always been the responsible one—her defender. Red was like an avenging angel when anything threatened. Annie missed her sister. But maybe it really did help Red, having her there to nudge her along sometimes—at least she'd like to think they'd mutually helped each other.

She passed Tatyana's house and thought of how they'd always swung by to pick her up for school. More often than not, she'd been waiting at the bottom of her driveway, a tad impatiently. She was now off to Johns Hopkins this year and Annie had no doubt she'd make it into medical school. She was an overachiever and a dedicated friend. Annie missed her, too.

And then, Annie thought as she walked, they'd usually met up with the bubbly Uma and serene Gabriella, further along their walk. Uma had obtained a cheerleading scholarship to the University of Maryland, and she wasn't sure where Gabriella ended up—likely Ivy League, as smart as she was. She missed the gang. Both Tatyana and Uma had, thankfully, fully recovered from their ordeal at the hands of the cult members.

So Annie walked alone. But in all honesty, it was nice to have the solitude. With her recent heartache, she was much happier walking alone, listening to bird calls from the trees, the open sky above that seemed to reach up to the heavens. She'd once wondered if anything was really up there; now, there was no doubt. She knew this day and every day were just one kind of thing, and that there were also other kinds of things, or realities, or places.

She began to wax philosophical in these solitary walks to school each day. Red had been the gregarious one and had been the magnet for the formation of their walking buddies. Annie was a person who tended to have one friend. Well, one friend in each port of call, anyway. She had Carrie, her childhood companion, still in the periphery of her life. In elementary and middle school, she'd had Olivia. Oh, she had other special friends, but she knew her tendencies were to deal with one person at a time. And she was glad she had this time to herself and equally glad that at the end of the walk, she had Nyah.

Nyah's route to school didn't overlap hers, so they just met up at school every morning and shared lunch together. They often spent time together after school as well, studying at either her house or Nyah's. Of all of her close friends, Nyah seemed the most brilliant—not so much that she had a particular talent— she played piano and had a great singing voice; she read profusely and made straight A's—but it was more than that. She had somewhat of a regal air or carriage. She was wise in both a down-to-earth way and a leadership way. Annie wasn't sure how to describe it; she just knew she was glad they'd found each other and felt lucky she got to spend time with her—she sensed Nyah would do great things in this life.

As she walked along in this deep reverie, still breathing deeply and enjoying the cool, delicious fall air, it entered her mind that it wasn't just Moon acting strangely—something was up today. Something about this day was new. The cool air seemed so clean and there were even a few early leaves turning golden. She loved spring, but this was really her favorite time of year. In spring, one felt the rebirth, but in fall, one felt the cleansing of old ideas and limitations, a time to delve within into the mysterious depths of the infinite. The summer's work was over and the harvest was at hand. Even all the schoolwork couldn't take away that sense within her that it was a magical time for dancing and for being thankful to have a mind. That was it, she thought; it was a time of the mind.

She was in this deep discourse with herself when she met up with Nyah at school. "Girl, I gotta get you out of all this serenity. I mean, I'm glad you're happy and all, but you need some energy, some excitement in your life," Nyah declared. "We're only young once, you know."

"Yeah, I know. But really, I'm not sad, just in a deep sort of mood." Annie waited as Nyah put some things into her locker and took out a tablet.

"You need to meet somebody new, like that new kid, Ian."

Annie started to shake her head, dismissive of the idea of any new guy in her life. But the sound of the name made her stop. "What did you say his name was?" she asked with heightened intensity.

"Oh, I don't know exactly. Something like Ian Angeli? Or Angelo? Something like that. Sounded Greek or Italian. Anyway, I caught a glimpse of him and he looked pretty f—Annie, what's wrong?"

On hearing a name that sounded so much like Aaan, Annie felt such a shock that she dropped her books and was on the verge of hyperventilating. Her extreme reaction caught her off guard.

Nyah seemed to be caught off guard, too, unsure of what was happening. "Are you sick? Need me to take you to the nurse's office?"

Annie forced herself to be calm. She began picking up her books. "No, no, I—I'm fine. I just thought of something. Where did you see this new kid?"

"It was out front." Nyah's voice dropped to a whisper. "Don't look now, but he's coming this way."

Annie wasn't sure how she managed to turn around, but somehow she kept her cool. She turned and saw a very handsome guy with sun-bronzed skin, and an impossibly messy, sexy shock of golden curls. He had bulging muscles, as if he'd just disembarked from crewing a large ship. He was Verrocchio's David personified. And his bright green eyes bored straight into hers as he sauntered toward her, one book carelessly held in a swinging hand—a mere prop. He was obviously coming for her, not caring one iota for the rest of the school, books, teachers, anything.

Annie stood, mesmerized, drawn to him like a moth to a flame. He was now standing directly in front of her. "I-Ian Angeli?" she managed.

"No ... *Aaan* Angeli," he said gently and with understated calmness.

Annie could neither move nor speak.

After a moment, he said in a whisper just to her, "Remember, you have right-of-refusal, like I said ... " but Annie cut off the rest of it by tackling him, springing as high as she could jump and holding onto his neck for dear life.

He lifted her off the ground in his strong embrace and swung her around and after one full revolution, they had their first kiss. It was unlike anything Annie had ever before imagined. His smell, the amazing taste of his mouth on hers, the feel of his breath on her cheek ... she was just where she wanted to be if offered every possibility in all the universe.

Annie heard Nyah clear her throat. "Um, Annie. Um, did I miss something? I mean, people are starting to stare. Annie. *Annie!*"

But Annie couldn't really answer. She just clung to Aaan and felt his arms around her, tears streaming down her face, unwilling to open her eyes for fear this might be a dream.

"Annie, I think, um ... " Nyah sounded uncertain at first but then gave a huff of decisive breath and Annie felt her gently push them through a doorway behind some lockers. Annie vaguely sensed that Nyah stood in front to block them from view as the hall filled with a thick crowd of students filing by.

Then, Nyah must have figured it out, because all at once she, too, was screaming and bouncing as she hugged both of them.

Annie hugged Nyah back excitedly, wanting to share her joy.

"Um, Annie, I somehow don't think you're in any shape to attend school today. Listen, I'll tell the office that both of you are out sick. So scram," Nyah said.

"I don't want to get you in trouble," Annie protested.

"Annie, if you don't get outta here now, *I'm* going to leave with him."

Annie giggled uncontrollably for the first time in many weeks as she and Aaan slipped out the nearest door. They held hands and ran away from the school.

They didn't stop until they reached the towpath. Finally able to slow down, Annie still felt like she was walking on air as they went for a long walk.

Annie learned what had happened in the angel realm since that day in July—July 16, a day she had thought would live on in infamy as the day she lost her true love, but could now take a place in a different list of merely sucky days.

It seemed that when the ethereal troop embarked on their journey with Eriel and the captured demon, who was very ancient and strong, they went first to the palace where Aaan had first met Eriel. This palace, Aaan told her, was somewhere in the angel realm and normally inaccessible to beings such as himself without the aid of the stones.

The demon had been as slippery as a jellyfish and had been very difficult to subdue. Eriel had summoned a team to follow him and to try reasoning with him as he searched for an exit back to Earth. Eventually, a member of Eriel's team had counseled with leaders further up in the hierarchy and a very powerful angel had confronted the demon. For whatever reasons, the demon had relented ever so slightly, probably awed by the presence of the angel. But it had been enough to get a spiritual toehold, Eriel had later explained, and there was some small degree of hope that the demon might be prevailed to recant evil, though Eriel thought it would take a very long time and wasn't very optimistic.

This had been the first order of business, followed closely by Daanak's reform. Aaan had described it in such a way that Annie thought it was akin to something like going to rehab or to a training camp. Aaan's father would need a lot of time and help to recover from ages of evil influence and bad choices. Getting him started on his road to recovery had been the second order of business.

Finally, Aaan and Zaak had been granted audience. Aaan said he had felt like Dorothy making her request to the wizard, and almost expected to discover a sham behind the curtain.

But his initial instincts about Eriel had been correct. Eriel had come through. Aaan had learned that his kind, half-angels, had been viewed by most of the more orthodox angels in much the same way as a human passing a beggar on the street. They tended to feel themselves too busy to be bothered and to assume the beggar was likely either a fake or had done something to bring this upon themselves—just not their problem. And with no guardian angel to be their champion in the angel realm, the half-angels had simply been overlooked for ages of time.

Another important reason the half-angels had been overlooked was their small numbers. Only a few had ever been brought into existence; no one really knew how many there were, how to collect information on them, or how to round them up if needed. Ancient scriptures mentioned the 'sons of Anak' as half-angels and giants, but he was the only angel who fathered offspring with humans who was mentioned by name in human documents—and angels did not keep any record of this. Apart from him, Eriel thought there were only a handful of others, such as Daanak, who had mated with humans before the practice was stopped.

"Stopped?" Annie asked. "Before, when I wanted to kiss you, you said it was forbidden." Annie was fascinated about Aaan's existence and wanted to know everything and understand all.

"It was discouraged before, but then, after the flood, it was absolutely forbidden," Aaan said thoughtfully, seeming to have difficulty explaining this. "It was so forbidden and the flood had shown the magnitude of its forbiddance. A huge change came about in the angel realm then. You see, Anya, before the flood, it was not unusual for humans and angels to interact. It would have been unheard of for a human to deny the existence of angels. It would be like denying the existence of trees or water. But after the flood, humans could go hundreds or even thousands of years without being visited by an angel, at least to their knowledge. As we have discussed before, guardian angels are always on duty, much like Marines or Navy Seals. They are very dedicated and part of that dedication is avoiding notice unless given special permission to convey a message. In fact, all angels operate under that understanding. Few even have retained the knowledge of how to materialize themselves in such a way as to be comprehended by humans. I worked for centuries on my technique, read everything I could get my hands on, and practiced. You would not want to know how many hours I practiced."

Annie giggled. "So, tell me what's going to happen now and how you came to have a—" she swallowed hard "—body now, and why it doesn't look like you."

Aaan looked a little sad and Annie thought he even seemed uncomfortable in what he had to say. "Sorry, Anya, there wasn't any way we could figure out how to have my old body back. But if you don't like this one ... "

Annie slapped him playfully on his shoulder. "Don't be silly. You're gorgeous. I mean, you were gorgeous before, too, when you materialized. But I like this one just fine. I can touch it. I can hold your hand and do this ... " Annie stopped walking and gave him a long kiss.

They looked for a long time into each other's eyes. Annie thought it seemed natural to look into these eyes. The color didn't matter, nor did the shape of the eyelid. She knew who was behind them and that's all that mattered.

Then she had a thought, fighting a smile. "Angeli—really?"

Aaan laughed. "Hey, who has a better right to use that name?"

Annie had to acknowledge the point.

He drew her hand up to his lips and kissed it tenderly and that led to another on the lips.

They eventually continued their walk. "So, as I was saying, we had a meeting with Eriel and other angels—you might call it a council. We explained our plight, how we were forever doomed to walk the earth, being reincarnated from time to time but never able to move forward to any kind of afterlife or go where our loved ones go." Annie heard his voice start to break here and gave his shoulder an affectionate squeeze as she waited for him to go on.

When he gathered control of his emotions, he stopped walking and took both of Annie's hands in his. "Anya, I told them I had finally and irrevocably fallen in love with a woman and yet was forbidden from ever kissing or holding her. And that I just wanted to be whatever she was and go wherever she goes after this life." He kissed Annie tenderly and then held her for a time. Annie thought it was amazing to feel his beating heart next to her own.

"And?" Annie was getting anxious to hear the verdict.

"Well, at first, they said they were sad for me but were not sure what they could do and were about to dismiss the issue. But do you remember that I once said that I thought I might know of a way to solve the dilemma? I mean, it is not like I have not had time to think about it. So, I suggested it to them and amazingly, they bought it." He stopped to laugh gleefully. "Okay, I hope this doesn't repulse you, but I need to tell you how this came about. I convinced them to allow me to ... reanimate a corpse."

She stared at him. "You did what?"

"I needed to find one that was freshly brain dead so the organs would still work but I would not be invading any other soul's domain. I had to wait until the soul left the body and then jump in," he said hastily. "It turned out that Eriel thought this would be great fun helping me find such an opportunity.

"We decided that having a body lost at sea would be best—in cold water, so that no ... well ... decomposition," Aaan cleared his throat, "would have taken place. So, we hung around Norwegian fishing fleets for a while and Eriel was able to engage several angel colleagues to be on the lookout for an opportunity, and finally this opportunity came about. I thought the physical form was good, pleasant and strong. The former owner of this body went to his afterlife and the body was lost at sea—I understood he fell victim to a night of cards and vodka. He simply toppled overboard while walking back to his cabin. I do not know the young man's name nor anything about his family. And since he was from another country, I expect no one who ever crosses my path will recognize him. So, the body is mine. I reanimated it before the fish could eat it and there were no memories left, so the only memories are mine," he said, looking at her with a slightly worried expression on his face. "Anya, this is nothing like possessing someone with a soul still *in situ*."

He looked sideways at her as they walked, anxious to hear her reaction but obviously giving her time to process the new information. She looked over at him a few times and started to tease him and then changed her mind.

Aaan was obviously getting nervous.

Eventually, she started laughing uncontrollably.

She found a sunny patch of grass nearby and plopped down on it. She couldn't help but roll over laughing.

Aaan sat on the ground beside her and laughed too, but soon stopped and said gently, "Anya, I feel a little uncomfortable laughing about it—I am thinking of the poor man who died."

Finally, she stopped laughing, sat up, dried her eyes, and tried to talk, though she did have some difficulty getting it out without an occasional giggle. "Aaan, Aaan, Aaan," she began, "I've spent the past many months since we first met thinking about this, too. And I always came to the conclusion that there was no feasible answer and that we would just have to be, to exist, and pretend it didn't matter that we couldn't be lovers as long as we were together. I decided long ago that I would be willing to wait for you to grow up if you became reincarnated as a baby. My only worry was how we'd find each other. I thought about how your little brain would have to develop so your spirit could let it know to find me. But then, what if you never remembered and never came to find me? I've had nightmares about dating younger men for the rest of my life, trying to find you."

She took his hand and continued. "And that's the best of all the plans I came up with. The others all went downhill from there. I thought of trying to seduce some weak-minded, yet good-looking bloke so you and I could trick him into allowing you to possess him so we could be together. That one left me feeling like I needed to take a mental bath. That was just so yucky. And it would make you a demon, and me ... I don't know

277

if even Hollywood has a name for what I would be," she said. "I thought I had thought of everything, but I guess I only had a little over a year to think about this. You've had how many years to work this out?"

"Anya, I really don't think you want to go there. I mean, since these years were not consecutive due to the reincarnations, I have not really kept up with the time," Aaan said.

"There's no way you're going to get out of this one. Dish. How old *are* you?"

Aaan finally relented. Chuckling to himself, he announced, "Let us just say that it is in the six digits. And that is as much as I shall say."

Annie came toward him with tickling fingers and had a blast pretending to try to get more information out of him by tickle torture. He seemed to know just how to react to her teasing. She was delighted. She really didn't care how old he was. He was Aaan, and that was all that mattered.

After the laughter subsided, Aaan confessed, "Anya, your playful attitude when you heard what I had done has made me love you even more, if that were possible. I have been so worried you might be totally repulsed by how I obtained this body, but this has made me feel so warm and accepted that my heart is so full it might burst."

Annie still felt playful and said, "No, don't do that, we just got it."

"Anya, as you know, I have played many roles in past lives, but this tender romance is something I never had. In all my lives, times were either too hard for tenderness or the priorities were simply different. I was in command or busy with some activity that took my attention away from any kind of human feelings. I did very much love my sister and daughter, but in a different way.

"And Anya, I have had erotic relationships, or at least moments of pleasure. But never, ever have the two gone together. Never have I been in love and been loved in turn."

Annie laid her head in his lap and he stroked her hair for a long time. The sound of the mighty Potomac echoed the deep beating of her heart.

Annie eventually looked up and smiled. "Aaan, I love you with all my heart."

"And I you, my Tiny Bold Maiden. I feel that I have been born into a truly new existence. I have a man's body and a woman I love and who loves me." He bent down and kissed the top of her head. "Anya, just the smell of your hair is heavenly. I could no more say no to you than a drowning man could say no to air."

Annie turned her face upward again and kissed him.

"Anya, are you sure you like this set up? You know all you have to do is say the word and I will disappear," he said, and she could hear the vulnerability in his voice.

Time to put a stop to that, Annie decided. She stood up, placing her hands on her hips, and towered over him as he still sat in the grass. "Aaan Angeli, if you say that one more

279

time, I will take you to one of those piercing places and get us matching body piercings so we're connected by a chain."

Annie was glad to see he looked shocked.

She continued, "Now stop it. I'm having the best day I ever had."

And with this she sat back down, this time in his lap, and kissed him hungrily.

When she finally took a breather from showing him just how much she liked his new body, he grinned impishly and said, "So, Anya, tell me more about these connected piercings." He raised one eyebrow.

Annie's giddiness from this whole amazing day threatened to make her guffaw again. "You know, Aaan, I think I'd like to change the subject now."

He smiled. "You and I shall have a lifetime to explore all those innuendos and see what we want to try, but today, I need to get you home before your parents forbid me from seeing you anymore."

As they strolled back toward Annie's house, they discussed whether they'd tell her parents and Red that it was really him. At first, Annie thought it might be best to pretend this was someone new, then realized there was just no way anyone in her closest circle of friends or family would believe Annie could love again so quickly. So she headed back to her house with Aaan, intending to just blurt it all out and let the chips fall where they may.

As they approached the mansion, Aaan spoke again. "Oh, yes, and one more thing. Eriel and the council decided it was high time the plight of the half-angels and their afterlife was raised up the chain and discussed with ... well, I hesitate to say it so casually, and to be honest, I don't know how things transpire as one moves higher up the chain of command ... but let's just say there is finally some hope that when I die this time, I'll move on and won't go back to my cave—as much as I love it," he said this, Annie thought, with a tiny hint of sarcasm.

Annie felt ecstatic for him and decided tonight would be a celebration at the mansion like no other. This day had brought Aaan back to her and though there were no guarantees of how long either of their lives would be, they'd live it together.

Epilogue

Annie took time to luxuriate in her bath before getting ready for the homecoming dance. She thought about her life and how lucky she was. She knew she was now at risk of becoming silly with happiness. Her biggest worry now was how to control the giggling that threatened to erupt in response to pretty much everything. Her morning toast popped up, she chuckled; if she almost tripped on a stone, she laughed until tears came. And oh, it was painful to remember how she had guffawed at every joke on *Saturday Night Live* last weekend.

Maybe she was still in shock. It was like one day, despair with peaceful existence as the only real thing to hope for, and the next day, euphoria. If she'd tried to plan a happy time, she knew she couldn't have invented this. She just wouldn't have thought of someone like Aaan coming into her life. His love was so selfless. He'd been through so much more than anyone she knew.

With all she'd seen and heard over the past couple of years, however, she knew one thing—she'd never really understand the whole picture, at least not here in this state of existence. She was determined to be open now, open to reading diverse ideas and experiences, open to listening for that still, small voice. And open to love. She'd base her existence on loving others, especially Aaan, but not him exclusively. How could she *not* love him? His soul called to hers and hers to his. He was as much a part of her existence now as the air she breathed.

With her new awareness and all the love she felt for and from Aaan, she wanted to share the love. She thought particularly of Red and Nyah. So she'd been making an effort to text Red every day, though she knew her sister had her hands full with her own life right now. They were both growing up and experiencing love and Annie knew that even if it all ended tomorrow, somehow lightning had struck twice in the same family. Who could have guessed that two sisters could have formed such unlikely attachments to ethereal beings and have it work out?

And Nyah—well, that was another story. Annie sighed. Nyah had become like a sister to her. Nyah knew her secret: that the one she loved was a half-angel. Yet she didn't make her feel like it was anything weird. She had helped her so much during those frantic days of trying to decipher Aaan's cave-wall writings—what she'd thought to be the tongue of angels. She snorted at how naïve she'd been.

Then she shook her head in awe when she thought of how far she'd come in her knowledge of the angel realm since those days. And Nyah had been right there by her side. She'd even helped amass supporters on the day of the great battle between good and evil. Annie was sure that the prayers, songs, and chants of those standing for good that day had made a difference. Since their first meeting in the lunchroom at Churchill, Nyah had been there for her.

She got out of the tub, wrapped herself in a towel, and started working on her hair, still thinking of Nyah. She wanted for Nyah to have what she'd found in Aaan. She knew it was dangerous to play matchmaker, but she'd tried to make suggestions to Nyah. Nyah had just scolded her, asking if she was trying to get rid of her, to pawn her off on some guy so she could focus only on Aaan. Annie hoped she'd been able to truly squelch that notion.

She loved every moment she spent with Aaan, but Aaan was so deep and wise he'd never ever interfere with her friendships. She still studied with Nyah, which was great because it would've been a huge disappointment to study with Aaan. Aaan attended high school, but didn't have to study—at all. He did read, however, and was rapidly coming up to speed on computer technology, having never had much opportunity to explore computers in the past. *Not many electrical outlets in his cave,* Annie thought wryly.

No, she didn't want to distance herself from Nyah—she needed her friends as much as before. It was just that she wanted happiness for her friend, happiness similar to her own now that she knew it was possible. She felt a little guilty of having such bounty.

Nyah had dates. Nyah was beautiful. She was a tall, willowy girl with café-au-lait skin and rich, golden-bronze cat eyes that were the same color as her hair. She had teeth that weren't perfect, but were imperfect in an awesome, interesting way, with the tiniest suggestion of prominent canines. Annie had been a little surprised that Nyah had agreed to go to the dance with Tyson Smith, captain of the football team, one of the many offers she'd received. She'd giggled with Nyah at how cliché this was. She knew Nyah wasn't really interested in him or anyone else; she just wanted to have fun. Annie didn't like him—he seemed too smooth and shallow. But to keep things light for Nyah, they'd arranged to go as a foursome tonight.

Annie smiled to herself, thinking how amazing it felt to not have to worry about a date to the dance—or for any event. Not that she would ever really have worried about it, but still, it was nice. She was glad her parents had been pretty cool about accepting that Aaan was in her life. Yesterday, though, her mom had expressed some concern that she might later regret being so committed at such a young age, but she failed to see what age had to do with anything. So what if she was sixteen and he was, well ... older? He seemed like a vulnerable teen in some ways. And she knew no other man could even come close to tempting her. Aaan was by far the hottest guy at school, in the state, in the country, heck, even in the universe. The youth who perished in the northern seas had taken care of his body—it was beautiful.

But more than that, it was like having someone you love put on a different shirt or get a new haircut—the thing she loved was that this was Aaan. And no matter that his physical form was gorgeous, her mind's eye still saw him as he'd looked when he manifested himself into his ancient form there at the Swan Hole.

She'd been fascinated to read about the Sons of Anak and the speculations people had made on what they must have looked like. Annie didn't have to speculate—she knew. He wasn't a son of Anak, but of Daanak—and like those legends of old, she was sure there had been some exaggerations about their size when someone had described them by using the simile that other men were like grasshoppers to them. But she knew that Aaan had been large. He'd needed to make a conscious effort during his manifestations to be a more reasonable size so as not to scare her. But once he'd forgotten himself and appeared to her as if he had been nine or ten feet tall. And his glow. She remembered how she had to keep reminding him to tone it down at Uncle Alistair's wedding. She smiled dreamily, remembering those times.

She was yanked from her reverie by Aaan's special tone on her iPhone, alerting her to a text message. *Are you ready? I am on my way over.*

She shook her head, thinking how formal he still sounded. She made a mental note to work with him to sound more like a teenager. *K*, she texted back.

She knew he'd be here momentarily because he'd only be coming from next door.

She thought about how much she owed to her aunt and uncle for helping Aaan to be accepted into the fold. When she'd brought home a new Aaan to meet the family, her parents had initially been a little freaked out. But Uncle Alistair had vouched for him and Aunt Zsofia so fully embraced him that her parents soon followed suit.

Thankfully, the topic had been broached as to just where he was staying and how he'd acquired paperwork that allowed him to enroll in school. The paperwork had been no problem, he'd assured them—having long been able to watch how such documents were made, he knew exactly how to fake them and where to go for the proper materials.

Annie smiled, remembering how Aaan had assured her parents that being phony wasn't something he enjoyed, and reasoned that he truly was creating this new citizen and so in a sense the documents were not false.

Aaan had explained that before the team of angels had embarked on their quest to procure a body for him, they'd helped him take care of many details, including securing the cave, arranging the papers, and moving critical pieces of his belongings to a safe-deposit box. He'd rented a furnished apartment via the Internet. But at the time, the rented lodgings had been uncertain, especially since no one knew how long the wait would be for the right body. So, he sheepishly admitted he had given his address as Aunt Zsofia's house, knowing that to be admitted to Churchill, the address needed to be close but not the same as Annie's.

At the mention of his giving Aunt Zsofia's address as his own, her aunt and uncle had whispered for a moment and then joyfully announced that Aaan should let the apartment go and actually move into Aunt Zsofia's cottage, since they didn't need it anyway; they spent most of their time housed in Alistair's master suite when they weren't traveling the world using the ghost transformation. And so, now Aaan lived just next door.

She slipped on her spiky heels and peeked out the window in time to see him approaching, so she rushed downstairs and flung open the door before he could even knock.

She was glad no one else was close by so she could enjoy the greeting with no distractions as she embraced him.

She began to realize how important their first real dance in public was to him when she stepped back to look at him. He looked amazing in a black-and-gray suit she was sure had come from Italy.

Once inside the door, he pulled from his pocket something wrapped in black velvet and held it out to her.

"For you," he said with smiling eyes.

"Aaan, you didn't have to bring a gift." She was excited to open it but speechless when she saw that inside was a dazzling sapphire-and-diamond necklace and earrings. These were obviously real jewelry. Not something from any store that operated in this century. She'd suddenly felt underdressed in her tiny black dress and spiky heels. This ensemble would have delighted royalty.

"Aaan, I don't know what to say. I—I absolutely love them, but these are too much. I don't have a gift for you, and even if I did, I could never give you something like this."

"Anya, what you've already given me is valued far above anything I could ever give you."

"And I can say the same for what you've given me." She didn't know what to do. She thought she should put them on to keep from hurting his feelings, but she wasn't sure how the other students would react if she wore crowned jewels to a high school dance.

Aaan, with his beautiful soul, seemed to recognize her dilemma and explained. "Love, please don't despair. This gift is something I have longed to give you for a long time and this is the first real opportunity I have had. It is yours to do with as you please. You can simply place it in the safe if you don't wish to wear it tonight, or wear any or all pieces as you see fit. I know that if you choose to wear it tonight, you will likely be the only person there with jewels such as these. And therefore, there is an argument for not wearing it, or perhaps only the earrings. But I do confess that I would dearly love to see how those sapphires try to compete with the beauty of your brilliant blue-green eyes. Actually, I do not wonder at all—I just wish to see them try."

At this, he kissed her hand, and she blushed and said playfully, "Hey, if you think you can sweep me off my feet with jewelry, you've made a good start. They really are stunning."

"Anya, you must know that all I have, all I am, is yours."

Annie thought her heart would totally stop beating. When she could breathe again, she ventured, "They really do look like jewels royalty would have. They couldn't have come from the mall. Do they have a story?"

"They are indeed antique, and part of a collection from an ancient fallen dynasty located in what is now Eastern Europe."

Annie held them appreciatively and admired the intricate artwork and brilliant jewels. "Hey, maybe we can do some web research on them."

"Perhaps we can travel to the location someday to do research in the local libraries and ruins — just for fun. A quest."

Annie nodded enthusiastically. Life with Aaan was going to be exciting, she knew. They wouldn't have to worry about money, though Aaan clearly didn't value his material treasure half so much as the treasured memories of loved ones. She knew he'd been a collector over the ages and had found ways to stash some of the treasure in secure places, not so much to hoard it, but more because he appreciated something about its beauty, grace, or history. He'd told her that usually when he'd hidden treasure in places throughout the world, it had been to protect it from being lost during times of social upheaval. Many times, he'd returned after an upheaval and found a way to make sure the treasure just happened to turn up by being found by a deserving person. This was one of his favorite activities. Annie wondered if he'd been the source of some of the Santa Claus and good elf legends.

"But Aaan, there's something I don't understand. I know you've collected treasures, but I thought your ability to manipulate material objects when you're out-of-body only developed recently. So how did you stash all this stuff?" she inquired.

He laughed and shook his head. "Remember, dear one, you and I have very different definitions of *recent*."

Annie thought of the first time she'd seen all the jewels in his cave. It suddenly made her remember her commitment to Missy and Billy. "Aaan, I have a favor to ask."

"Anything for you, my love."

She blushed but trudged on. "You remember Missy and Billy? The couple that lived in the little travel trailer next to the Swan Hole? It was Missy who was with me when you first saw me." She added the last part to build her case that Missy had as much right to any treasure "found" in the Swan Hole.

She continued, "Well, I made a promise to myself the day I first entered the cave that if I ever retrieved any of the jewels, I'd give Missy her share." She quickly added, "That is, of course, before I realized the cave was occupied." She blushed. It felt like she was giving away his treasure. "I know now the treasure belongs to you, but the fact is that I purposefully didn't invite Missy back to the cave after I saw the treasure. I knew she hadn't seen it because she didn't go as far in as me. I mean, I think I had a good reason—I wanted to protect the cave and keep it intact and I was afraid most people wouldn't feel that way, and with Missy and Billy so poor, I was afraid someone might exploit them and take the treasure for themselves. I had visions of a theme park built around it."

Unable to gauge his reaction, she added, "Now that you've actually given me some of the treasure, I feel I need to ask that a treasure of similar value be given to Missy and Billy." After blurting all this out, she waited.

Aaan took a moment to respond. "Anya, I am not angry at you for asking me to give away my—um, our—treasure. It does feel a little odd to have the cave viewed as an archeological find. But mostly I agree with you. They seem like good, honest people and it will be good to give them a break in life. After all, had it not been for their help, my Tiny Bold Maiden might not have entered my cave, and thus, my heart. I do have a readily accessible bracelet that would work well, I think. But since I cannot leave his body without risking its final death, it will be challenging to figure out how to hide the bracelet in a place that would suggest to them that they merely found it. I will figure out a way to accomplish this the next time I am there."

Annie was perhaps more pleased with his promise than her own beautiful gift. She adored the sapphires but thinking about the difference such a valuable treasure would make in the lives of Missy, Billy, and their baby was priceless. Oh, how she loved this man.

She decided to wear the exquisite earrings to the dance and place the necklace in the safe for another occasion. Soon she was ready to leave and caught a glimpse of the two of them in a mirror downstairs. She couldn't believe she was part of this handsome, happy couple. Her mom and dad came into the foyer and her mom snapped a few pictures of them before wishing them a pleasant evening.

They picked up Nyah and her date and soon arrived at the high school.

The music was loud and Aaan offered his hand as an obvious signal that he wanted to dance. In a manner befitting any Jane Austen character, Annie thought, she gave her hand into his and was drawn onto the dance floor. The lights dimmed and the air was now filled with strains of a slow dance. Annie never would have expected to enjoy a dance so much, but Aaan was the perfect dance partner, both fun and attentive. His eye didn't rove around the room looking at every girl. She truly felt that he only had eyes for her.

But the same was not the case for poor Nyah. Somewhere about halfway through the dance, it became clear that Nyah's date expected this to be more than just a casual social engagement. Annie watched him try to dominate every dance, and when slow dances came, he really put the moves on Nyah and she could tell that Nyah was getting annoyed. Aaan offered to act as her defender and let the young man know the lady was ready to go home—alone. Annie knew Aaan, true to his angel half, was ultimately a peaceful being, but was quite capable of championing a cause when needed. Annie hoped it wouldn't come to that and asked Aaan to hold off saying anything until she could talk to Nyah.

Annie felt bad for Nyah, who glowed like a model in her short, one-shoulder, formal dress in deep persimmon with matching spiky heels. She looked so beautiful and yet so sad. Annie took her hand and pulled her to the ladies room. Once inside, she gave her a hug.

Nyah seemed to appreciate the hug, but assured her that she was fine and could handle any bozo who tried to lay a hand on her. She acknowledged, though, that her date was being disrespectful and it was time to set him straight and let him know the date was over.

Annie felt herself tear up a little, "I just want you to be happy like I am. It's not fair. I have everything now and you don't."

Nyah took both of Annie's hands and said, "Annie, dear one. My time will come. Don't you worry. We all have to go through valleys in our lives. Need I remind you that not so long ago, it was me who was worried sick about you? I thought you'd never be back to the old Annie, and now look at you. You're better than the old Annie. Here you are with the love of your life. It doesn't take a rocket scientist to look at the two of you and see how happy you are. That's what I want. Well, after I get my medical degree and travel the world." They both laughed. "And after all, the night is young. You go out there and enjoy your beau."

Annie nodded and the two went back out together. Aaan was waiting with a glass of punch for each of them. She hesitated to reach for hers and looked at Aaan thoughtfully, having a surreal moment remembering Zaak handing her a similar glass at the dance in Transylvania.

"Where's Zaak when you need him?" she asked flippantly but didn't think anyone heard her over the music. She smiled, remembering how interested he'd been in Nyah.

Nyah's date joined them and Annie saw Nyah saying something into his ear. She braced for action when she saw him give Nyah an angry look. She saw Aaan straighten, too, eying the couple.

Luckily, her date seemed to give up and in a mocking jester of not touching her by throwing his hands up, backed away scowling. As if to prove something, he was already dancing with someone else within a few minutes.

Nyah shouted into Annie's ear that she was fine and was determined to enjoy the rest of the dance. She urged Annie to get back out on the dance floor.

After finishing her punch, Annie was in the process of excusing herself from Nyah to go back out with Aaan when she saw Nyah's mouth drop, her eyes staring over Annie's shoulder. Turning carefully so as not to appear to stare at whatever, or whoever, had caught her friend's eye, she saw the object of her gaze.

Annie watched as a bronze, statuesque man sauntered toward them with long, confident strides, his eyes only seeing Nyah, to the obvious dismay of many wallflowers around the room and several who had dates. His bulging muscles threatened the very fabric of his finely tailored gray suit. His perfectly chiseled jawline blended well with the determined character of his brow, his sharp, black eyes intense.

"What were you saying?" Nyah asked, without taking her eyes off him.

Annie couldn't remember. She looked at Aaan and saw that he, too, watched the approaching Olympian, but with a curious sideways grin. The athletic figure, a head taller than everyone else at the dance, even a couple of inches taller than Aaan, looked sideways at him and nodded. Annie was dumbfounded as she watched Aaan nod back, as though he recognized the stranger.

She wanted to ask him if he knew who the guy was, but couldn't do more than watch as the stranger walked up to Nyah, bowed, took her hand, and kissed it gallantly.

Nyah was obviously confused by his actions.

The music was now lower as a slow song began and Annie could hear the stranger say to Nyah, "May I be so bold as to introduce myself? I am a new student in this fine establishment as of Monday. My name is Zaak Angeli."

Annie gasped. Now it all made sense. He must have had help from Eriel. Now both brothers had a way out as well as a chance at a lifetime with one they loved—at least that's what it was beginning to look like, though with Zaak and Nyah it was way too early to tell.

"Zaak Angeli," Nyah repeated the words, seemingly incapable of forming any other thoughts right now but merely repeating what she'd heard.

Zaak slowly nodded, watching her eyes, and seemed to be waiting for recognition to take place. "You may call me Zak. That's what my friends call me. And may I ask your name?"

Nyah cleared her throat as though unable to remember her name. Annie had never before seen her friend taken aback by anything and tried nudging her. Nyah eventually snapped back to reality and murmured, "Oh, my name is Nyah Harrison."

"Would you make me the happiest man here by honoring me with this dance?" he asked smoothly as he offered her his arm.

She took it, her eyes not leaving his, and seemed to glide toward the dance floor. After a moment she glanced back at Annie and shrugged.

Annie shrugged back, her brows lifted, totally amazed by this new occurrence but giddy with happiness for her friend. She and Aaan followed them onto the dance floor. She saw Aaan shake his head and laugh, as if he weren't surprised at all.

Afterword

T his series was at least in part influenced by the work of C.S. Lewis. Through his brilliant writings he shared joy and helped me to better understand my own journey. He is my favorite author and in a couple of places he suggested that he wanted to see more new writers write fiction that openly treats the supernatural as reality. He knew how to finesse a good novel on supernatural subjects so that it was fun and joyful without sounding judgmental or legalistic; as others have said, he knew the difference between a fiction novel and a sermon. One place he alluded to this was in <u>Out of the Silent Planet</u> when Ransom explains, "What we need for the moment is not so much a body of belief as a body of people familiarized with certain ideas."[3] The other was something he wrote in a 1956 letter[4] to a young Narnia fan in Florida, "If you become a writer you'll be trying to describe the thing all your life: and lucky if, out of dozens of books, one or two sentences, just for a moment, come near to getting it across." In any case, this is the chief reason I added a supernatural dimension to this trilogy. I hope my own writings reflect even a hint of the playful way he viewed supernatural realms.

Endnotes

[1] Quote from: C. S. Lewis. 1943. *Perelandra*. The Bodley Head. London.

[2] Quote from: J.R.R. Tolkien. 1954. *The Lord of the Rings: The Two Towers*. George Allen and Unwin. New South Wales.

[3] Quote from: C.S. Lewis. 1938. *Out of the Silent Planet*. John Lane. London.

[4] Quote from: C.S. Lewis. 1956. Letter to a young Narnia fan in Florida, published by Lyle W. Dorset and Marjorie Lamp Mead. 1996. *C.S. Lewis' Letters to Children*. Touchstone. New York.